CARTOON HANGOVER

BRAVEST WARRIORS ™

CREATED by PENDLETON WARD

VOLUME EIGHT

www.boom-studios.com • www.youtube.com/cartoonhangover

ROSS RICHIE CEO & Founder • MATT GAGNON Editor-in-Chief • FILIP SABLIK President of Publishing & Marketing • STEPHEN CHRISTY President of Development • LANCE KREITER VP of Licensing & Merchandising
PHIL BARBARO VP of Finance • BRYCE CARLSON Managing Editor • MEL CAYLO Marketing Manager • SCOTT NEWMAN Production Design Manager • IRENE BRADISH Operations Manager • SIERRA HAHN Senior Editor
DAFNA PLEBAN Editor, Talent Development • SHANNON WATTERS Editor • ERIC HARBURN Editor • WHITNEY LEOPARD Associate Editor • JASMINE AMIRI Associate Editor • CHRIS ROSA Associate Editor
ALEX GALER Associate Editor • CAMERON CHITTOCK Associate Editor • MARY GUMPORT Assistant Editor • MATTHEW LEVINE Assistant Editor • KELSEY DIETERICH Production Designer • JILLIAN CRAB Production Designer
MICHELLE ANKLEY Production Designer • GRACE PARK Production Design Assistant • AARON FERRARA Operations Coordinator • ELIZABETH LOUGHRIDGE Accounting Coordinator • STEPHANIE HOCUTT Social Media Coordinator
JOSÉ MEZA Sales Assistant • JAMES ARRIOLA Mailroom Assistant • HOLLY AITCHISON Operations Assistant • SAM KUSEK Direct Market Representative • AMBER PARKER Administrative Assistant

BRAVEST WARRIORS Volume Eight, December 2016. Published by KaBOOM!, a division of Boom Entertainment, Inc. Based on "Bravest Warriors" ™ & © 2016 Frederator
Networks, Inc. Originally published in single magazine form as BRAVEST WARRIORS No. 29-32. ™ & © 2015 Frederator Networks, Inc. All rights reserved. KaBOOM!™ and
the KaBOOM! logo are trademarks of Boom Entertainment, Inc., registered in various countries and categories. All characters, events, and institutions depicted herein are
fictional. Any similarity between any of the names, characters, persons, events, and/or institutions in this publication to actual names, characters, and persons, whether
living or dead, events, and/or institutions is unintended and purely coincidental. KaBOOM! does not read or accept unsolicited submissions of ideas, stories, or artwork.

A catalog record of this book is available from OCLC and from the BOOM! Studios website, www.boom-studios.com, on the Librarians Page.

BOOM! Studios, 5670 Wilshire Boulevard, Suite 450, Los Angeles, CA 90036-5679. Printed in China. First Printing.

ISBN: 978-1-60886-922-0, eISBN: 978-1-61398-593-9

CREATED BY
PENDLETON WARD

WRITTEN BY
KATE LETH

ILLUSTRATED BY
IAN McGINTY

COLORED BY
LISA MOORE

LETTERED BY
COREY BREEN

SHORT MISSIONS

WRITTEN AND ILLUSTRATED BY
PRANAS NAUJOKAITIS

COVER BY
IAN McGINTY

WITH COLORS BY
FRED STRESING

DESIGNER
JILLIAN CRAB

ASSOCIATE EDITOR
CAMERON CHITTOCK

ORIGINAL SERIES EDITOR
REBECCA TAYLOR

COLLECTION EDITOR
SHANNON WATTERS

WITH SPECIAL THANKS TO BREEHN BURNS, ERIC HOMAN,
FRED SEIBERT, RUTH MORRISON, NATE OLSON, AND ALL OF
THE CLASSY FOLKS AT FREDERATOR STUDIOS.

CHAPTER
29

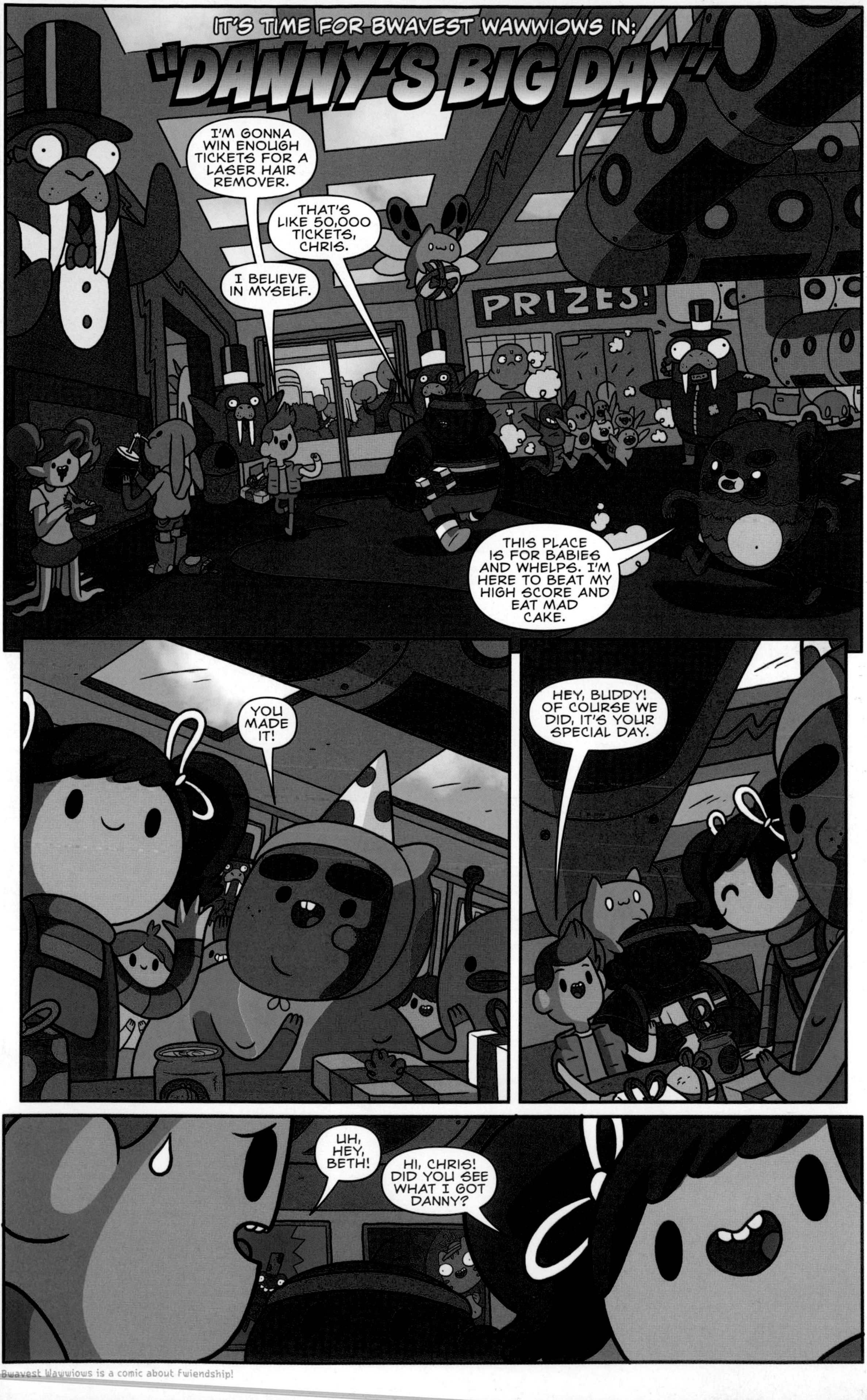
IT'S TIME FOR BWAVEST WAWWIOWS IN:
"DANNY'S BIG DAY"
I'M GONNA WIN ENOUGH TICKETS FOR A LASER HAIR REMOVER.
THAT'S LIKE 50,000 TICKETS, CHRIS.
I BELIEVE IN MYSELF.
PRIZES!
THIS PLACE IS FOR BABIES AND WHELPS. I'M HERE TO BEAT MY HIGH SCORE AND EAT MAD CAKE.
YOU MADE IT!
HEY, BUDDY! OF COURSE WE DID, IT'S YOUR SPECIAL DAY.
UH, HEY, BETH!
HI, CHRIS! DID YOU SEE WHAT I GOT DANNY?

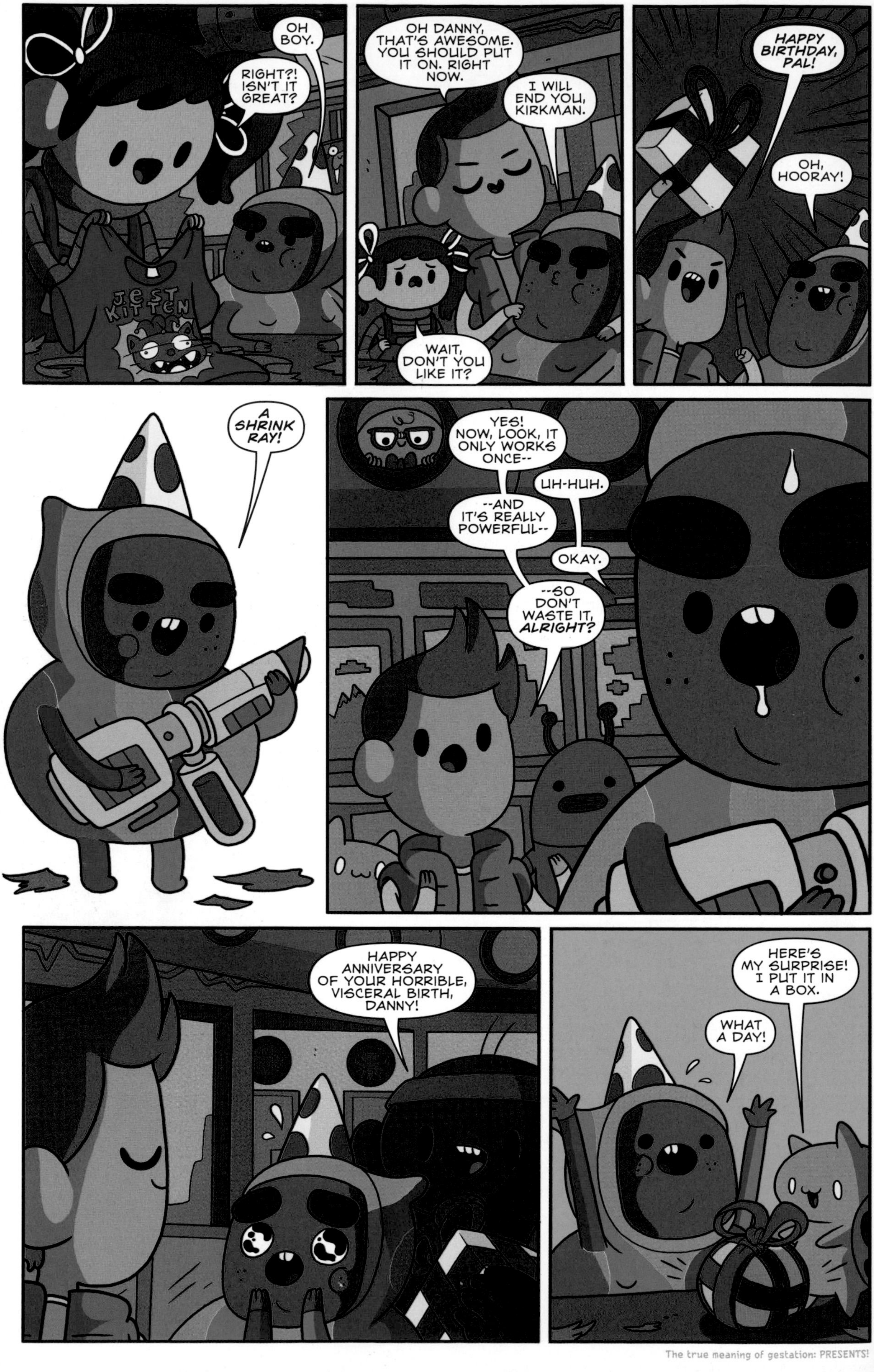
OH BOY.
RIGHT?! ISN'T IT GREAT?
JEST KITTEN
OH DANNY, THAT'S AWESOME. YOU SHOULD PUT IT ON. RIGHT NOW.
I WILL END YOU, KIRKMAN.
WAIT, DON'T YOU LIKE IT?
HAPPY BIRTHDAY, PAL!
OH, HOORAY!
A SHRINK RAY!
YES! NOW, LOOK, IT ONLY WORKS ONCE--
UH-HUH.
--AND IT'S REALLY POWERFUL--
OKAY.
--SO DON'T WASTE IT, ALRIGHT?
HAPPY ANNIVERSARY OF YOUR HORRIBLE, VISCERAL BIRTH, DANNY!
HERE'S MY SURPRISE! I PUT IT IN A BOX.
WHAT A DAY!

The true meaning of gestation: PRESENTS!

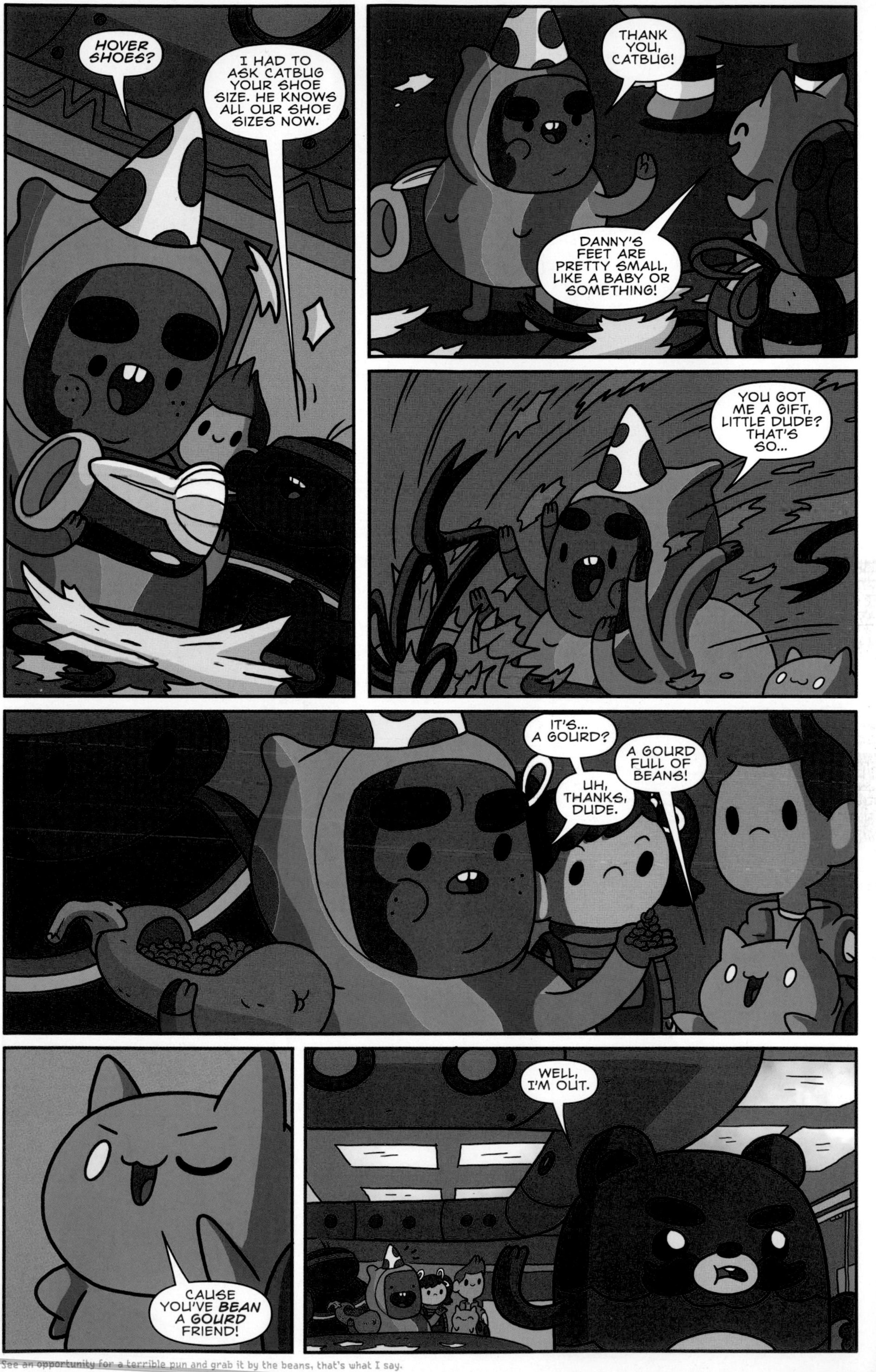
HOVER SHOES?
I HAD TO ASK CATBUG YOUR SHOE SIZE. HE KNOWS ALL OUR SHOE SIZES NOW.
THANK YOU, CATBUG!
DANNY'S FEET ARE PRETTY SMALL, LIKE A BABY OR SOMETHING!
YOU GOT ME A GIFT, LITTLE DUDE? THAT'S SO...
IT'S... A GOURD?
UH, THANKS, DUDE.
A GOURD FULL OF BEANS!
CAUSE YOU'VE BEAN A GOURD FRIEND!
WELL, I'M OUT.

See an opportunity for a terrible pun and grab it by the beans, that's what I say.

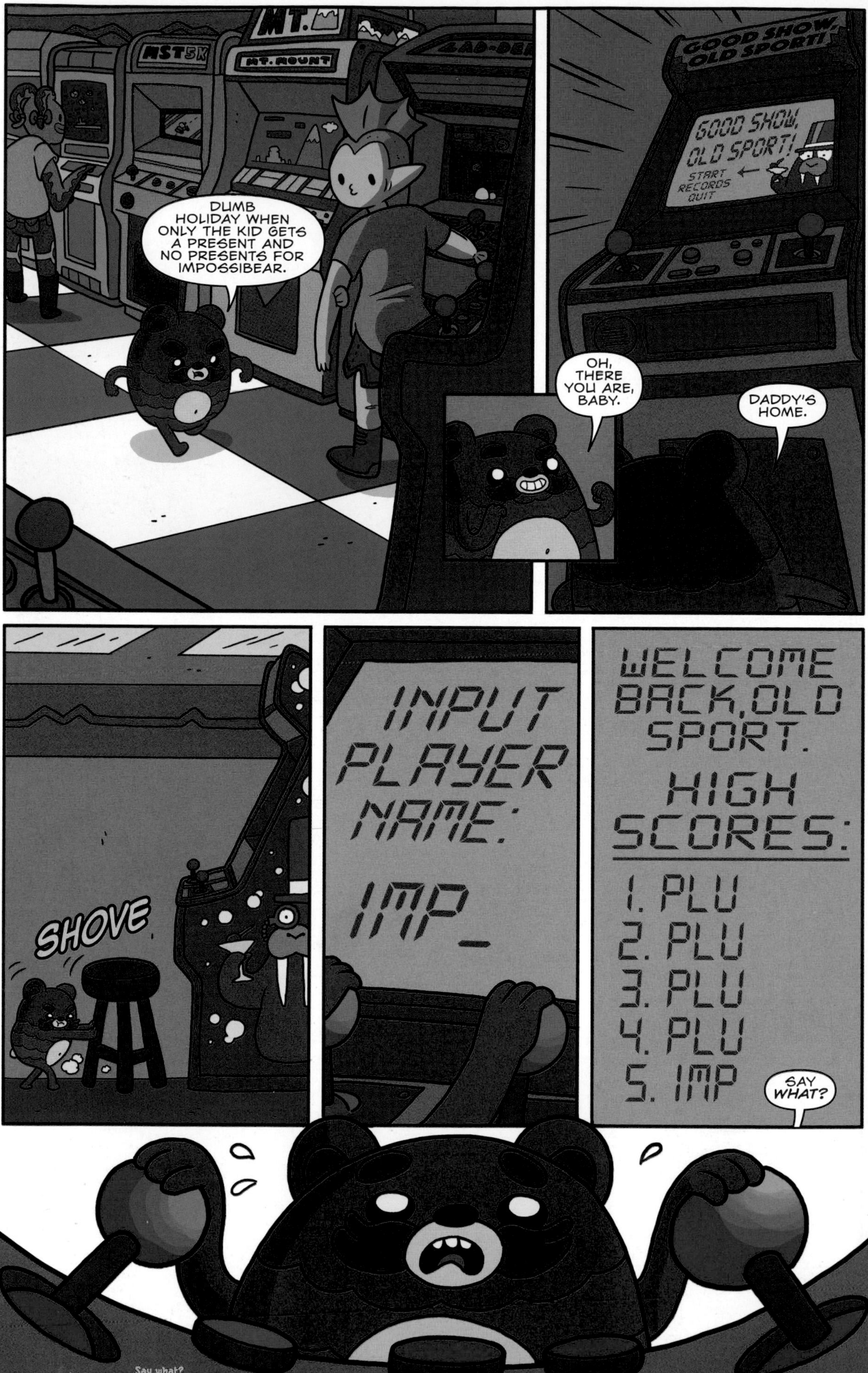
MST5K
MT. MOUNT
DUMB HOLIDAY WHEN ONLY THE KID GETS A PRESENT AND NO PRESENTS FOR IMPOSSIBEAR.
GOOD SHOW, OLD SPORT!
GOOD SHOW, OLD SPORT!
START
RECORDS
QUIT
OH, THERE YOU ARE, BABY.
DADDY'S HOME.
SHOVE
INPUT PLAYER NAME:
IMP_
WELCOME BACK, OLD SPORT.
HIGH SCORES:
1. PLU
2. PLU
3. PLU
4. PLU
5. IMP
SAY WHAT?
Say what?

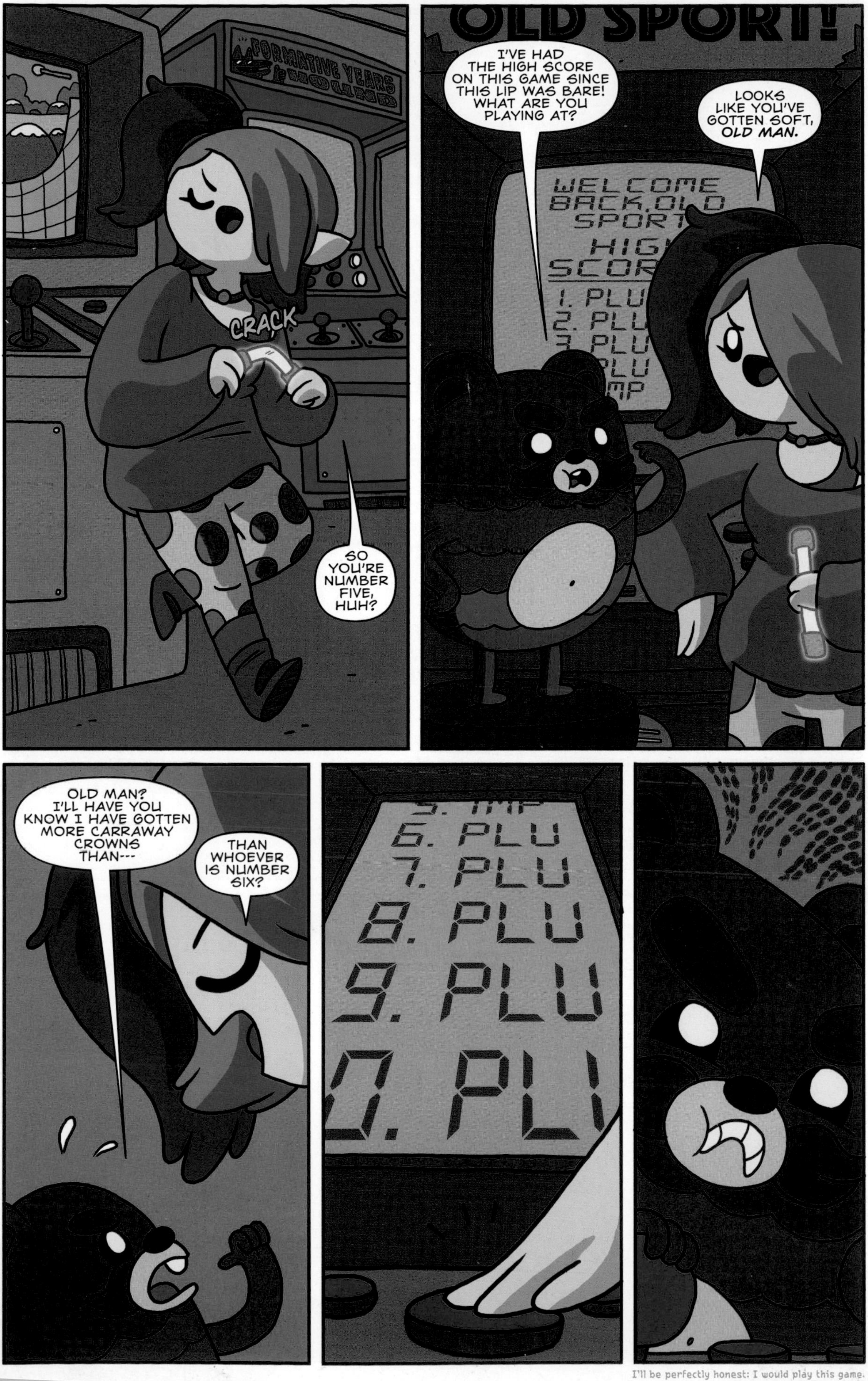
FORMATIVE YEARS
CRACK
SO YOU'RE NUMBER FIVE, HUH?
OLD SPORT!
I'VE HAD THE HIGH SCORE ON THIS GAME SINCE THIS LIP WAS BARE! WHAT ARE YOU PLAYING AT?
WELCOME BACK,OLD SPORT
HIGH SCOR
1. PLU
2. PLU
3. PLU
PLU
MP
LOOKS LIKE YOU'VE GOTTEN SOFT, OLD MAN.
OLD MAN? I'LL HAVE YOU KNOW I HAVE GOTTEN MORE CARRAWAY CROWNS THAN---
THAN WHOEVER IS NUMBER SIX?
6. PLU
7. PLU
8. PLU
9. PLU

I'll be perfectly honest: I would play this game.

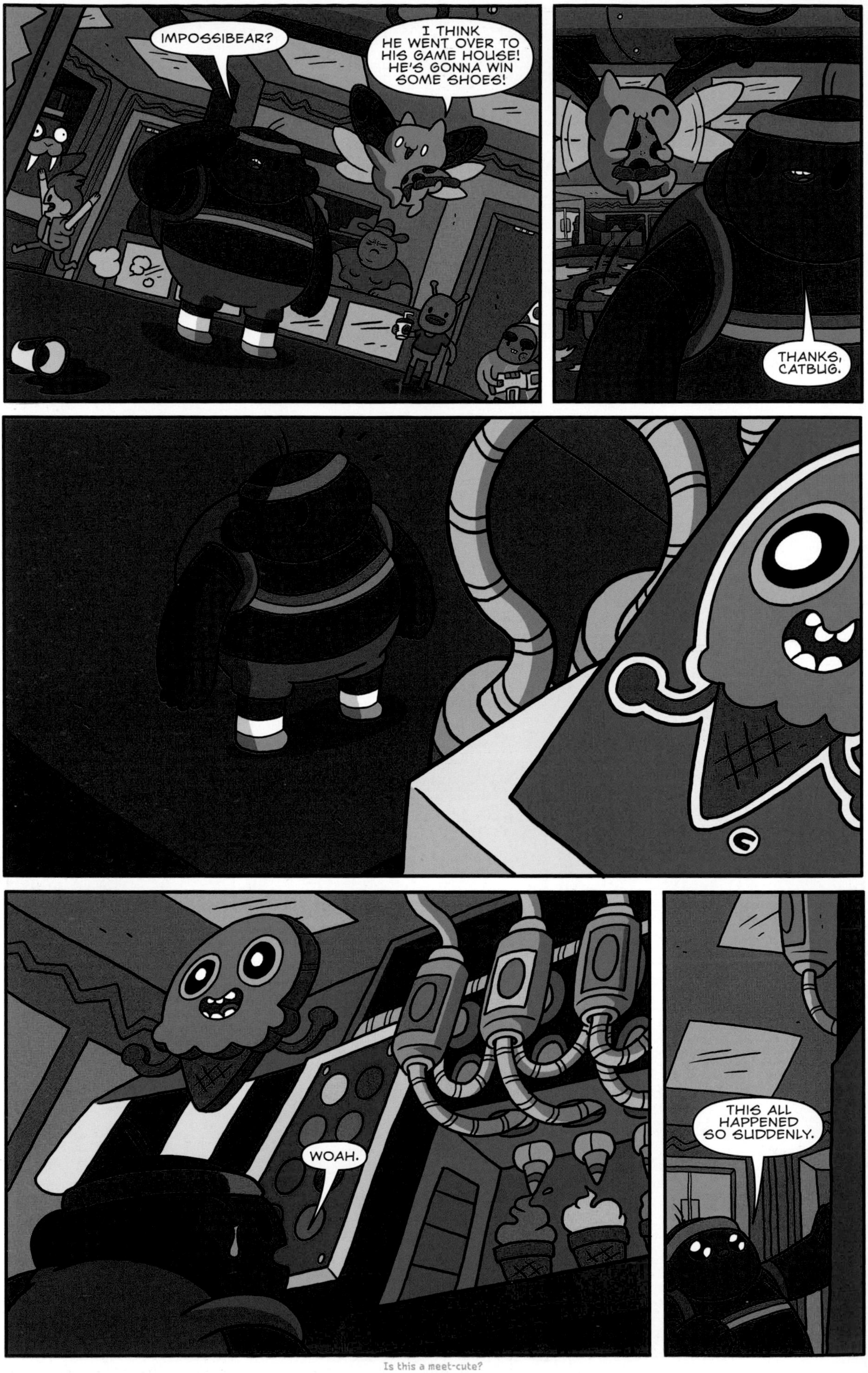
IMPOSSIBEAR?
I THINK HE WENT OVER TO HIS GAME HOUSE! HE'S GONNA WIN SOME SHOES!
THANKS, CATBUG.
WOAH.
THIS ALL HAPPENED SO SUDDENLY.

Is this a meet-cute?

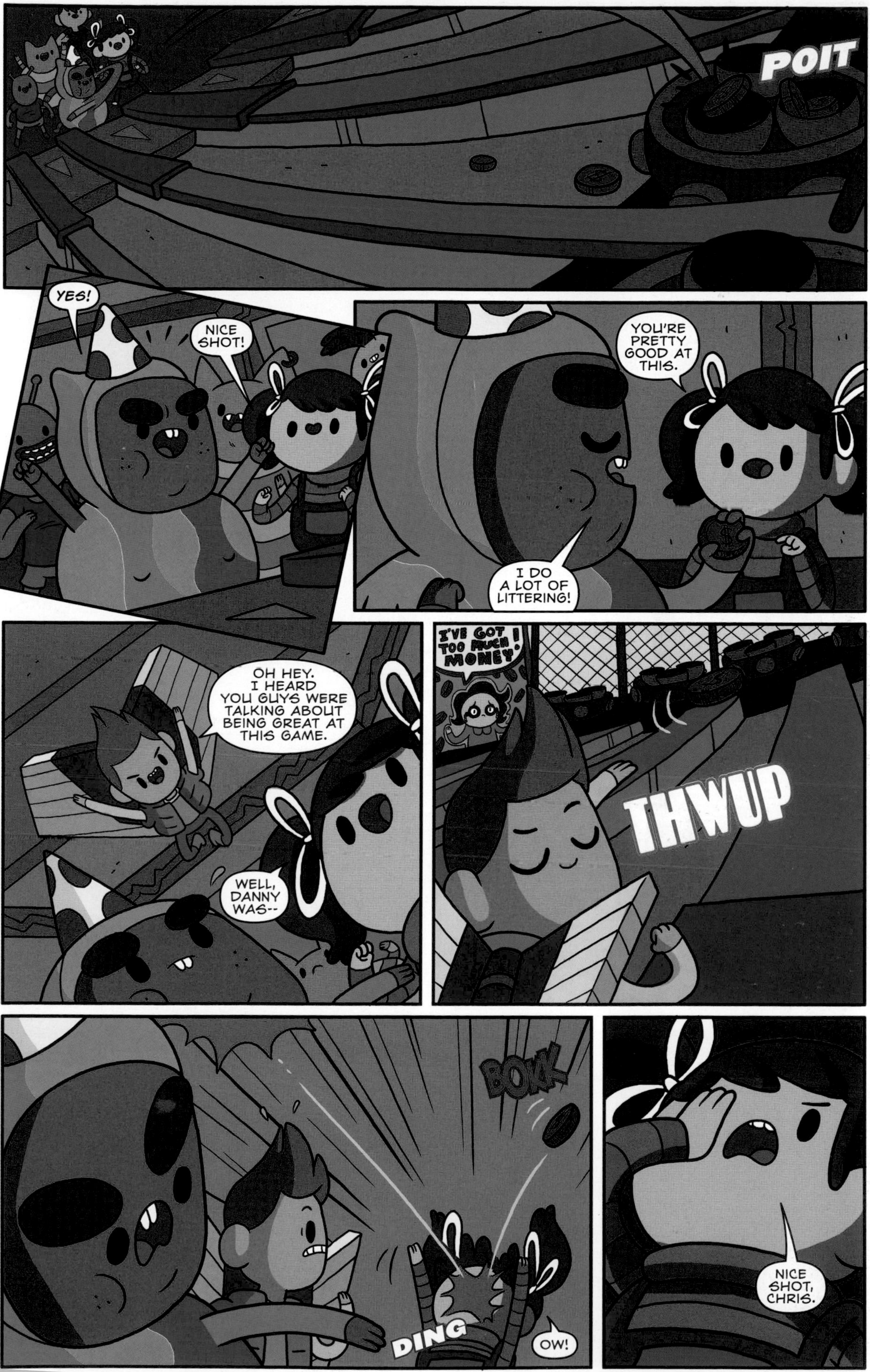
POIT
YES!
NICE SHOT!
YOU'RE PRETTY GOOD AT THIS.
I DO A LOT OF LITTERING!
OH HEY. I HEARD YOU GUYS WERE TALKING ABOUT BEING GREAT AT THIS GAME.
WELL, DANNY WAS--
I'VE GOT TOO MUCH MONEY!
THWUP
BOKK
DING
OW!
NICE SHOT, CHRIS.

So much violence! Nobody here has any respect for Friendship Time!

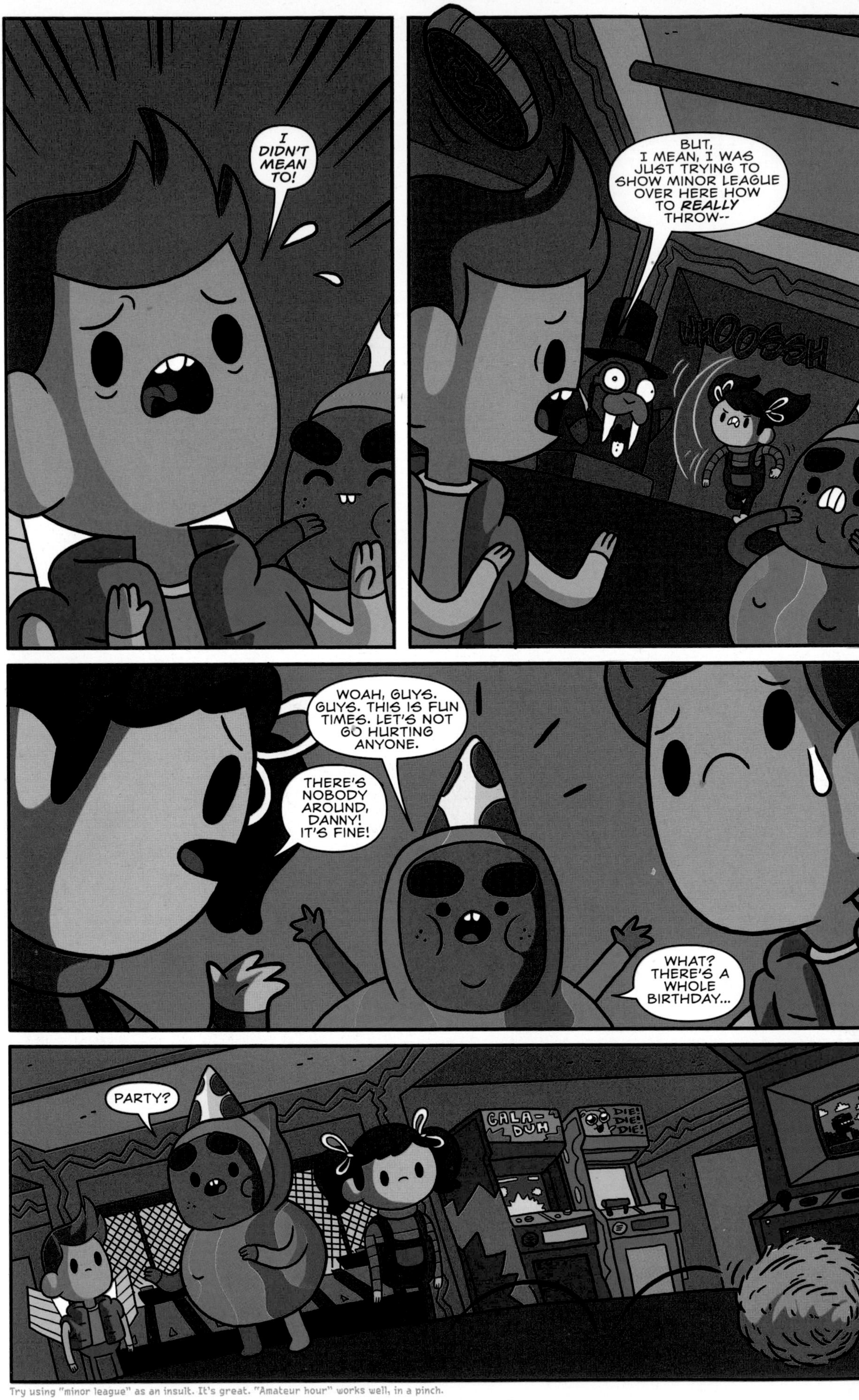
I DIDN'T MEAN TO!
BUT, I MEAN, I WAS JUST TRYING TO SHOW MINOR LEAGUE OVER HERE HOW TO *REALLY* THROW--
WHOOSSH
WOAH, GUYS. GUYS. THIS IS FUN TIMES. LET'S NOT GO HURTING ANYONE.
THERE'S NOBODY AROUND, DANNY! IT'S FINE!
WHAT? THERE'S A WHOLE BIRTHDAY...
PARTY?
GALA-DUH
DIE! DIE! DIE!

Try using "minor league" as an insult. It's great. "Amateur hour" works well, in a pinch.

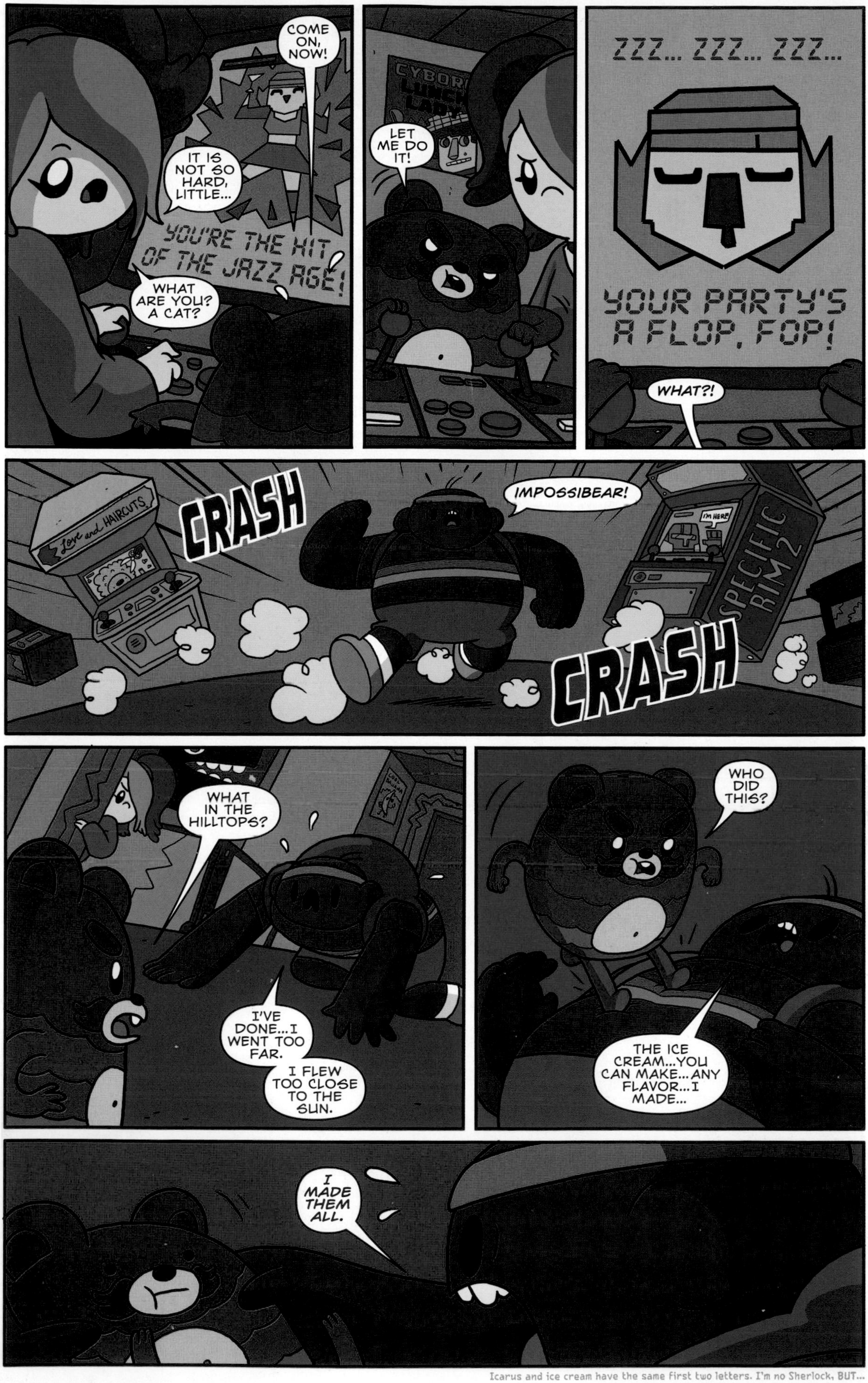
COME ON, NOW!
IT IS NOT SO HARD, LITTLE...
YOU'RE THE HIT OF THE JAZZ AGE!
WHAT ARE YOU? A CAT?
CYBORG LUNCH LADY
LET ME DO IT!
ZZZ... ZZZ... ZZZ...
YOUR PARTY'S A FLOP, FOP!
WHAT?!
CRASH
IMPOSSIBEAR!
Love and HAIRCUTS
I'M HERE!
SPECIFIC RIM 2
CRASH
WHAT IN THE HILLTOPS?
I'VE DONE...I WENT TOO FAR.
I FLEW TOO CLOSE TO THE SUN.
WHO DID THIS?
THE ICE CREAM...YOU CAN MAKE...ANY FLAVOR...I MADE...
I MADE THEM ALL.

Icarus and ice cream have the same first two letters. I'm no Sherlock, BUT...

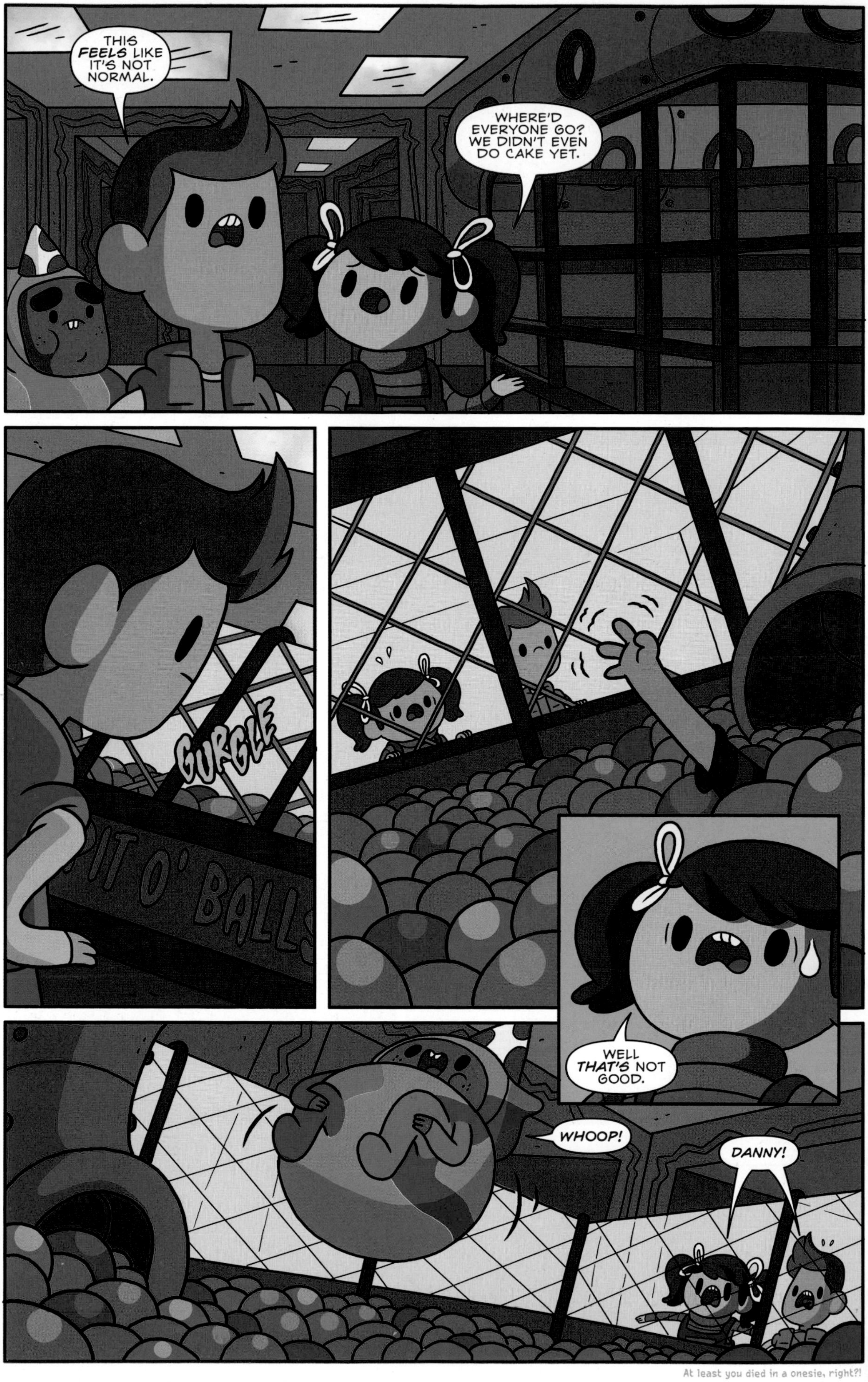
THIS FEELS LIKE IT'S NOT NORMAL.
WHERE'D EVERYONE GO? WE DIDN'T EVEN DO CAKE YET.
GURGLE
PIT O' BALLS
WELL THAT'S NOT GOOD.
WHOOP!
DANNY!

At least you died in a onesie, right?!

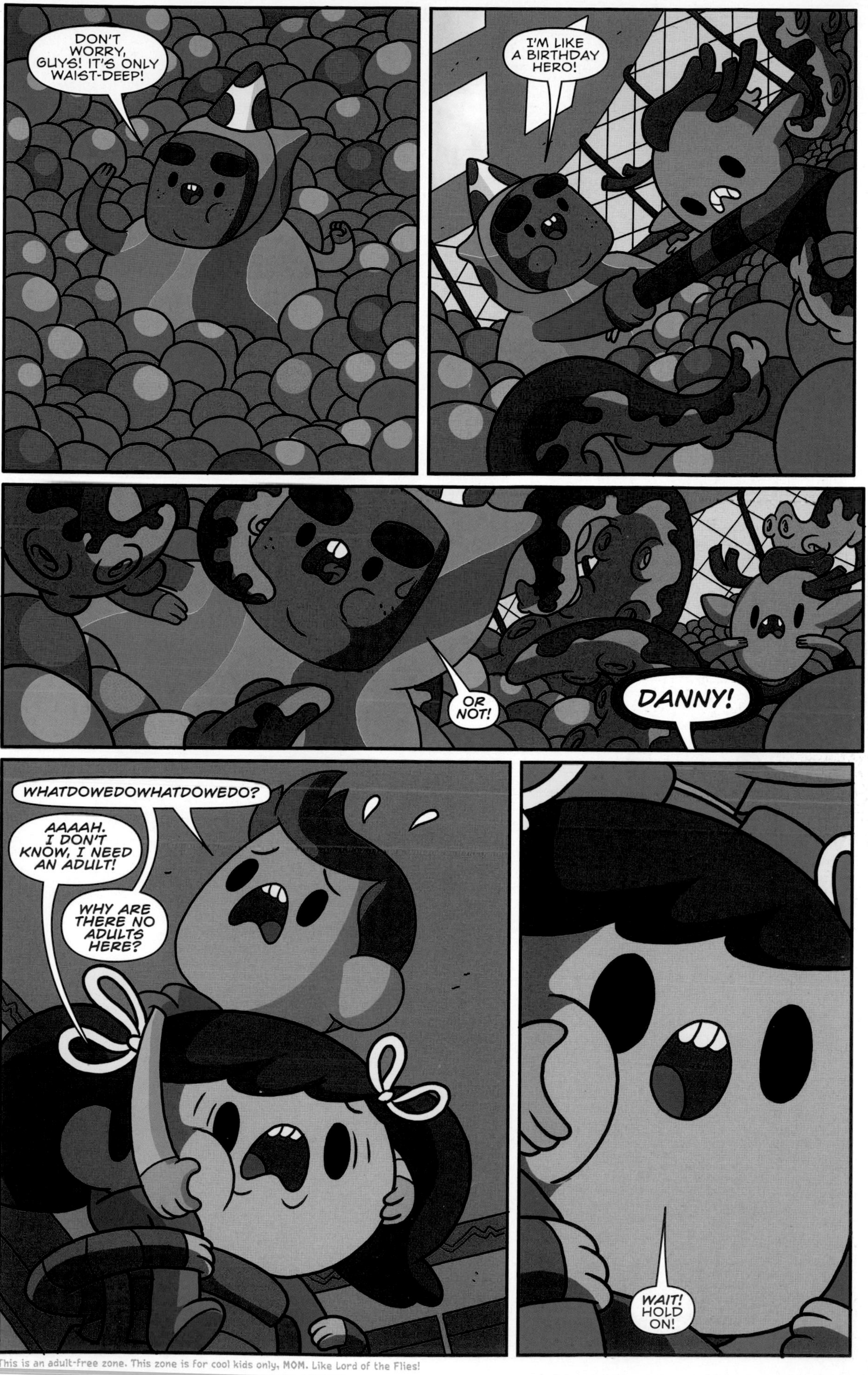
DON'T WORRY, GUYS! IT'S ONLY WAIST-DEEP!
I'M LIKE A BIRTHDAY HERO!
OR NOT!
DANNY!
WHATDOWEDOWHATDOWEDO?
AAAAH. I DON'T KNOW, I NEED AN ADULT!
WHY ARE THERE NO ADULTS HERE?
WAIT! HOLD ON!

This is an adult-free zone. This zone is for cool kids only, MOM. Like Lord of the Flies!

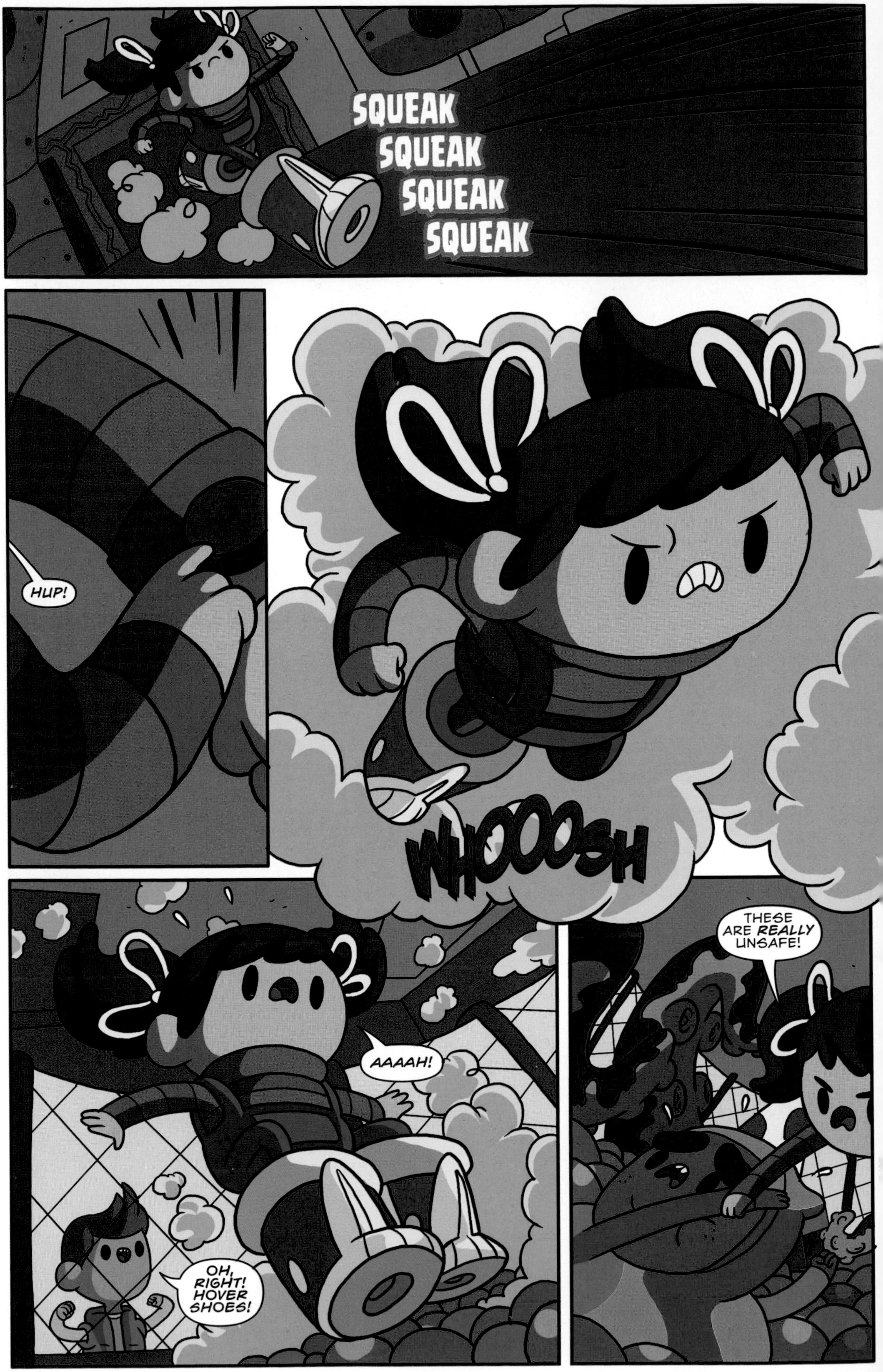
SQUEAK
SQUEAK
SQUEAK
SQUEAK
HUP!
WHOOOOSH
AAAAH!
OH, RIGHT! HOVER SHOES!
THESE ARE *REALLY* UNSAFE!

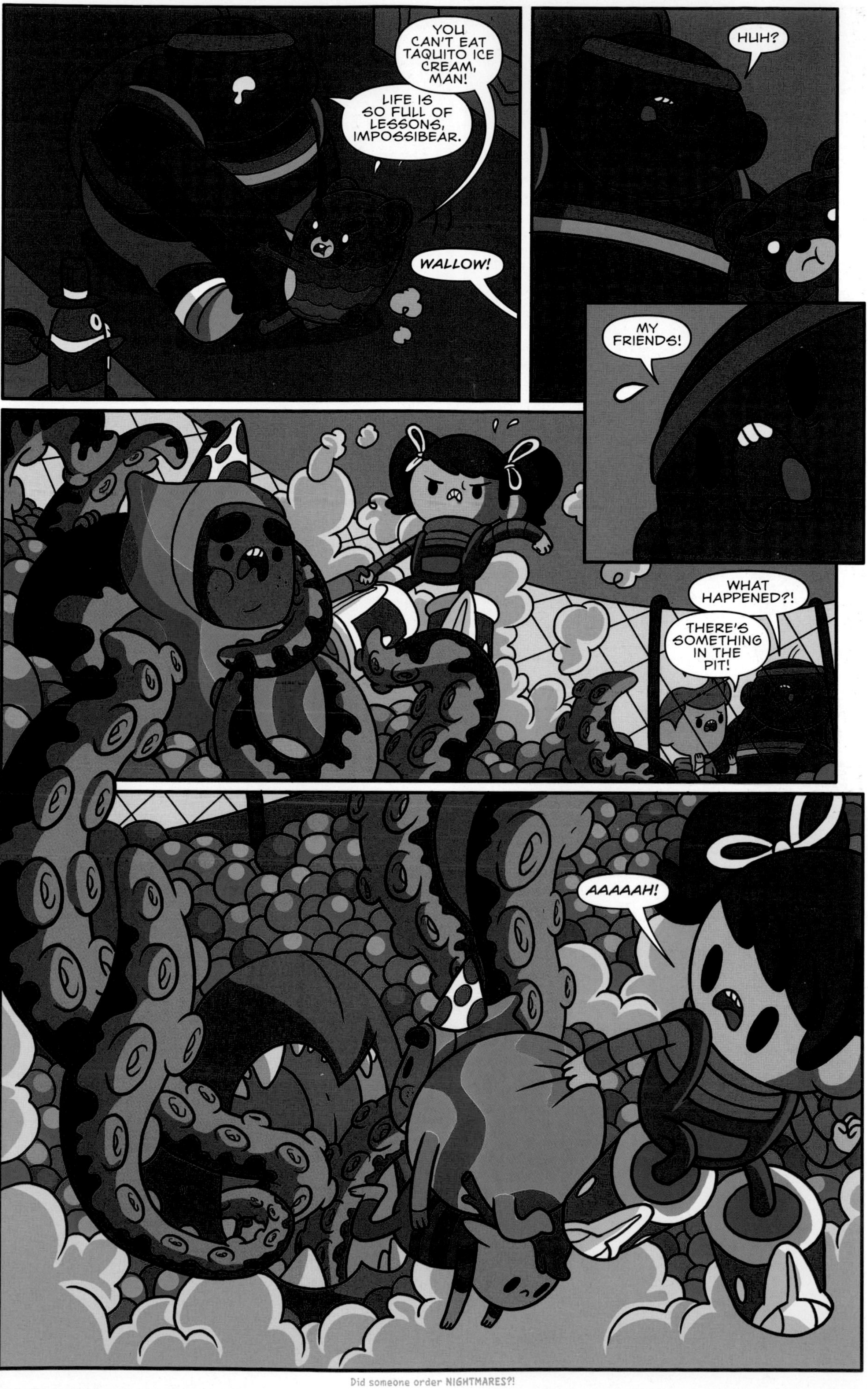
YOU CAN'T EAT TAQUITO ICE CREAM, MAN!
LIFE IS SO FULL OF LESSONS, IMPOSSIBEAR.
WALLOW!
HUH?
MY FRIENDS!
WHAT HAPPENED?!
THERE'S SOMETHING IN THE PIT!
AAAAAH!

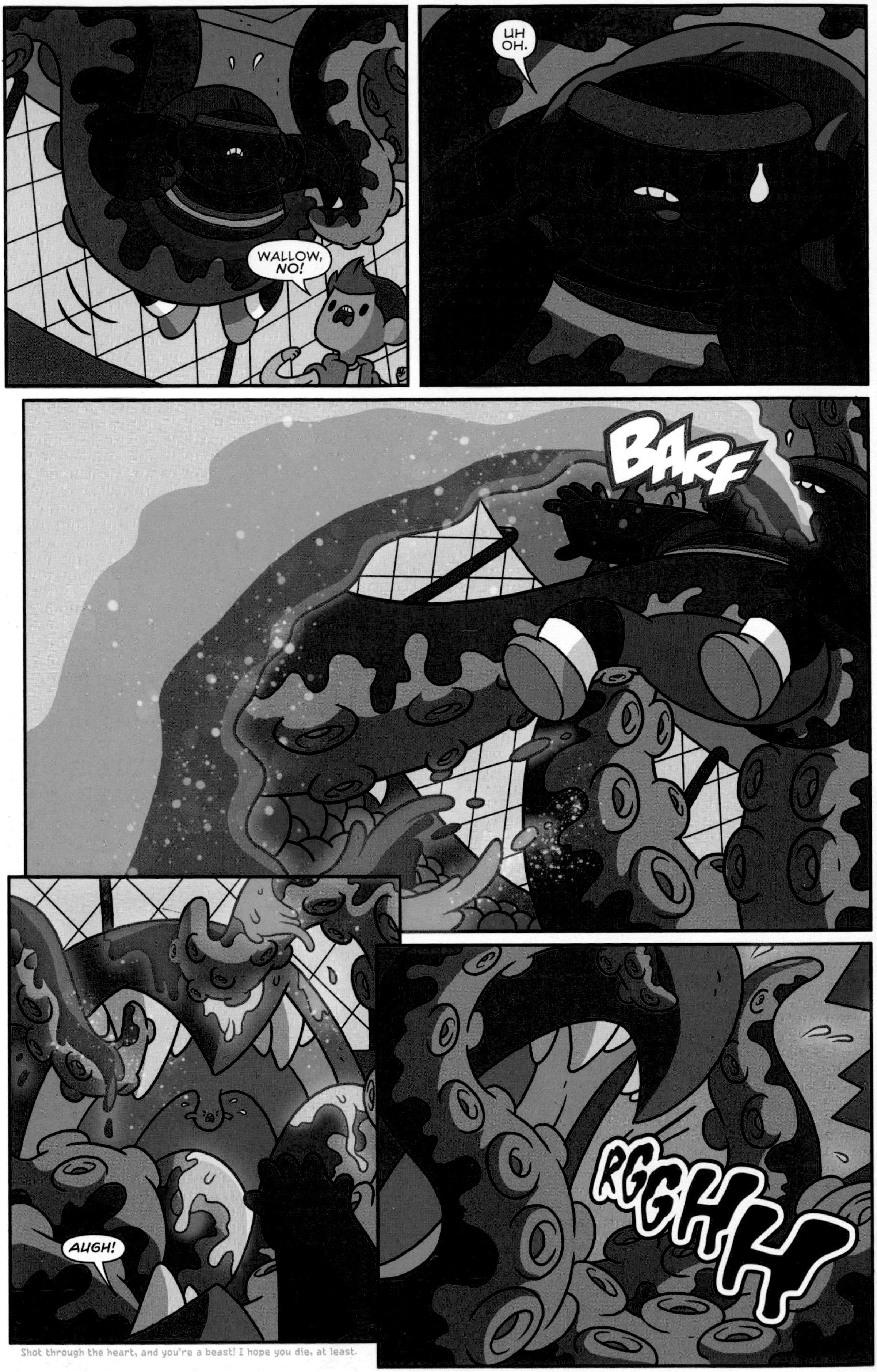
WALLOW, NO!
UH OH.
BARF
AUGH!
RGGHHH

Shot through the heart, and you're a beast! I hope you die, at least.

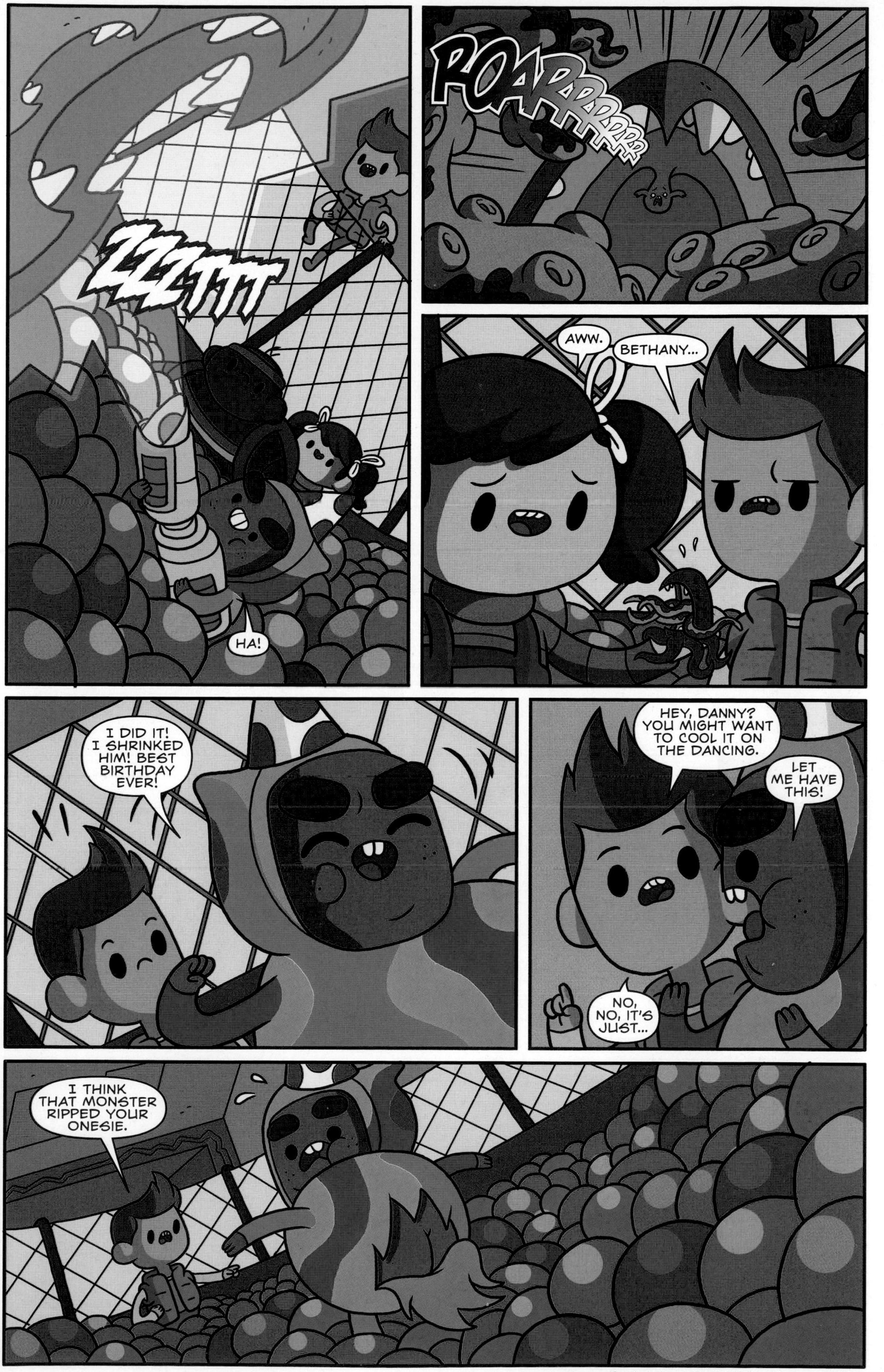

ZZZTTTT
HA!
ROARRRRRRR
AWW.
BETHANY...
I DID IT! I SHRINKED HIM! BEST BIRTHDAY EVER!
HEY, DANNY? YOU MIGHT WANT TO COOL IT ON THE DANCING.
LET ME HAVE THIS!
NO, NO, IT'S JUST...
I THINK THAT MONSTER RIPPED YOUR ONESIE.

Hfnnvi rh xlnrmt. Tvg lfg blfi hdrnhfrgh zmw izb tfmh.

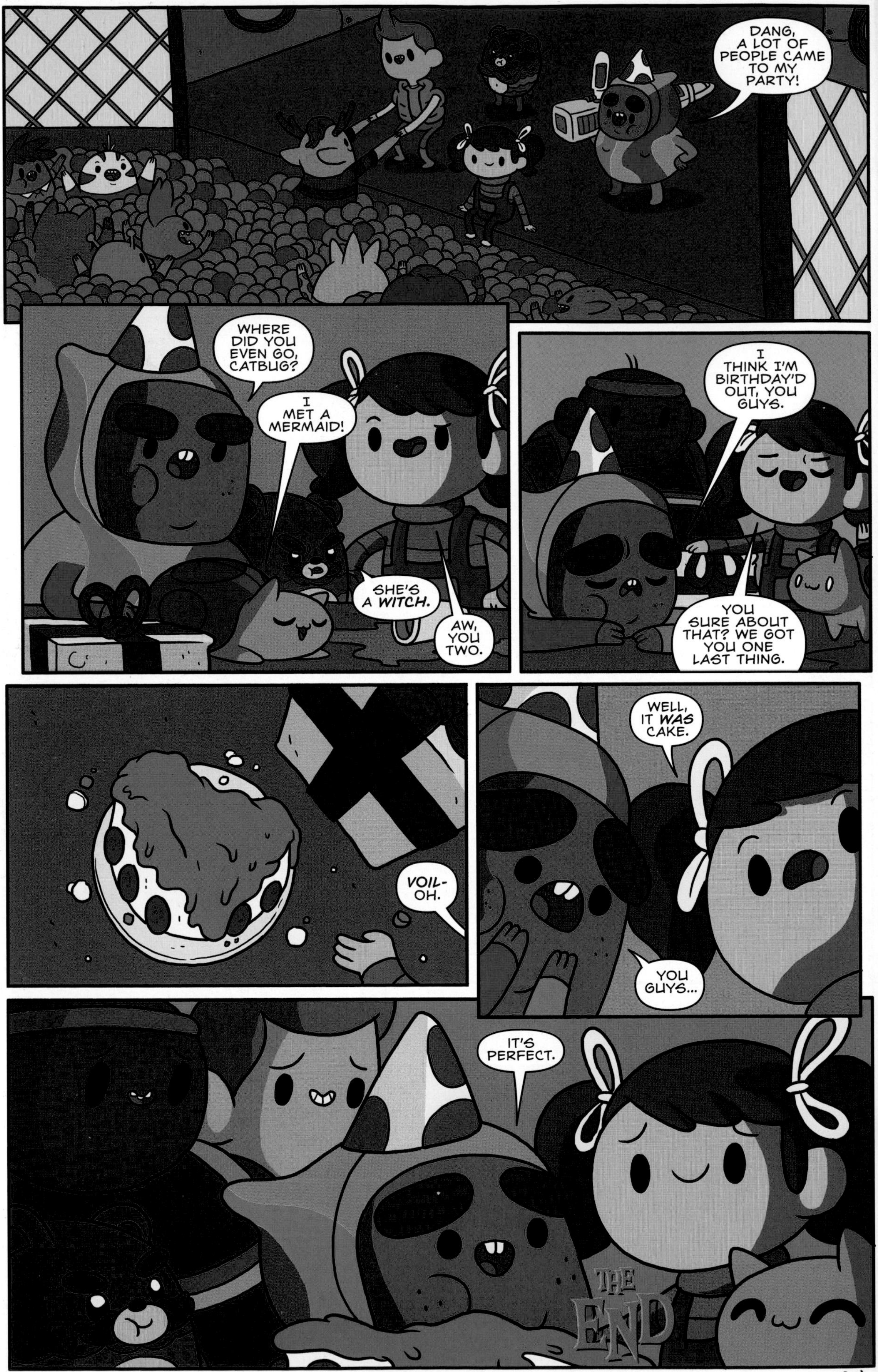

DANG, A LOT OF PEOPLE CAME TO MY PARTY!
WHERE DID YOU EVEN GO, CATBUG?
I MET A MERMAID!
SHE'S A *WITCH.*
AW, YOU TWO.
I THINK I'M BIRTHDAY'D OUT, YOU GUYS.
YOU SURE ABOUT THAT? WE GOT YOU ONE LAST THING.
VOIL-OH.
WELL, IT *WAS* CAKE.
YOU GUYS...
IT'S PERFECT.
THE END

Dv wvurmrgvob szevm'g hvvm gsv ozhg lu kvzxs...li lu yftxzg.

iAN!

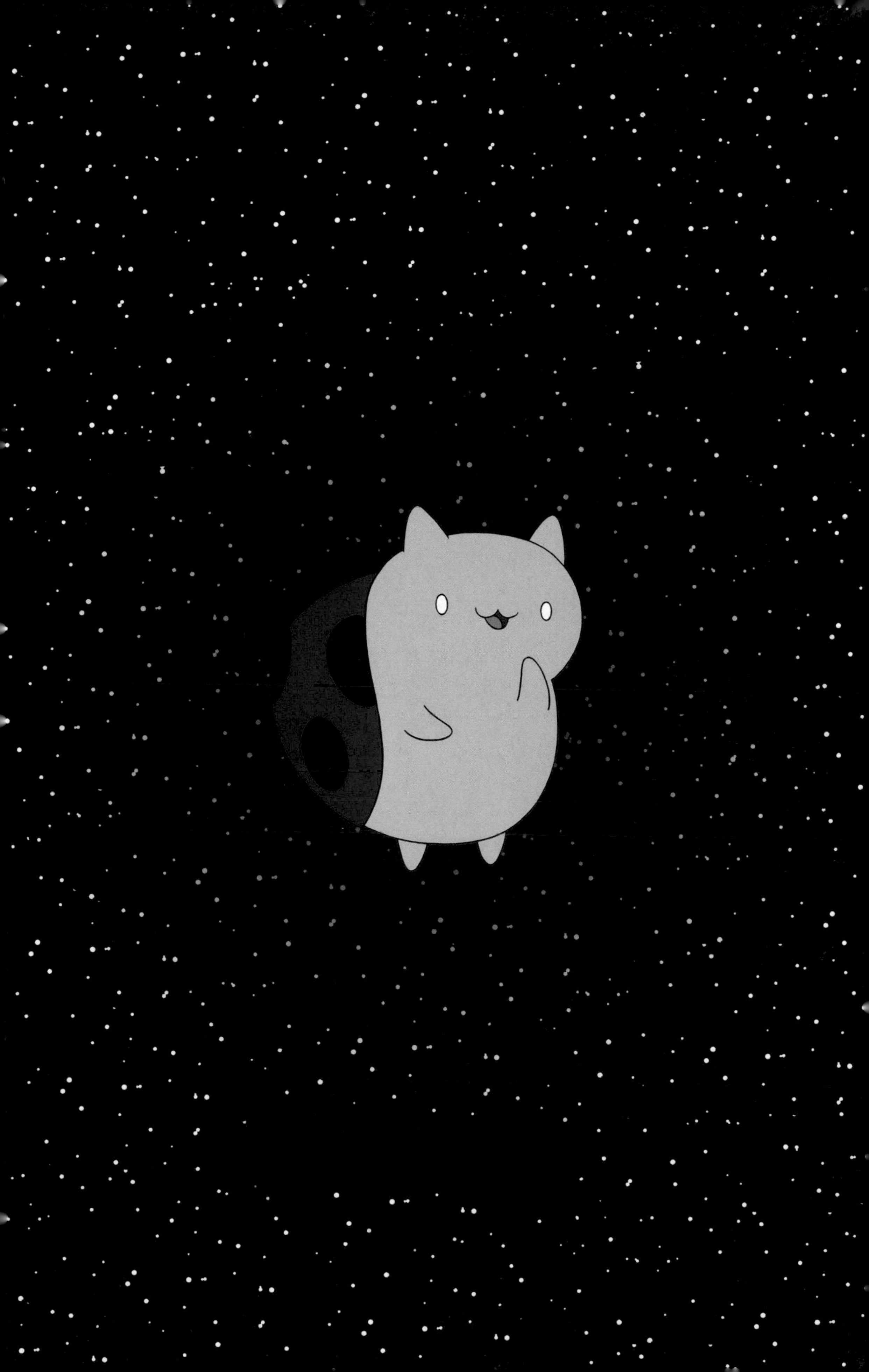

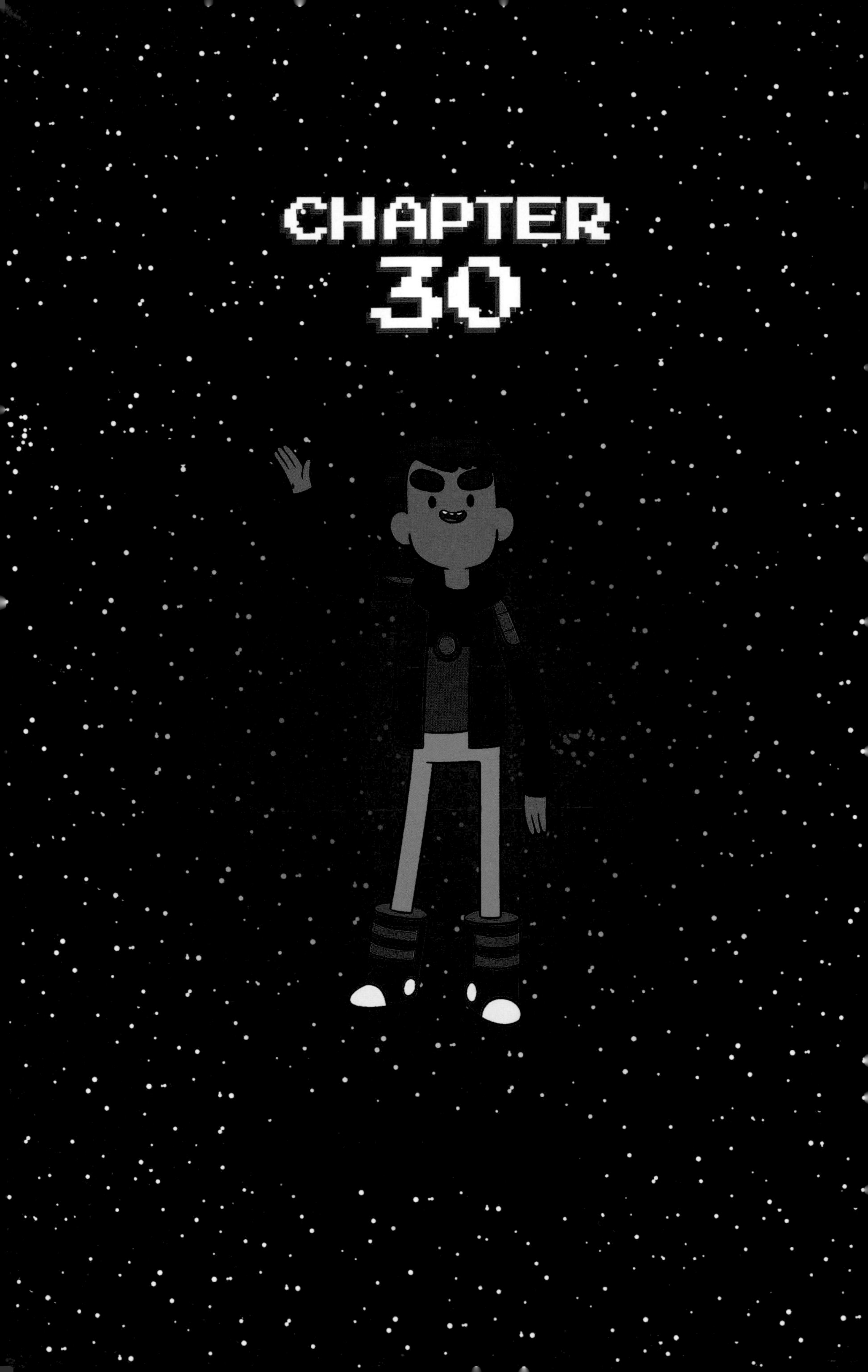
CHAPTER
30

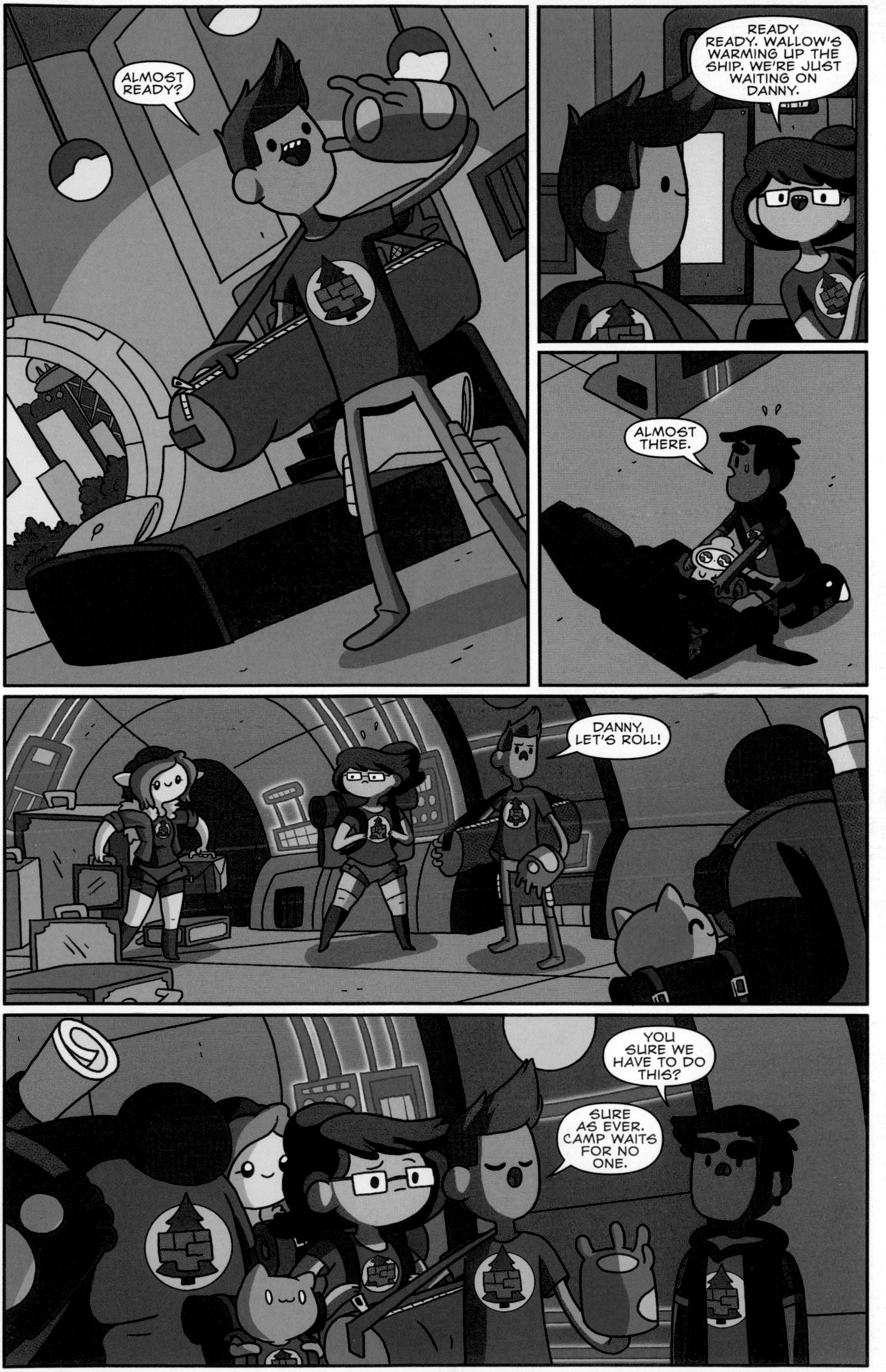
ALMOST READY?
READY READY. WALLOW'S WARMING UP THE SHIP. WE'RE JUST WAITING ON DANNY.
ALMOST THERE.
DANNY, LET'S ROLL!
YOU SURE WE HAVE TO DO THIS?
SURE AS EVER. CAMP WAITS FOR NO ONE.

It's really impatient that way! Hi again, everybody! Caesar Shift, N=13

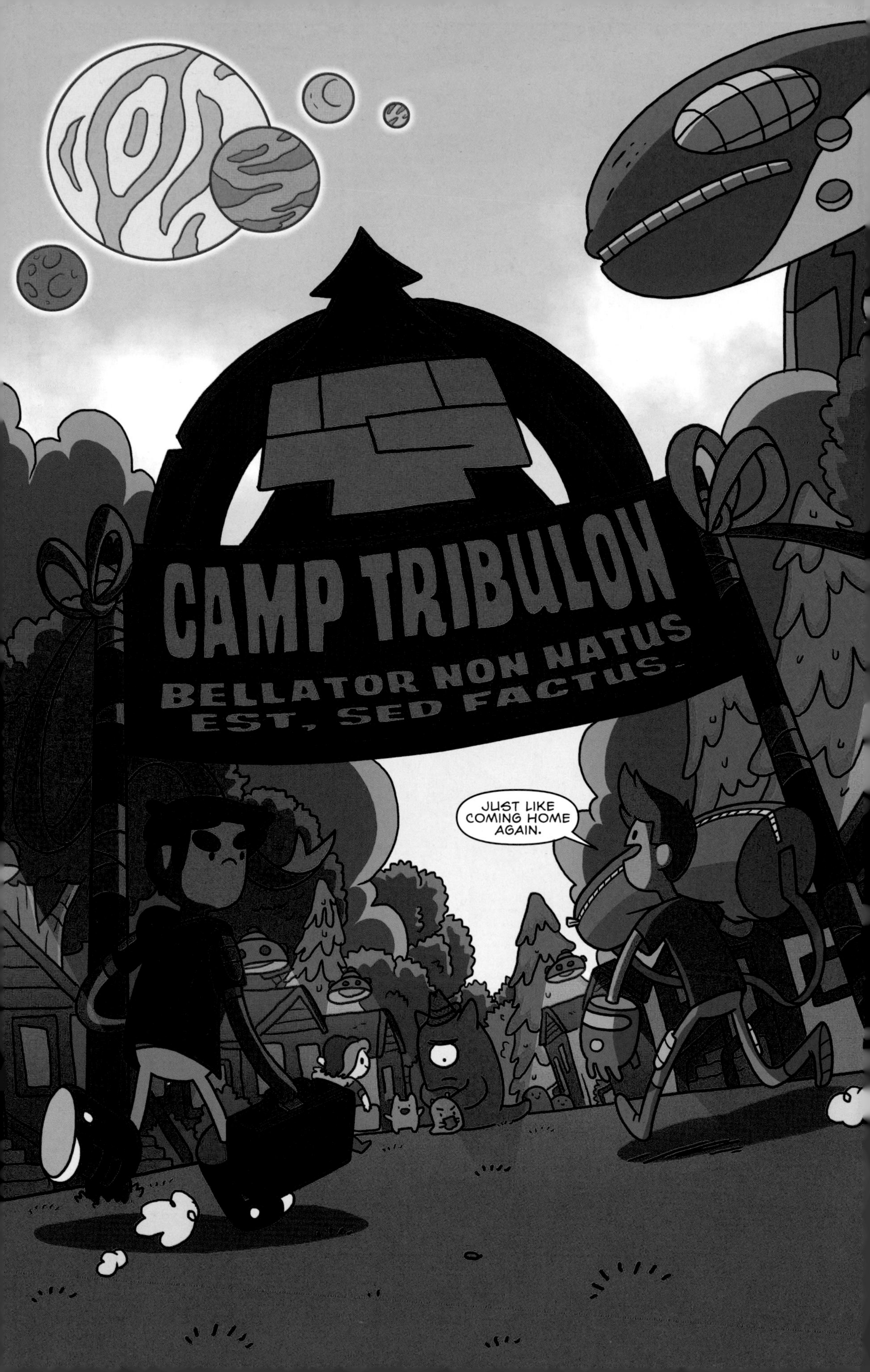
CAMP TRIBULON
BELLATOR NON NATUS EST, SED FACTUS.
JUST LIKE COMING HOME AGAIN.

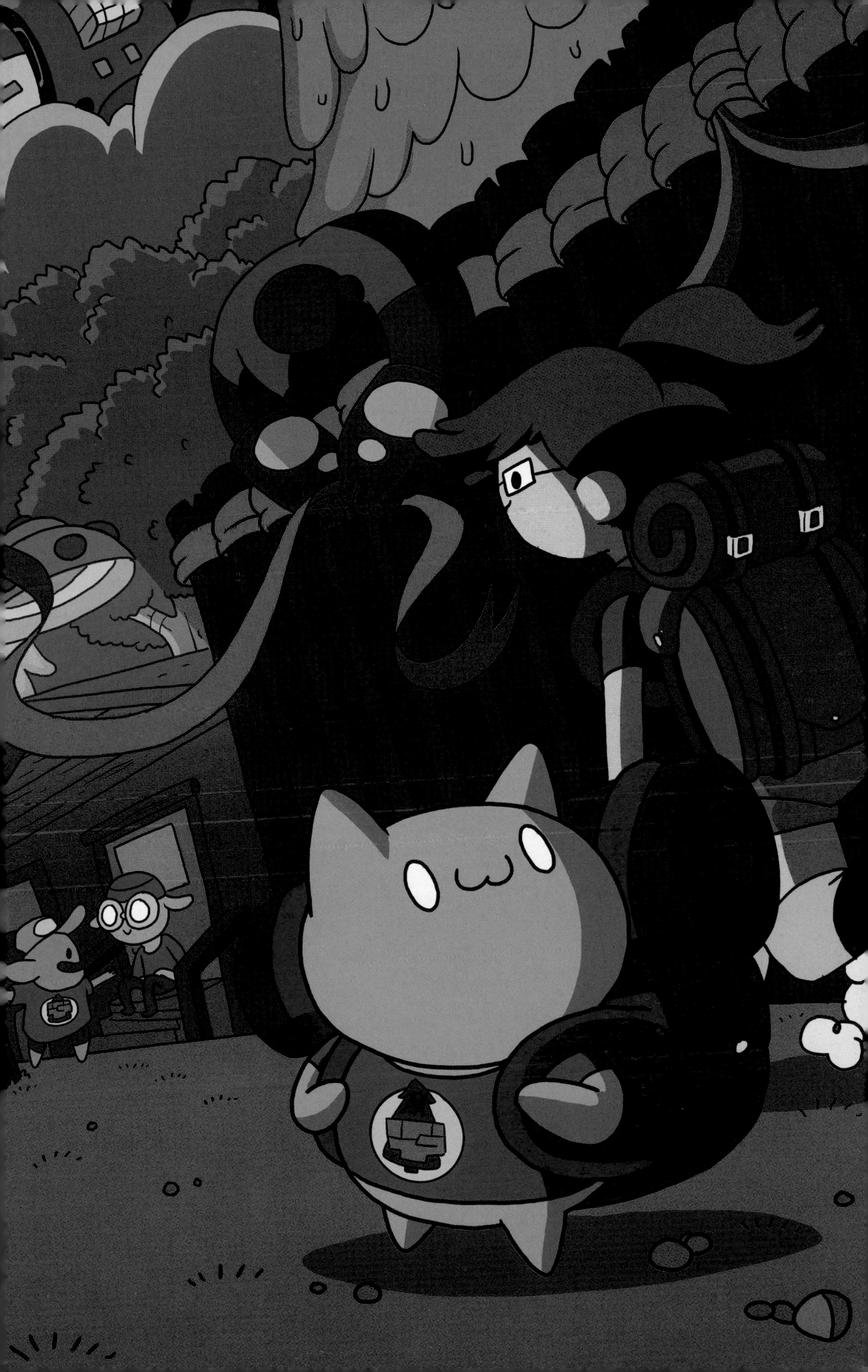

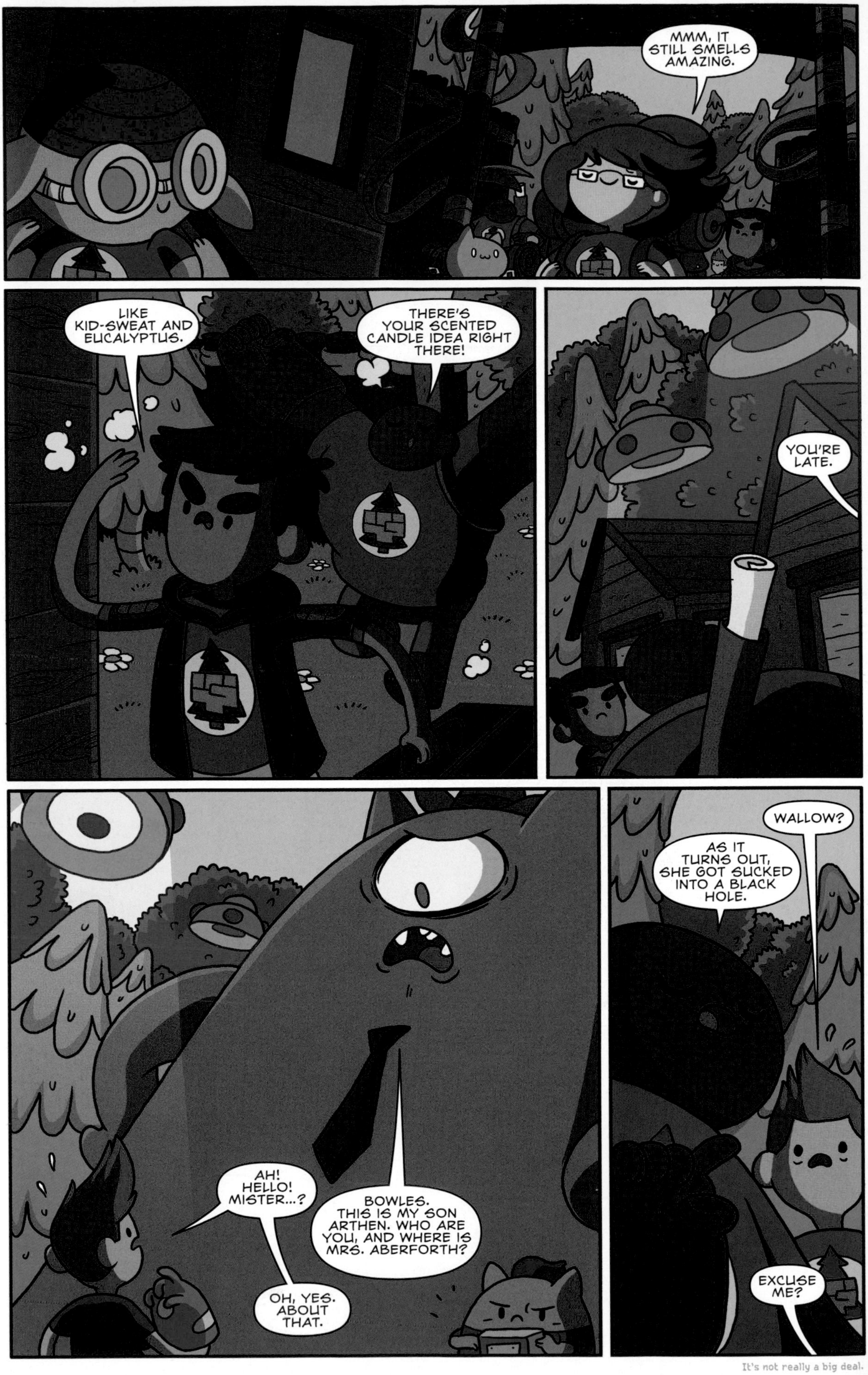
MMM, IT STILL SMELLS AMAZING.
LIKE KID-SWEAT AND EUCALYPTUS.
THERE'S YOUR SCENTED CANDLE IDEA RIGHT THERE!
YOU'RE LATE.
AH! HELLO! MISTER...?
BOWLES. THIS IS MY SON ARTHEN. WHO ARE YOU, AND WHERE IS MRS. ABERFORTH?
OH, YES. ABOUT THAT.
WALLOW?
AS IT TURNS OUT, SHE GOT SUCKED INTO A BLACK HOLE.
EXCUSE ME?

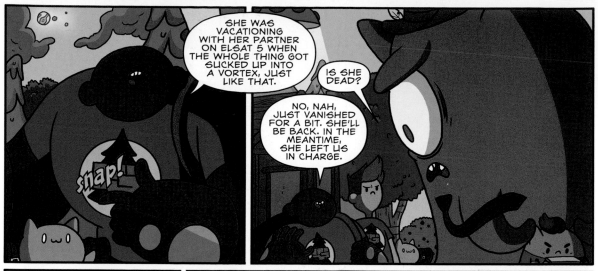

SHE WAS VACATIONING WITH HER PARTNER ON ELSAT 5 WHEN THE WHOLE THING GOT SUCKED UP INTO A VORTEX, JUST LIKE THAT.

IS SHE DEAD?

NO, NAH, JUST VANISHED FOR A BIT. SHE'LL BE BACK. IN THE MEANTIME, SHE LEFT US IN CHARGE.

snap!

AND WHO ARE YOU, EXACTLY?

THE **BRAVEST WARRIORS!**

ALSO, WE WENT TO CAMP HERE WHEN WE WERE KIDS.

MRS. ABERFORTH NAMED US EMERGENCY COUNSELORS, IN CASE OF HER DISAPPEARANCE OR DEATH.

WE SIGNED A BLOOD OATH!

RIGHT, WELL, WORKS FOR ME. HE'S ALLERGIC TO SHELLFISH. SEE YOU IN THREE WEEKS.

WHA--

DON'T FORGET YOUR OINTMENT, SON!

DAD!

For goodness sake, give him his ointment but NO LOBSTERS!

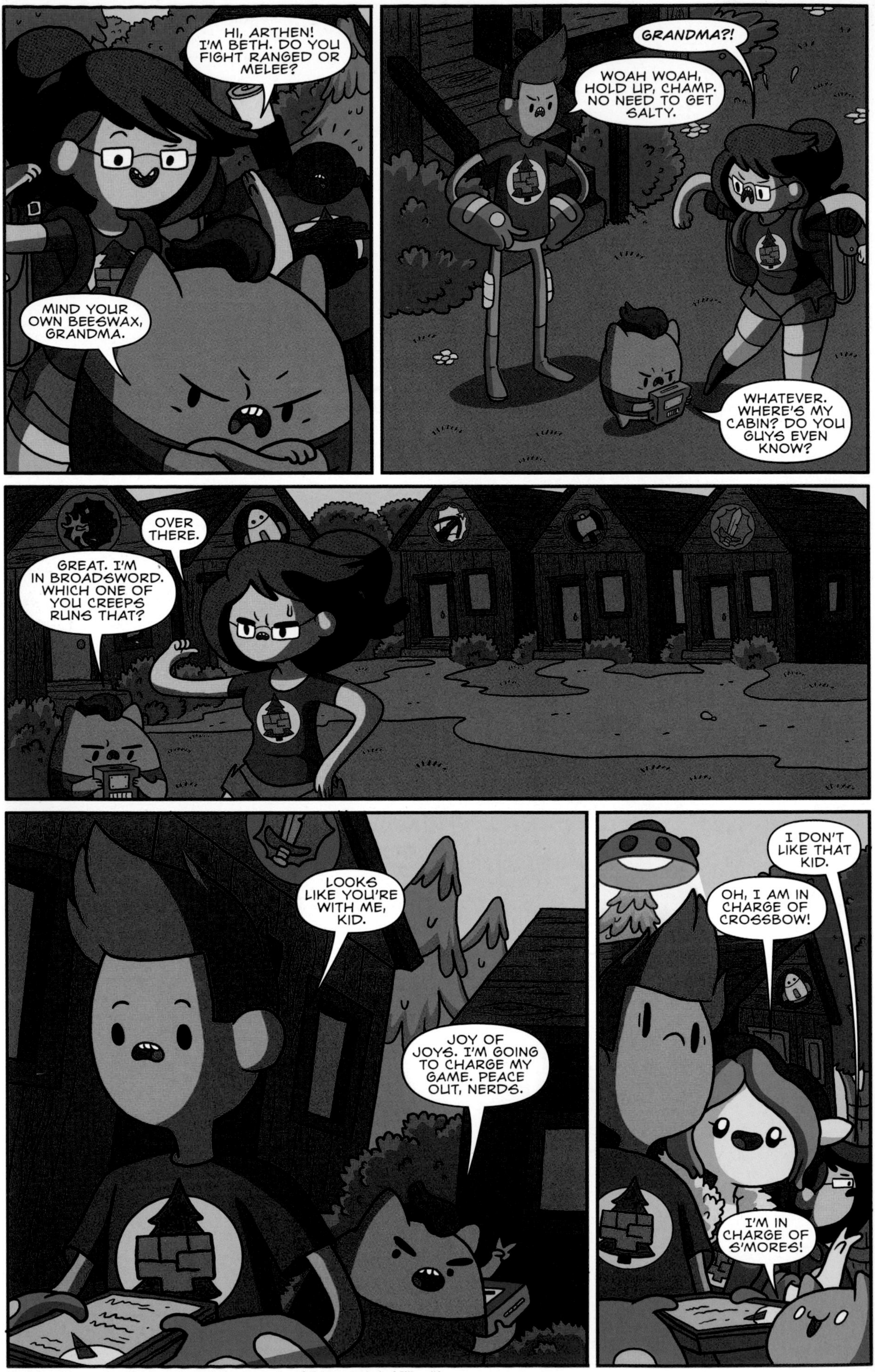
HI, ARTHEN! I'M BETH. DO YOU FIGHT RANGED OR MELEE?
MIND YOUR OWN BEESWAX, GRANDMA.
GRANDMA?!
WOAH WOAH, HOLD UP, CHAMP. NO NEED TO GET SALTY.
WHATEVER. WHERE'S MY CABIN? DO YOU GUYS EVEN KNOW?
OVER THERE.
GREAT. I'M IN BROADSWORD. WHICH ONE OF YOU CREEPS RUNS THAT?
LOOKS LIKE YOU'RE WITH ME, KID.
JOY OF JOYS. I'M GOING TO CHARGE MY GAME. PEACE OUT, NERDS.
I DON'T LIKE THAT KID.
OH, I AM IN CHARGE OF CROSSBOW!
I'M IN CHARGE OF S'MORES!

S'mores are so amazing. When was the last time you had one? Make some today! I'll wait!

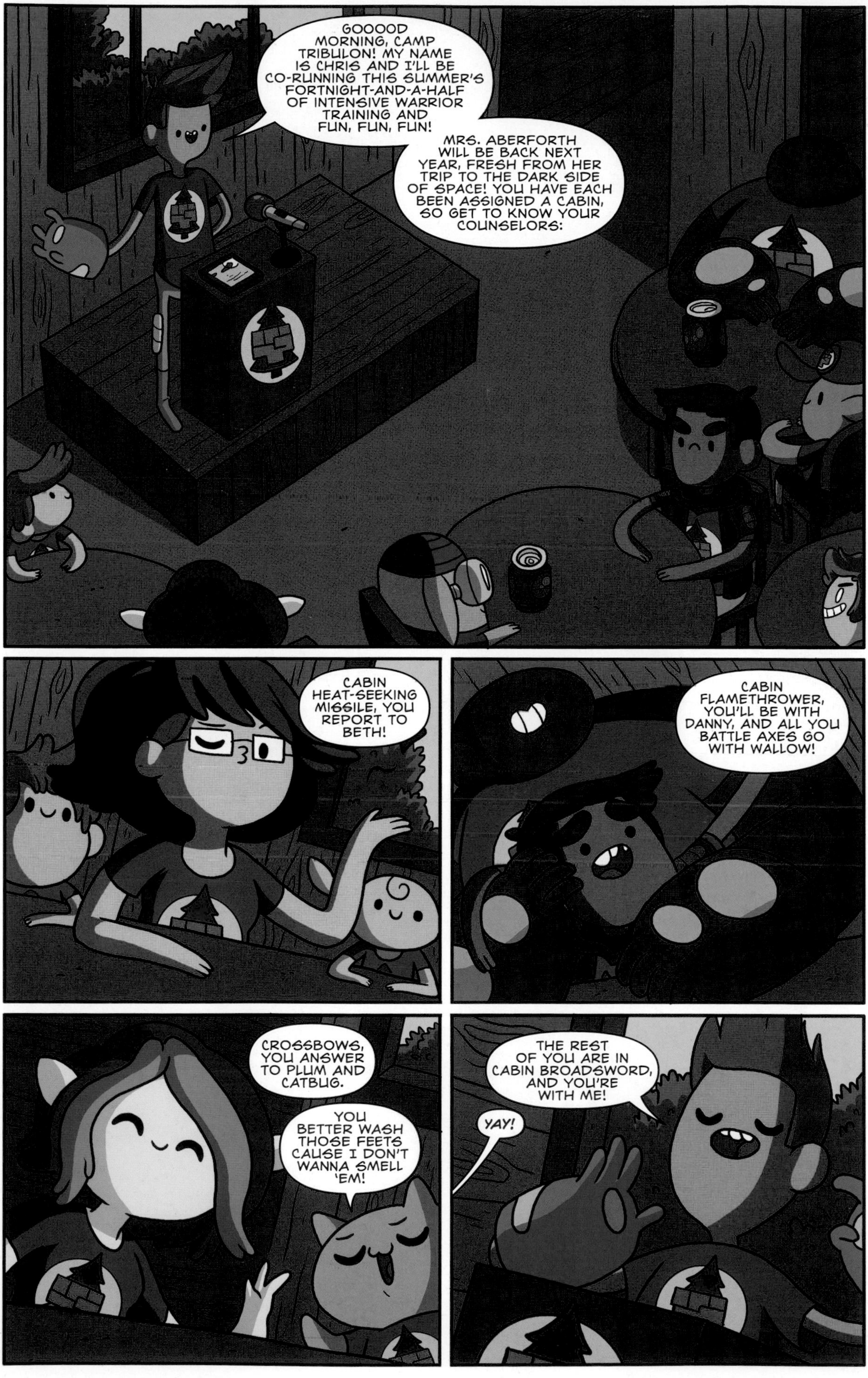
GOOOOD MORNING, CAMP TRIBULON! MY NAME IS CHRIS AND I'LL BE CO-RUNNING THIS SUMMER'S FORTNIGHT-AND-A-HALF OF INTENSIVE WARRIOR TRAINING AND FUN, FUN, FUN!
MRS. ABERFORTH WILL BE BACK NEXT YEAR, FRESH FROM HER TRIP TO THE DARK SIDE OF SPACE! YOU HAVE EACH BEEN ASSIGNED A CABIN, SO GET TO KNOW YOUR COUNSELORS:
CABIN HEAT-SEEKING MISSILE, YOU REPORT TO BETH!
CABIN FLAMETHROWER, YOU'LL BE WITH DANNY, AND ALL YOU BATTLE AXES GO WITH WALLOW!
CROSSBOWS, YOU ANSWER TO PLUM AND CATBUG.
YOU BETTER WASH THOSE FEETS CAUSE I DON'T WANNA SMELL 'EM!
THE REST OF YOU ARE IN CABIN BROADSWORD, AND YOU'RE WITH ME!
YAY!

Did you get those s'mores? Man oh man, wasn't I right?

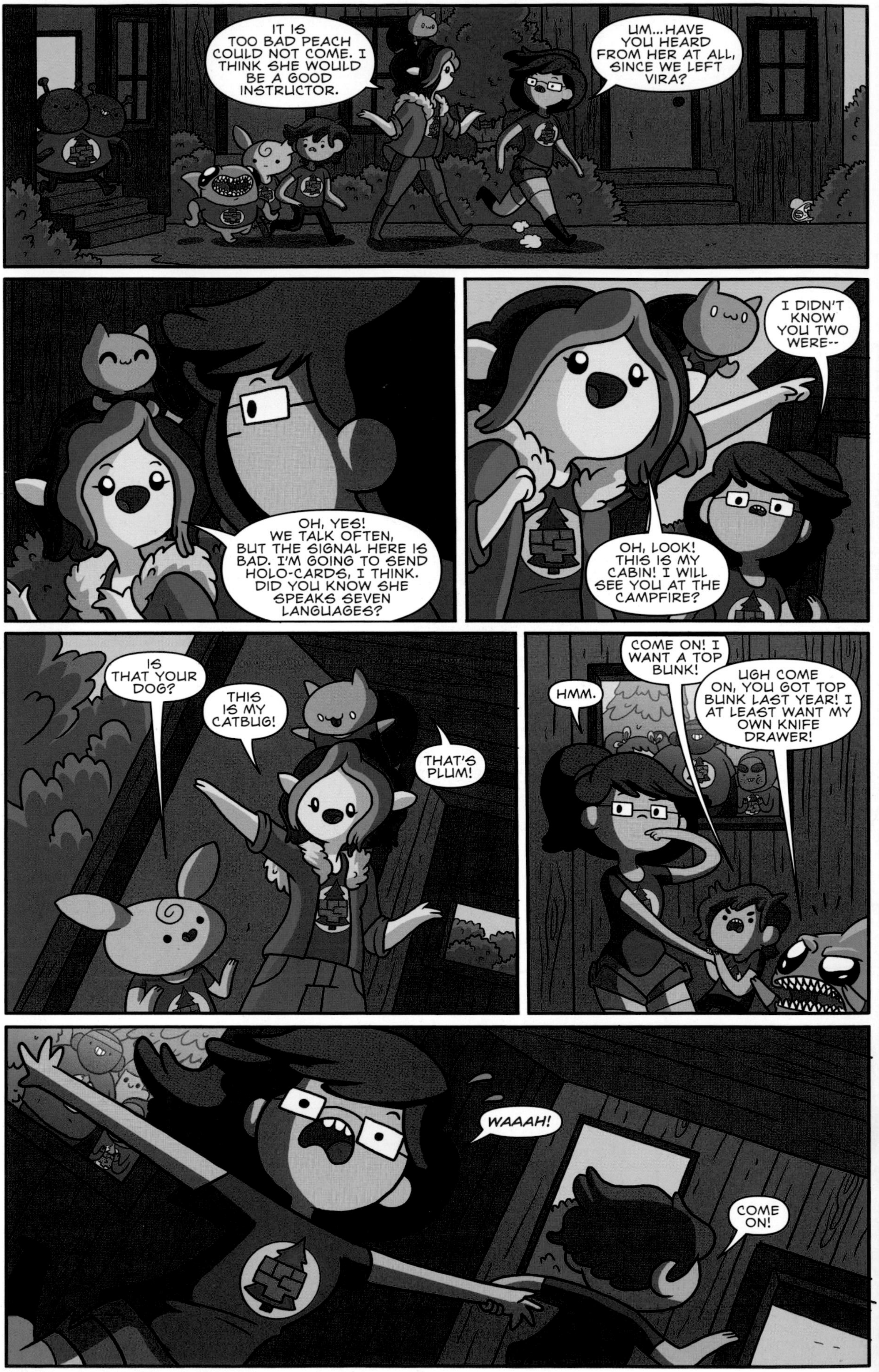
IT IS TOO BAD PEACH COULD NOT COME. I THINK SHE WOULD BE A GOOD INSTRUCTOR.
UM...HAVE YOU HEARD FROM HER AT ALL, SINCE WE LEFT VIRA?
OH, YES! WE TALK OFTEN, BUT THE SIGNAL HERE IS BAD. I'M GOING TO SEND HOLO-CARDS, I THINK. DID YOU KNOW SHE SPEAKS SEVEN LANGUAGES?
I DIDN'T KNOW YOU TWO WERE--
OH, LOOK! THIS IS MY CABIN! I WILL SEE YOU AT THE CAMPFIRE?
IS THAT YOUR DOG?
THIS IS MY CATBUG!
THAT'S PLUM!
HMM.
COME ON! I WANT A TOP BUNK!
UGH COME ON, YOU GOT TOP BUNK LAST YEAR! I AT LEAST WANT MY OWN KNIFE DRAWER!
WAAAH!
COME ON!

She's also very good at Scrabble and making omelets.

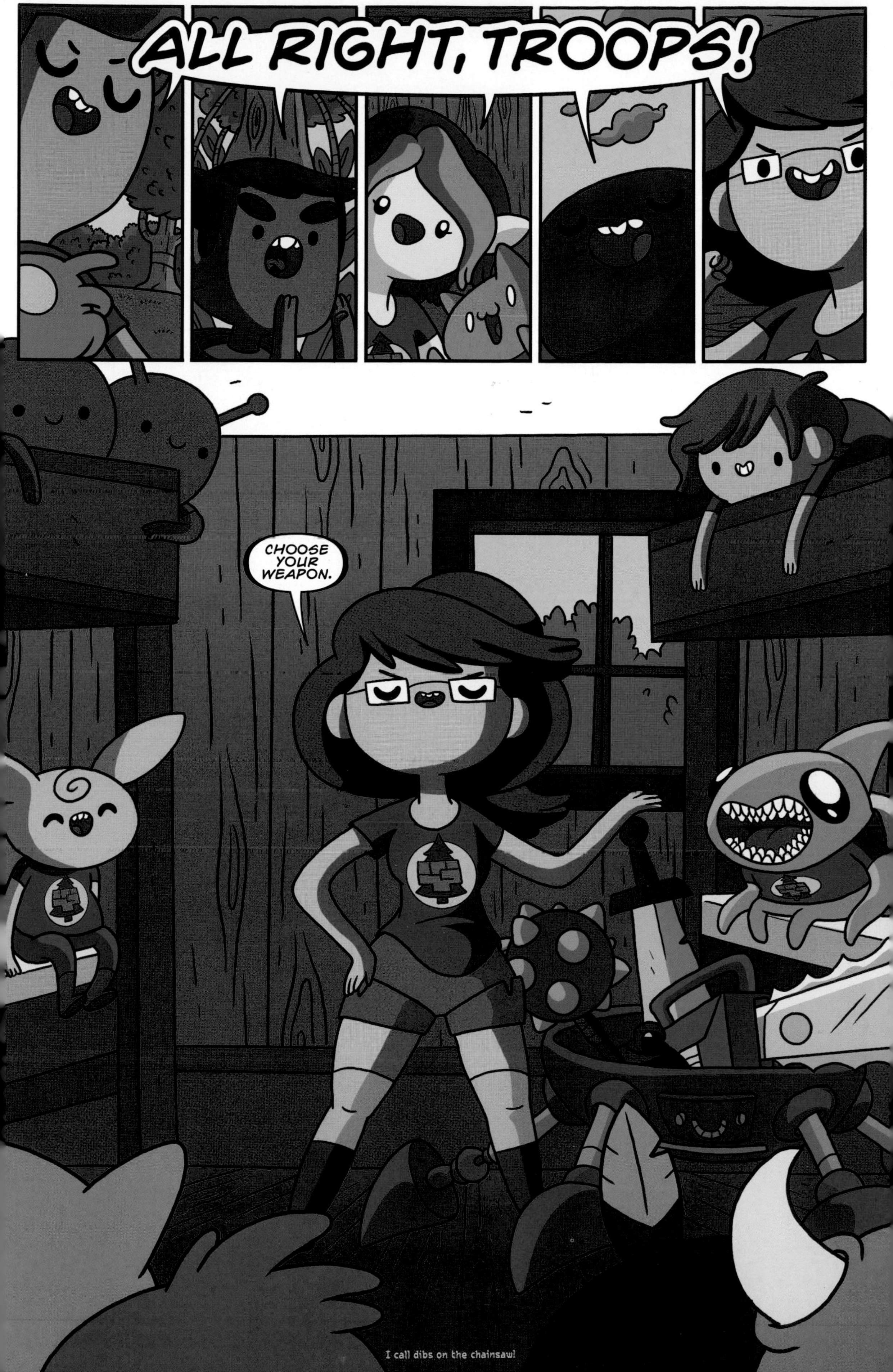
ALL RIGHT, TROOPS!
CHOOSE YOUR WEAPON.

I call dibs on the chainsaw!

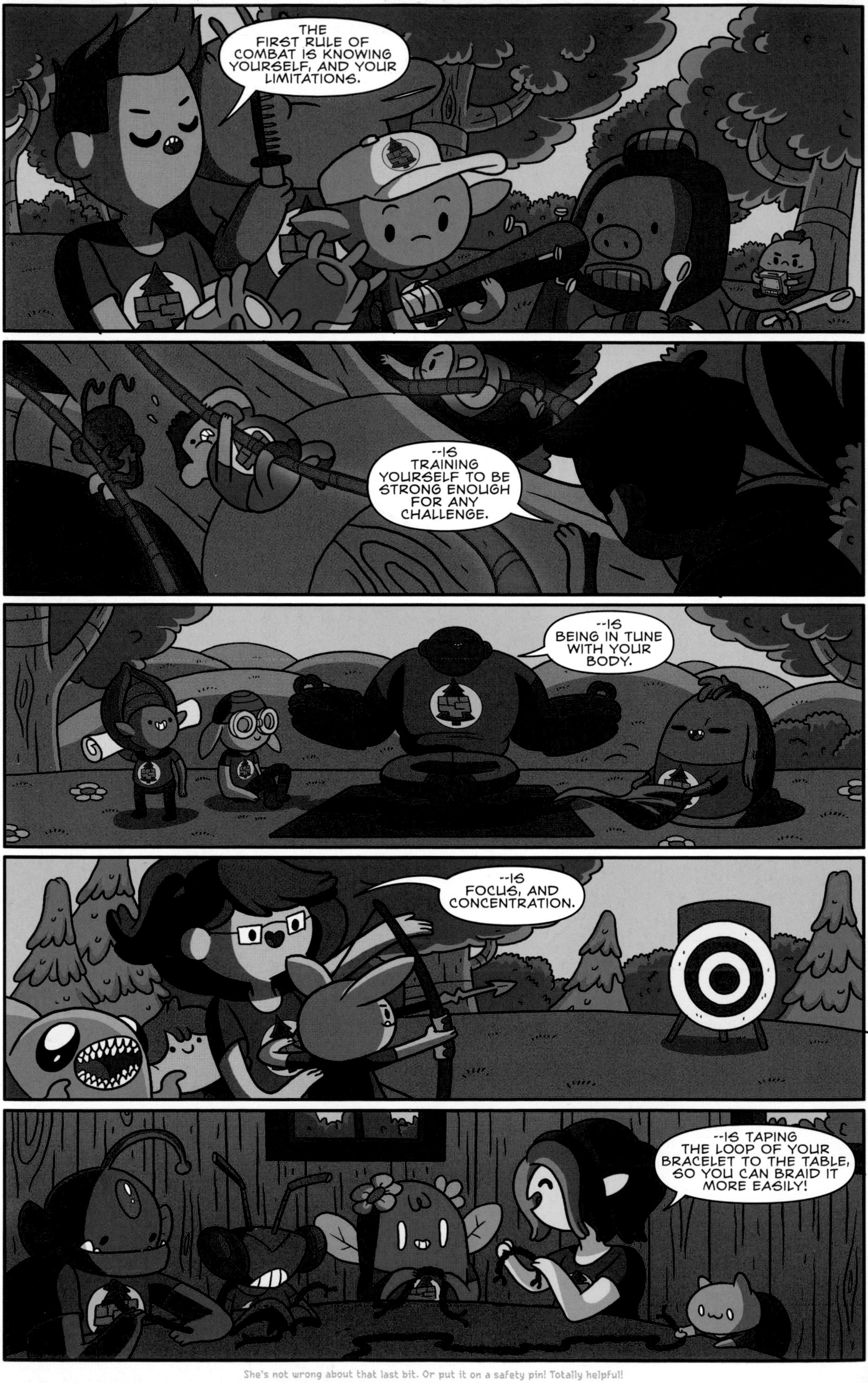
THE FIRST RULE OF COMBAT IS KNOWING YOURSELF, AND YOUR LIMITATIONS.
--IS TRAINING YOURSELF TO BE STRONG ENOUGH FOR ANY CHALLENGE.
--IS BEING IN TUNE WITH YOUR BODY.
--IS FOCUS, AND CONCENTRATION.
--IS TAPING THE LOOP OF YOUR BRACELET TO THE TABLE, SO YOU CAN BRAID IT MORE EASILY!

She's not wrong about that last bit. Or put it on a safety pin! Totally helpful!

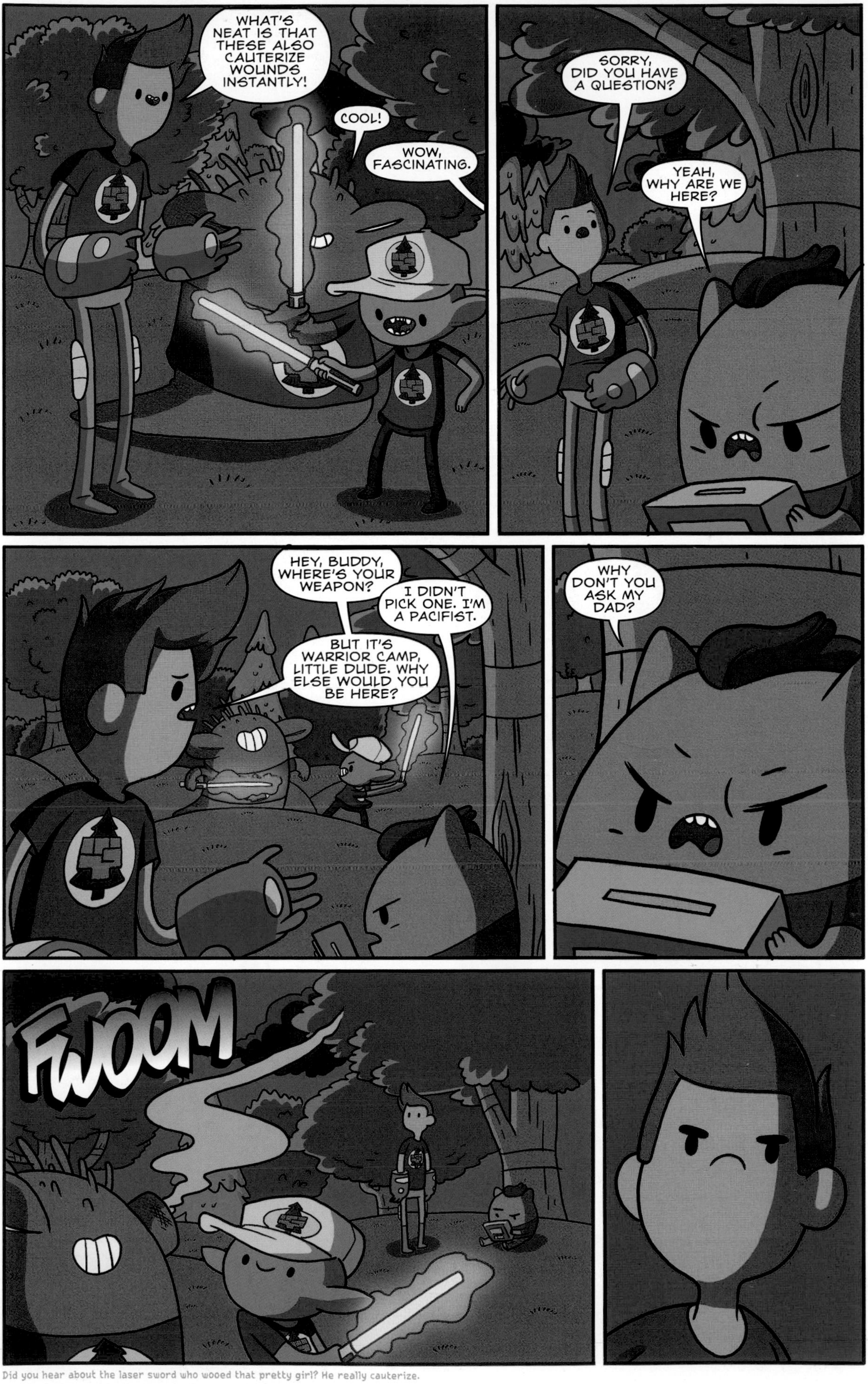
WHAT'S NEAT IS THAT THESE ALSO CAUTERIZE WOUNDS INSTANTLY!
COOL!
WOW, FASCINATING.
SORRY, DID YOU HAVE A QUESTION?
YEAH, WHY ARE WE HERE?
HEY, BUDDY, WHERE'S YOUR WEAPON?
I DIDN'T PICK ONE. I'M A PACIFIST.
BUT IT'S WARRIOR CAMP, LITTLE DUDE. WHY ELSE WOULD YOU BE HERE?
WHY DON'T YOU ASK MY DAD?
FWOOM

Did you hear about the laser sword who wooed that pretty girl? He really cauterize.

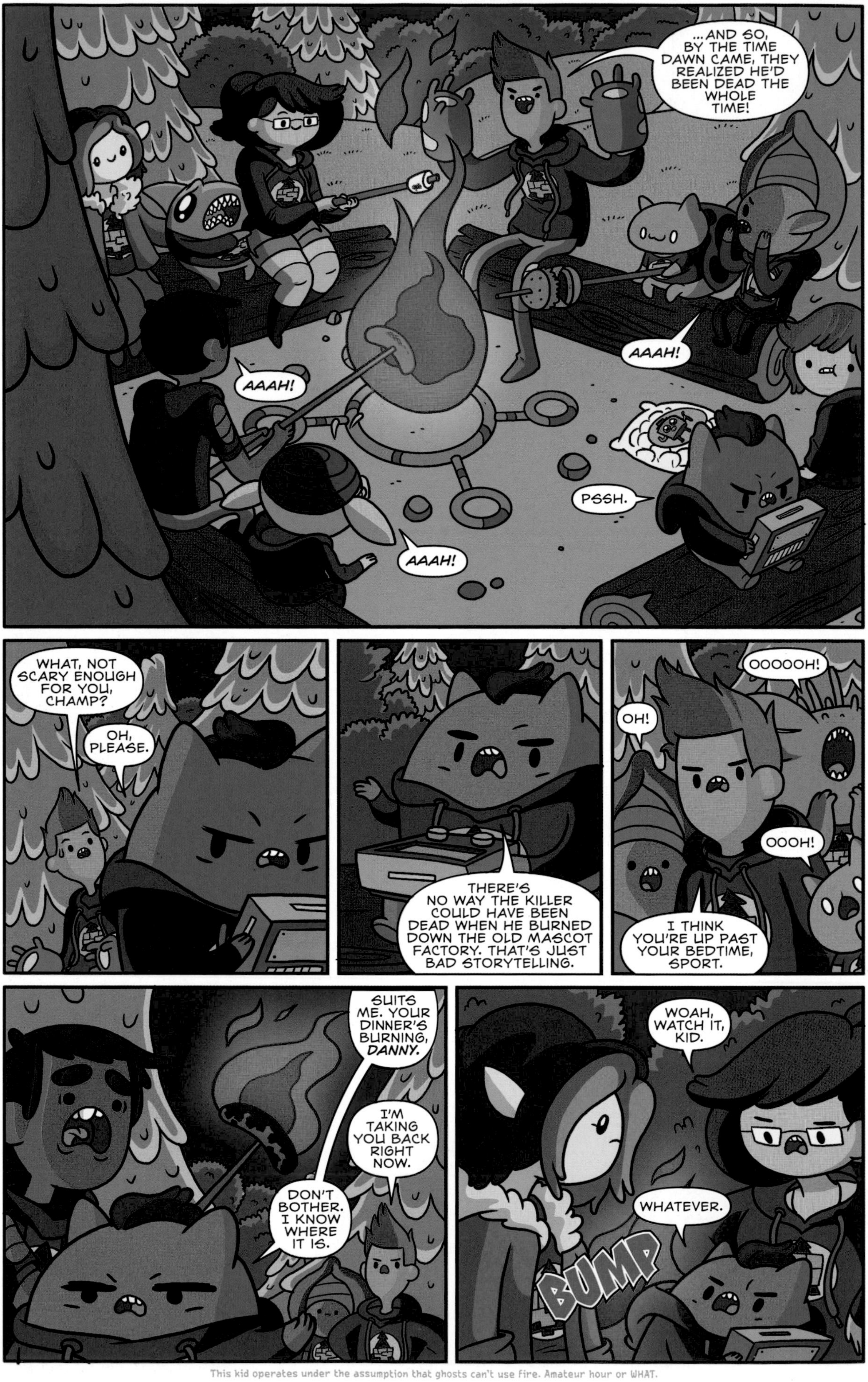
...AND SO, BY THE TIME DAWN CAME, THEY REALIZED HE'D BEEN DEAD THE WHOLE TIME!
AAAH!
AAAH!
AAAH!
PSSH.
WHAT, NOT SCARY ENOUGH FOR YOU, CHAMP?
OH, PLEASE.
THERE'S NO WAY THE KILLER COULD HAVE BEEN DEAD WHEN HE BURNED DOWN THE OLD MASCOT FACTORY. THAT'S JUST BAD STORYTELLING.
OOOOOH!
OH!
OOOH!
I THINK YOU'RE UP PAST YOUR BEDTIME, SPORT.
SUITS ME. YOUR DINNER'S BURNING, DANNY.
I'M TAKING YOU BACK RIGHT NOW.
DON'T BOTHER. I KNOW WHERE IT IS.
WOAH, WATCH IT, KID.
WHATEVER.
BUMP

This kid operates under the assumption that ghosts can't use fire. Amateur hour or WHAT.

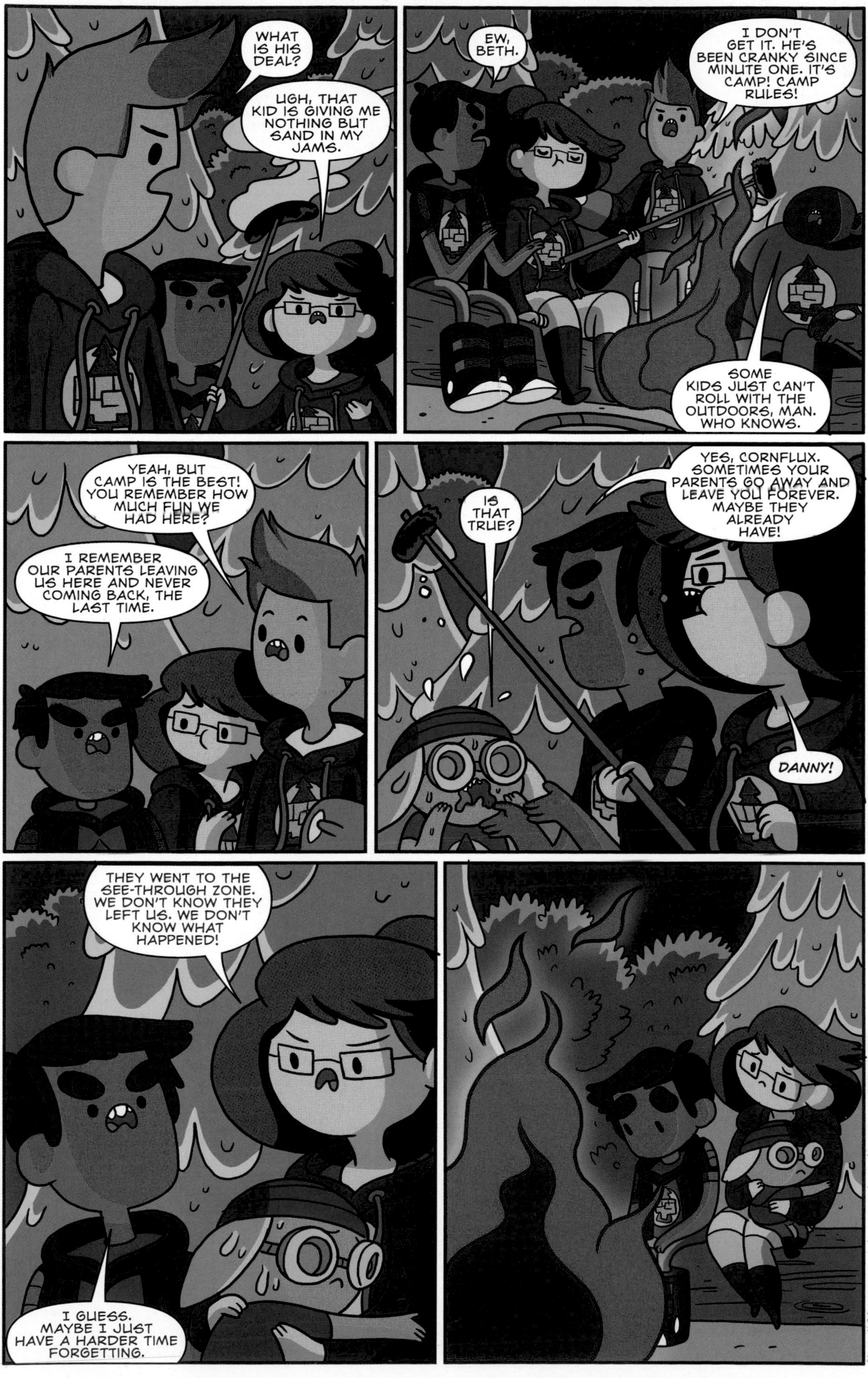
WHAT IS HIS DEAL?
UGH, THAT KID IS GIVING ME NOTHING BUT SAND IN MY JAMS.
EW, BETH.
I DON'T GET IT. HE'S BEEN CRANKY SINCE MINUTE ONE. IT'S CAMP! CAMP RULES!
SOME KIDS JUST CAN'T ROLL WITH THE OUTDOORS, MAN. WHO KNOWS.
YEAH, BUT CAMP IS THE BEST! YOU REMEMBER HOW MUCH FUN WE HAD HERE?
I REMEMBER OUR PARENTS LEAVING US HERE AND NEVER COMING BACK, THE LAST TIME.
IS THAT TRUE?
YES, CORNFLUX. SOMETIMES YOUR PARENTS GO AWAY AND LEAVE YOU FOREVER. MAYBE THEY ALREADY HAVE!
DANNY!
THEY WENT TO THE SEE-THROUGH ZONE. WE DON'T KNOW THEY LEFT US. WE DON'T KNOW WHAT HAPPENED!
I GUESS. MAYBE I JUST HAVE A HARDER TIME FORGETTING.

Oh gosh I hope you saved me some s'mores!

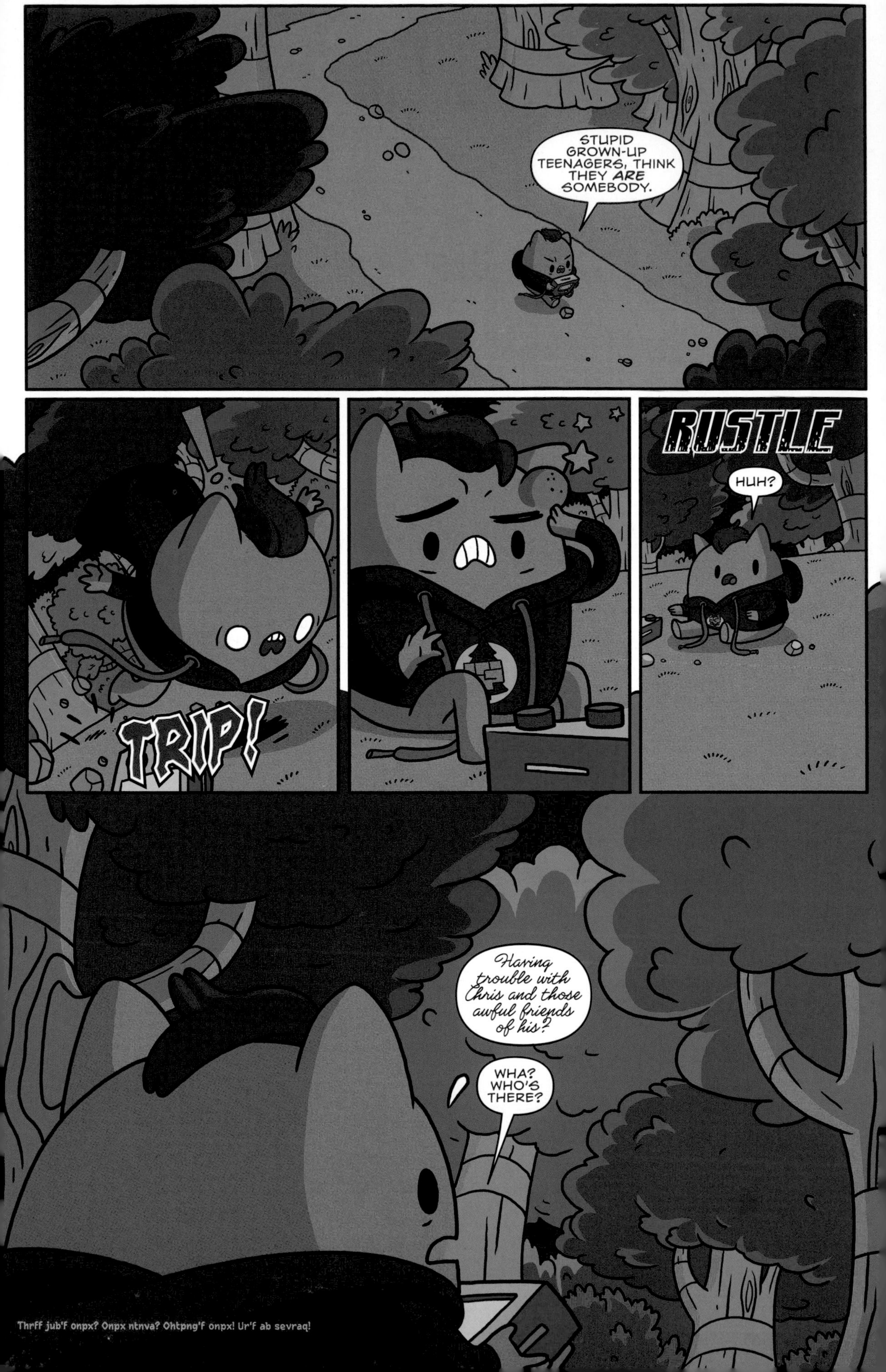
STUPID GROWN-UP TEENAGERS, THINK THEY ARE SOMEBODY.
TRIP!
RUSTLE
HUH?
Having trouble with Chris and those awful friends of his?
WHA? WHO'S THERE?

Thrff jub'f onpx? Onpx ntnva? Ohtpng'f onpx! Ur'f ab sevraq!

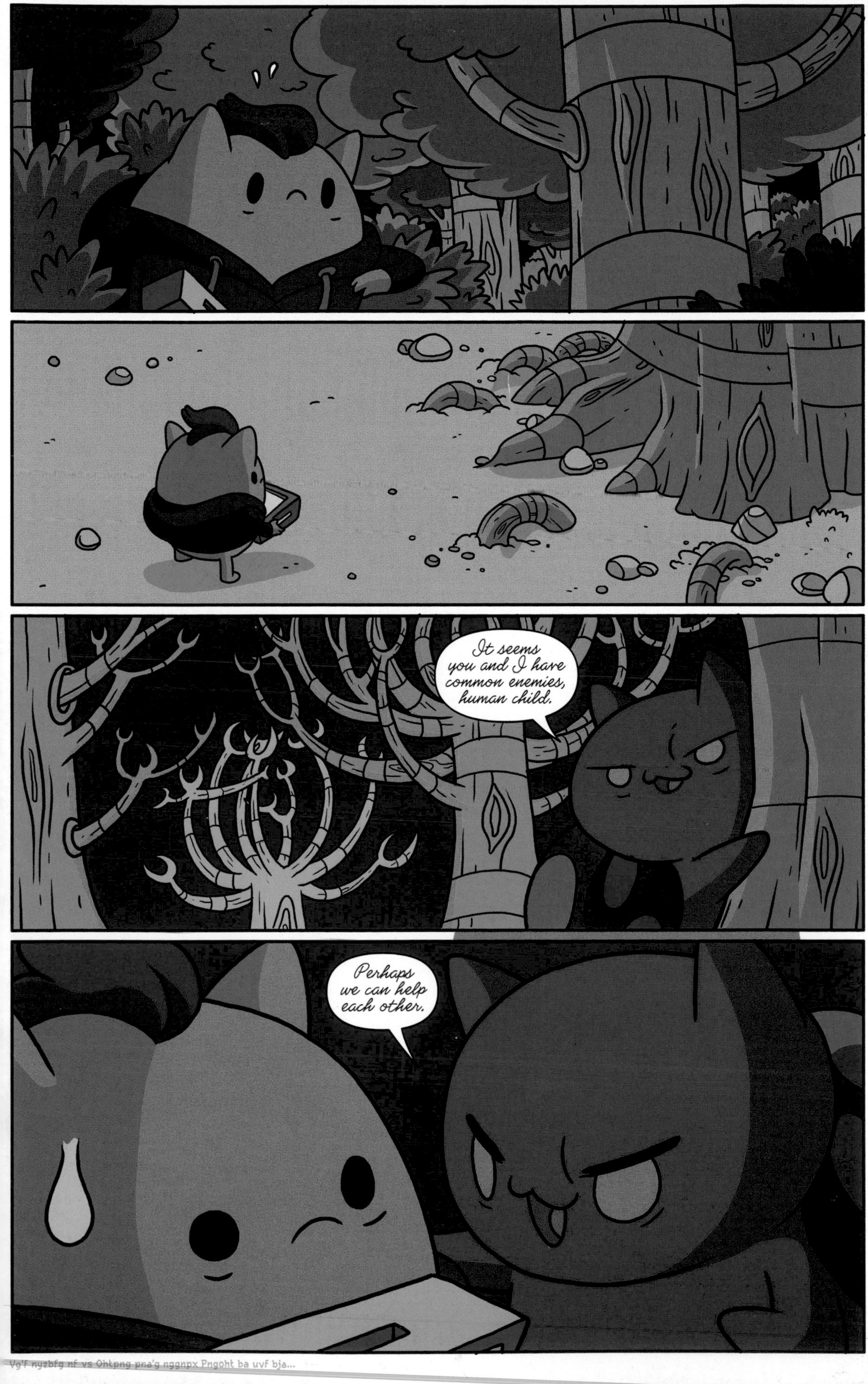
It seems you and I have common enemies, human child.
Perhaps we can help each other.

Vg'F nyzbfg nf vs Ohtpng pna'g nggnpx Pngoht ba uvf bja...

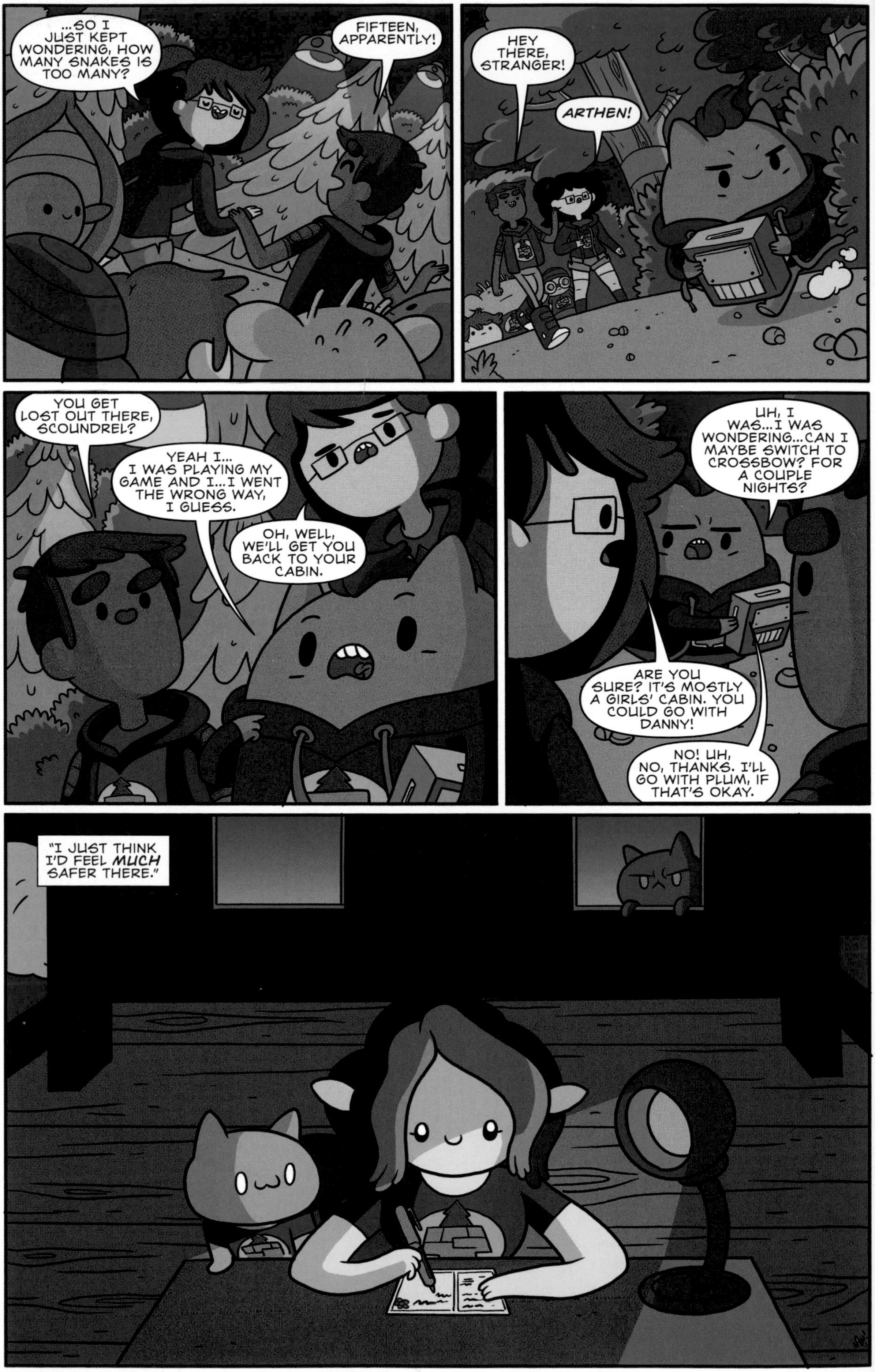
...SO I JUST KEPT WONDERING, HOW MANY SNAKES IS TOO MANY?
FIFTEEN, APPARENTLY!
HEY THERE, STRANGER!
ARTHEN!
YOU GET LOST OUT THERE, SCOUNDREL?
YEAH I... I WAS PLAYING MY GAME AND I...I WENT THE WRONG WAY, I GUESS.
OH, WELL, WE'LL GET YOU BACK TO YOUR CABIN.
UH, I WAS...I WAS WONDERING...CAN I MAYBE SWITCH TO CROSSBOW? FOR A COUPLE NIGHTS?
ARE YOU SURE? IT'S MOSTLY A GIRLS' CABIN. YOU COULD GO WITH DANNY!
NO! UH, NO, THANKS. I'LL GO WITH PLUM, IF THAT'S OKAY.
"I JUST THINK I'D FEEL MUCH SAFER THERE."

Negura ovgrf bss zber guna ur pna purj, naq pnzc'f nobhg gb trg zrffl!

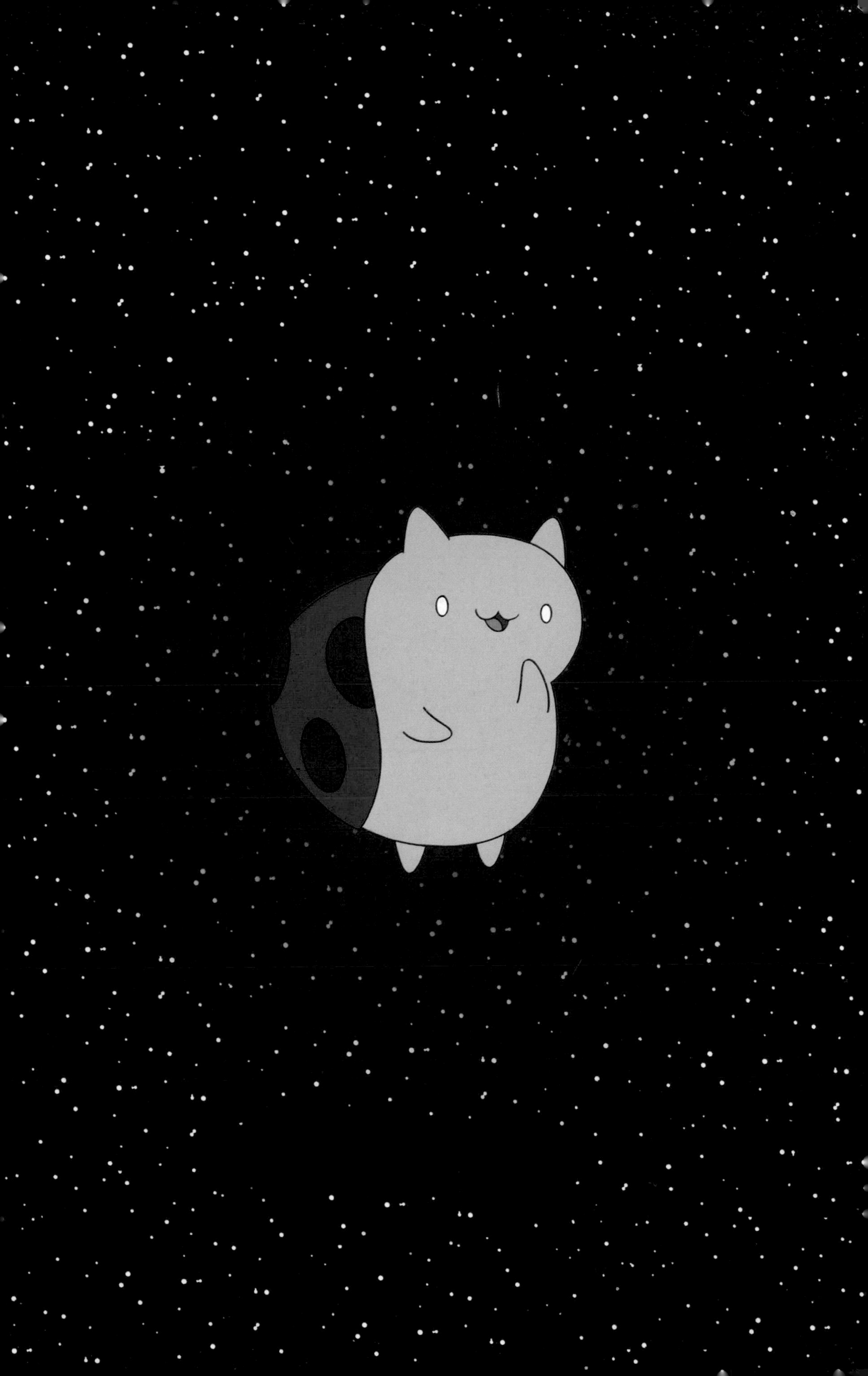

CHAPTER
31

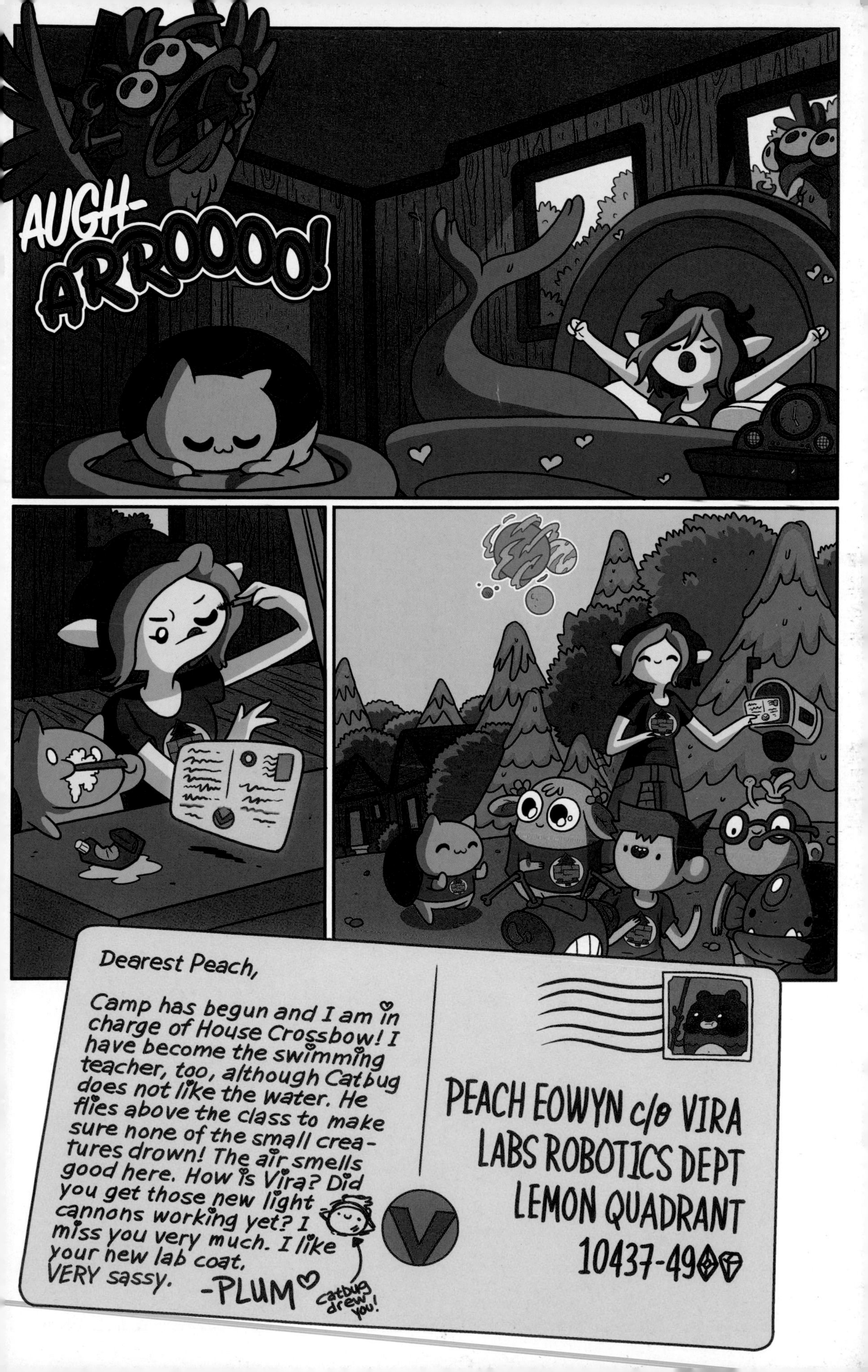
AUGH-ARROOOO!
Dearest Peach,
Camp has begun and I am in charge of House Crossbow! I have become the swimming teacher, too, although Catbug does not like the water. He flies above the class to make sure none of the small creatures drown! The air smells good here. How is Vira? Did you get those new light cannons working yet? I miss you very much. I like your new lab coat. VERY sassy.
-PLUM
catbug drew you!
PEACH EOWYN c/o VIRA
LABS ROBOTICS DEPT
LEMON QUADRANT
10437-49

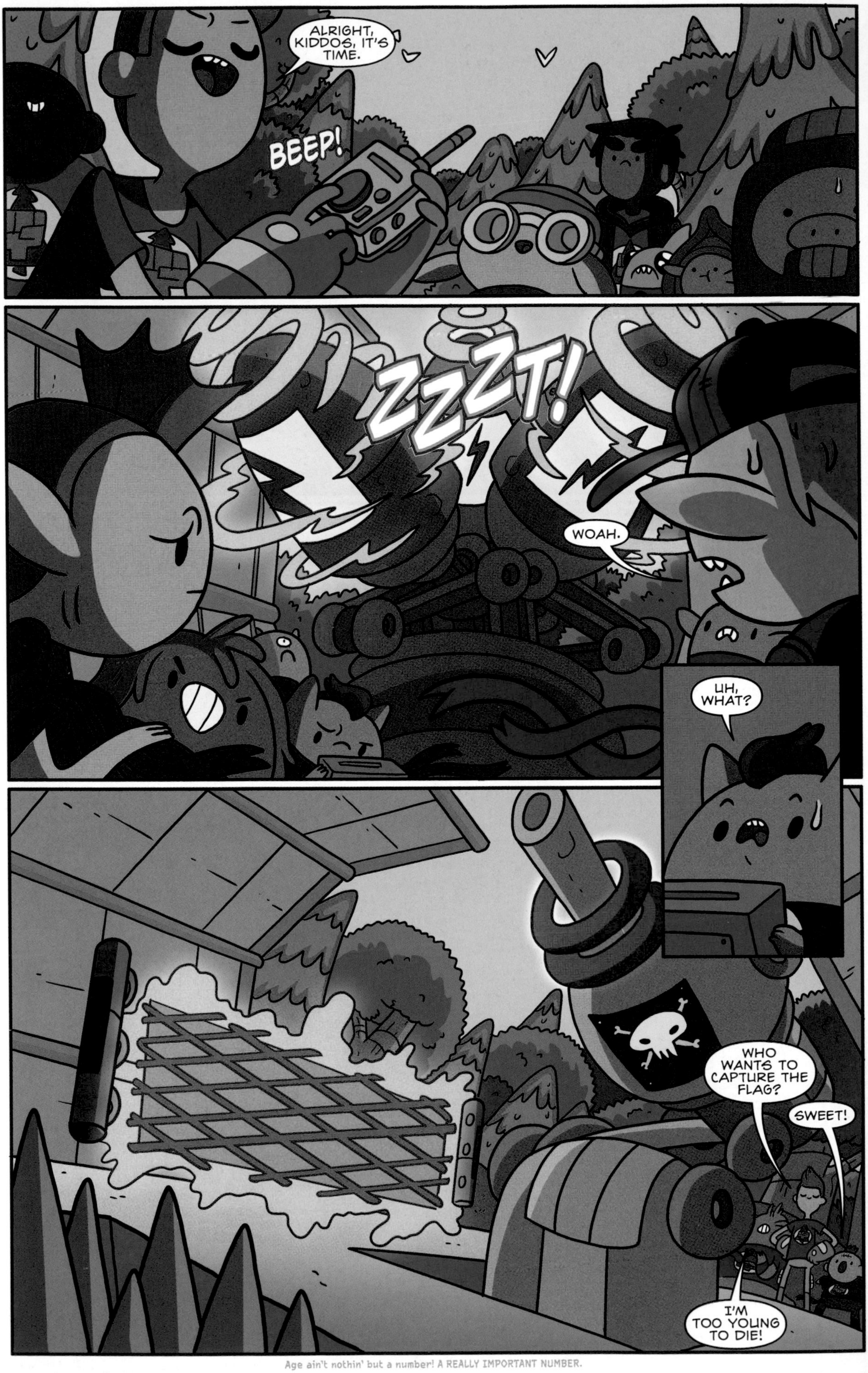
ALRIGHT, KIDDOS, IT'S TIME.
BEEP!
ZZZZT!
WOAH.
UH, WHAT?
WHO WANTS TO CAPTURE THE FLAG?
SWEET!
I'M TOO YOUNG TO DIE!

Age ain't nothin' but a number! A REALLY IMPORTANT NUMBER.

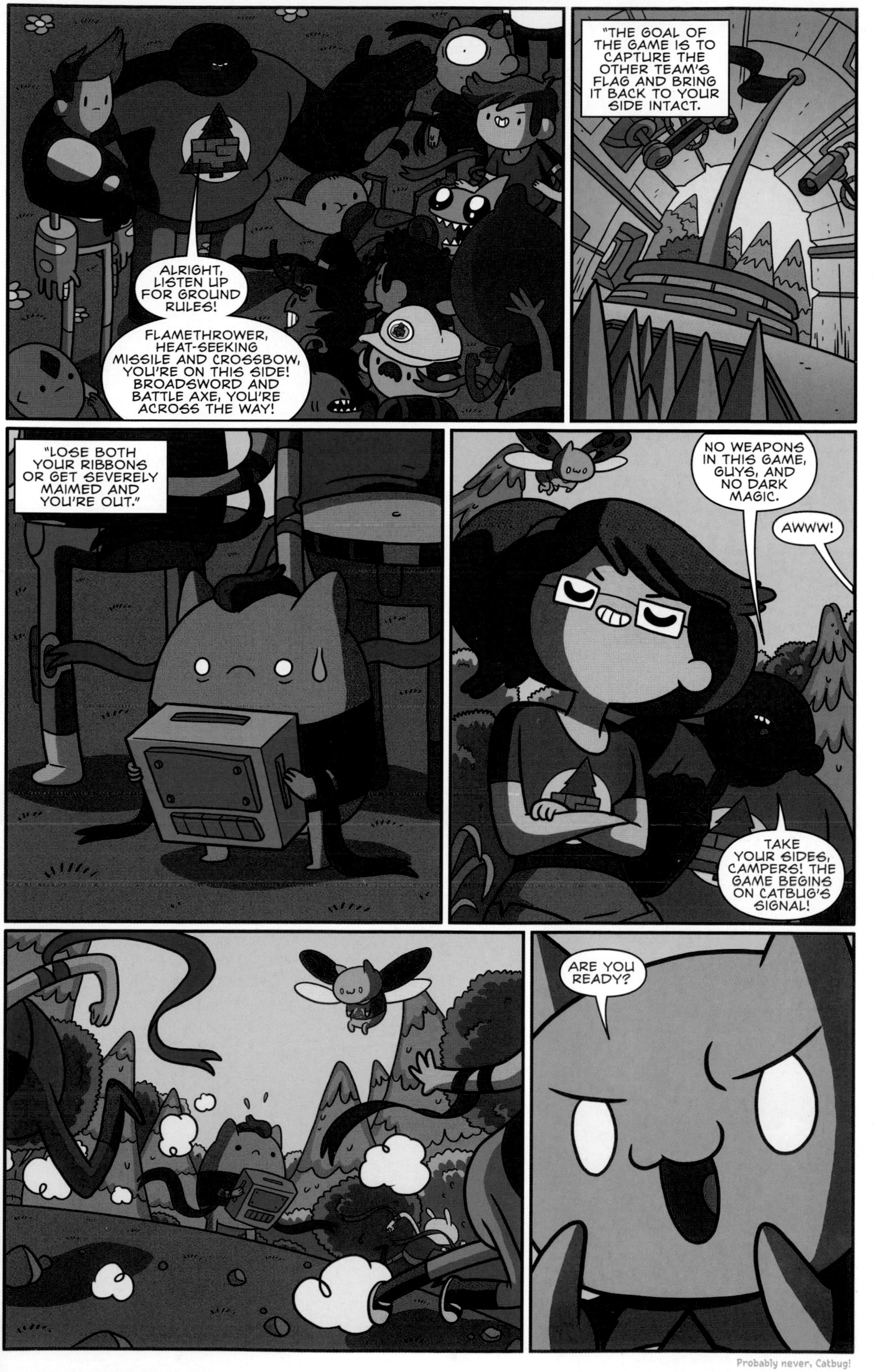
ALRIGHT, LISTEN UP FOR GROUND RULES!
FLAMETHROWER, HEAT-SEEKING MISSILE AND CROSSBOW, YOU'RE ON THIS SIDE! BROADSWORD AND BATTLE AXE, YOU'RE ACROSS THE WAY!
"THE GOAL OF THE GAME IS TO CAPTURE THE OTHER TEAM'S FLAG AND BRING IT BACK TO YOUR SIDE INTACT.
"LOSE BOTH YOUR RIBBONS OR GET SEVERELY MAIMED AND YOU'RE OUT."
NO WEAPONS IN THIS GAME, GUYS, AND NO DARK MAGIC.
AWWW!
TAKE YOUR SIDES, CAMPERS! THE GAME BEGINS ON CATBUG'S SIGNAL!
ARE YOU READY?

Probably never, Catbug!

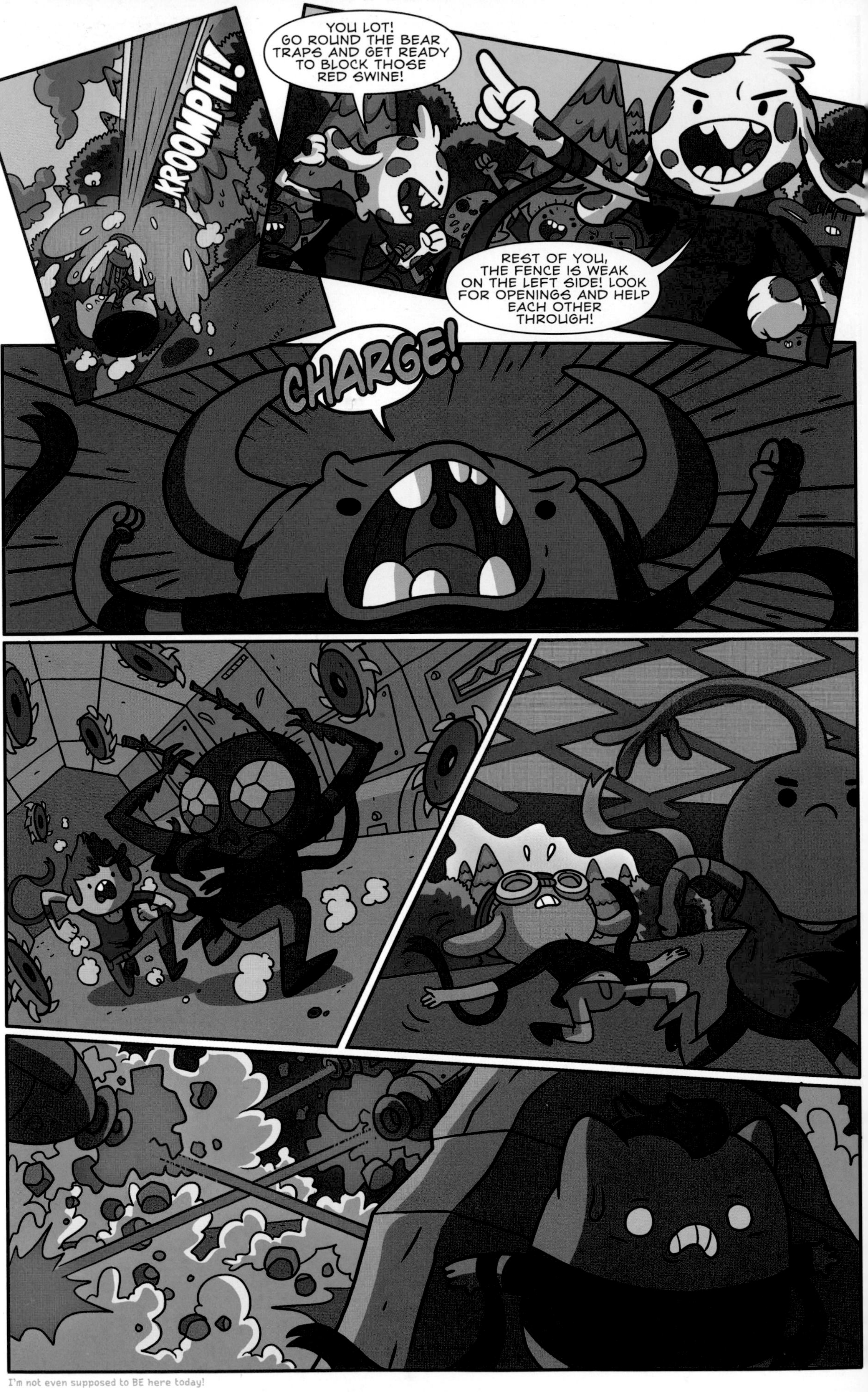
KROOMPH!
YOU LOT! GO ROUND THE BEAR TRAPS AND GET READY TO BLOCK THOSE RED SWINE!
REST OF YOU, THE FENCE IS WEAK ON THE LEFT SIDE! LOOK FOR OPENINGS AND HELP EACH OTHER THROUGH!
CHARGE!

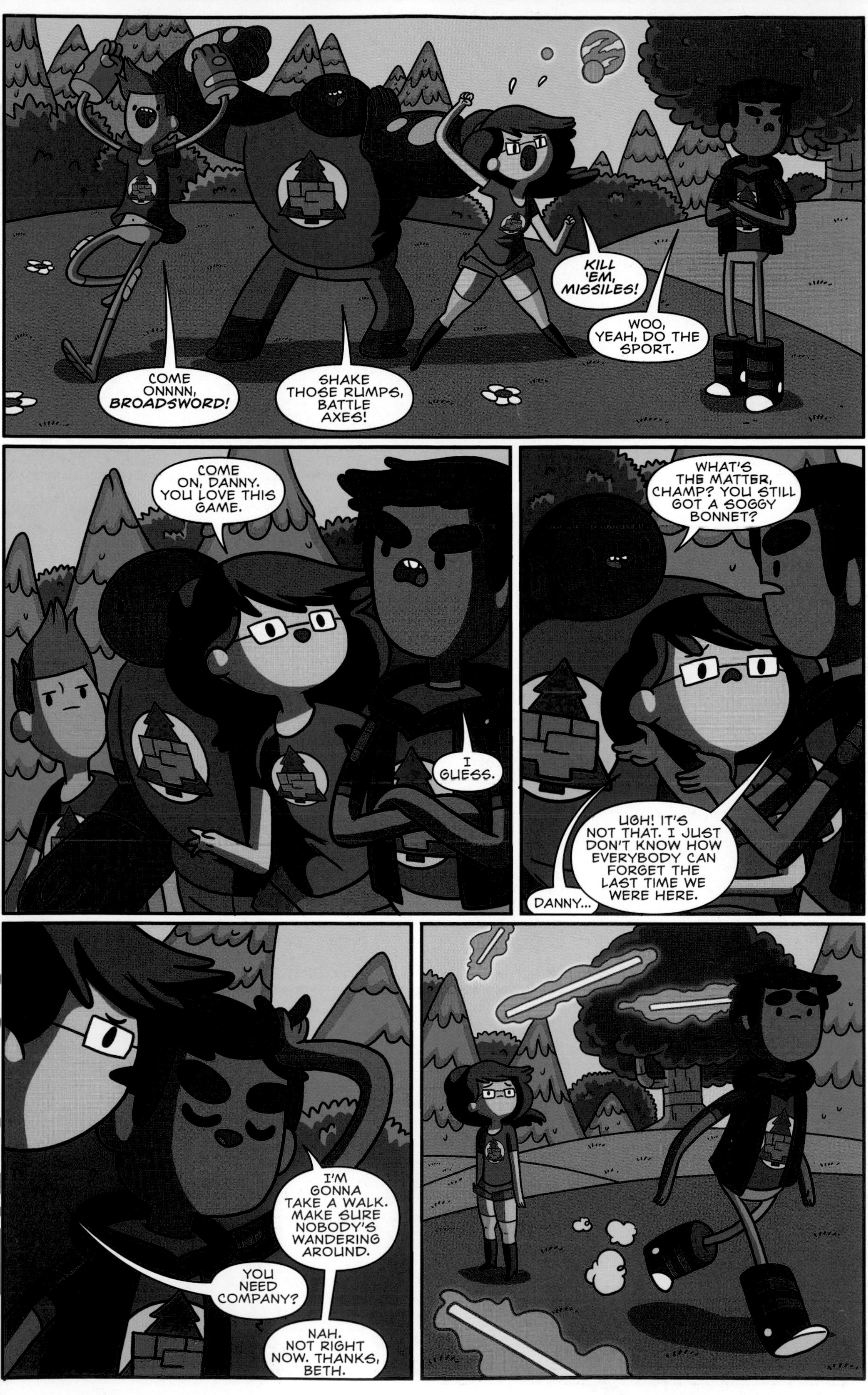
COME ONNNN, BROADSWORD!
SHAKE THOSE RUMPS, BATTLE AXES!
KILL 'EM, MISSILES!
WOO, YEAH, DO THE SPORT.
COME ON, DANNY. YOU LOVE THIS GAME.
I GUESS.
WHAT'S THE MATTER, CHAMP? YOU STILL GOT A SOGGY BONNET?
DANNY...
UGH! IT'S NOT THAT. I JUST DON'T KNOW HOW EVERYBODY CAN FORGET THE LAST TIME WE WERE HERE.
I'M GONNA TAKE A WALK. MAKE SURE NOBODY'S WANDERING AROUND.
YOU NEED COMPANY?
NAH. NOT RIGHT NOW. THANKS, BETH.

It's crazy that the chemicals in our brain make us sad! A cool mutant power would be to never cry.

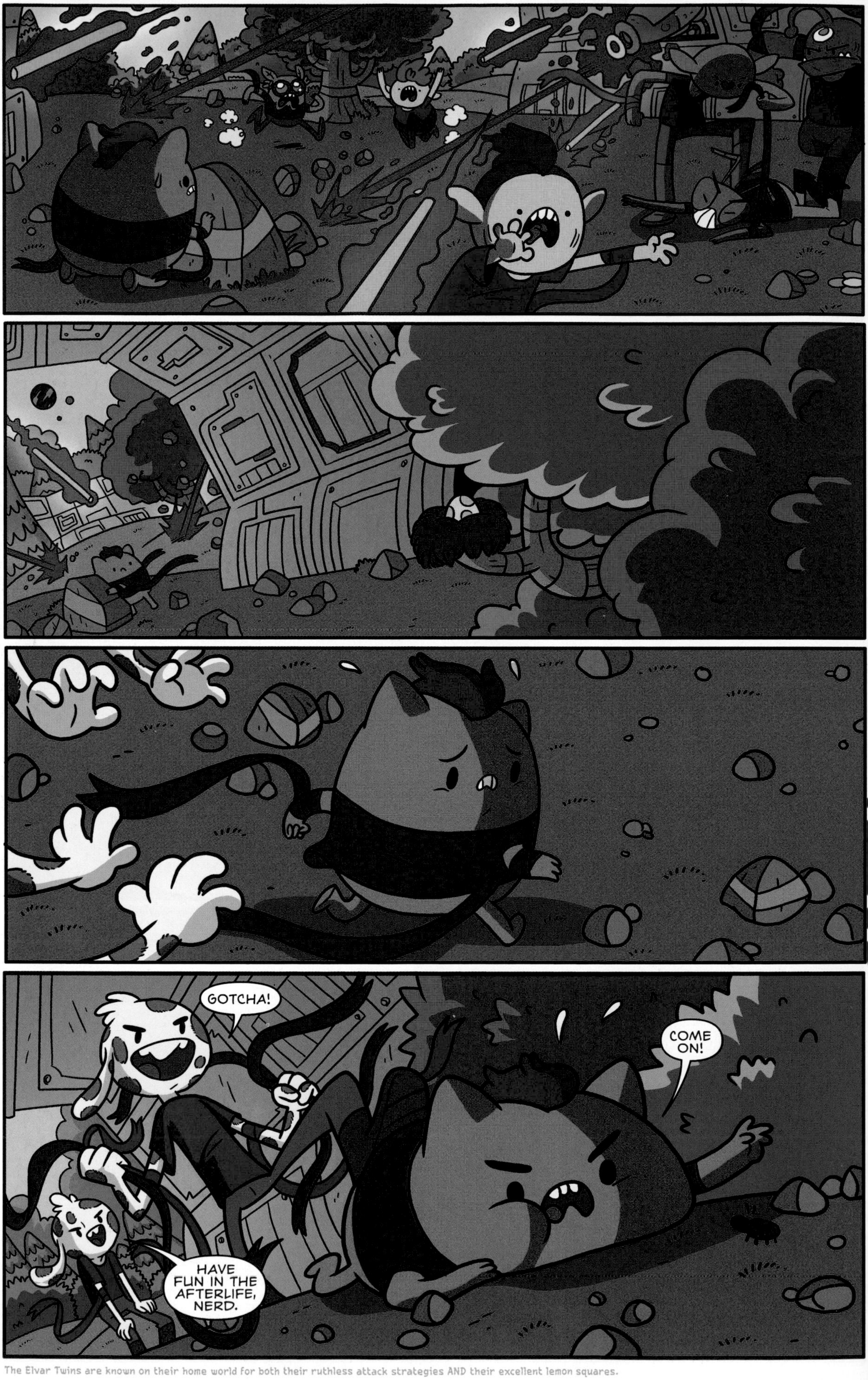
GOTCHA!
COME ON!
HAVE FUN IN THE AFTERLIFE, NERD.

The Elvar Twins are known on their home world for both their ruthless attack strategies AND their excellent lemon squares.

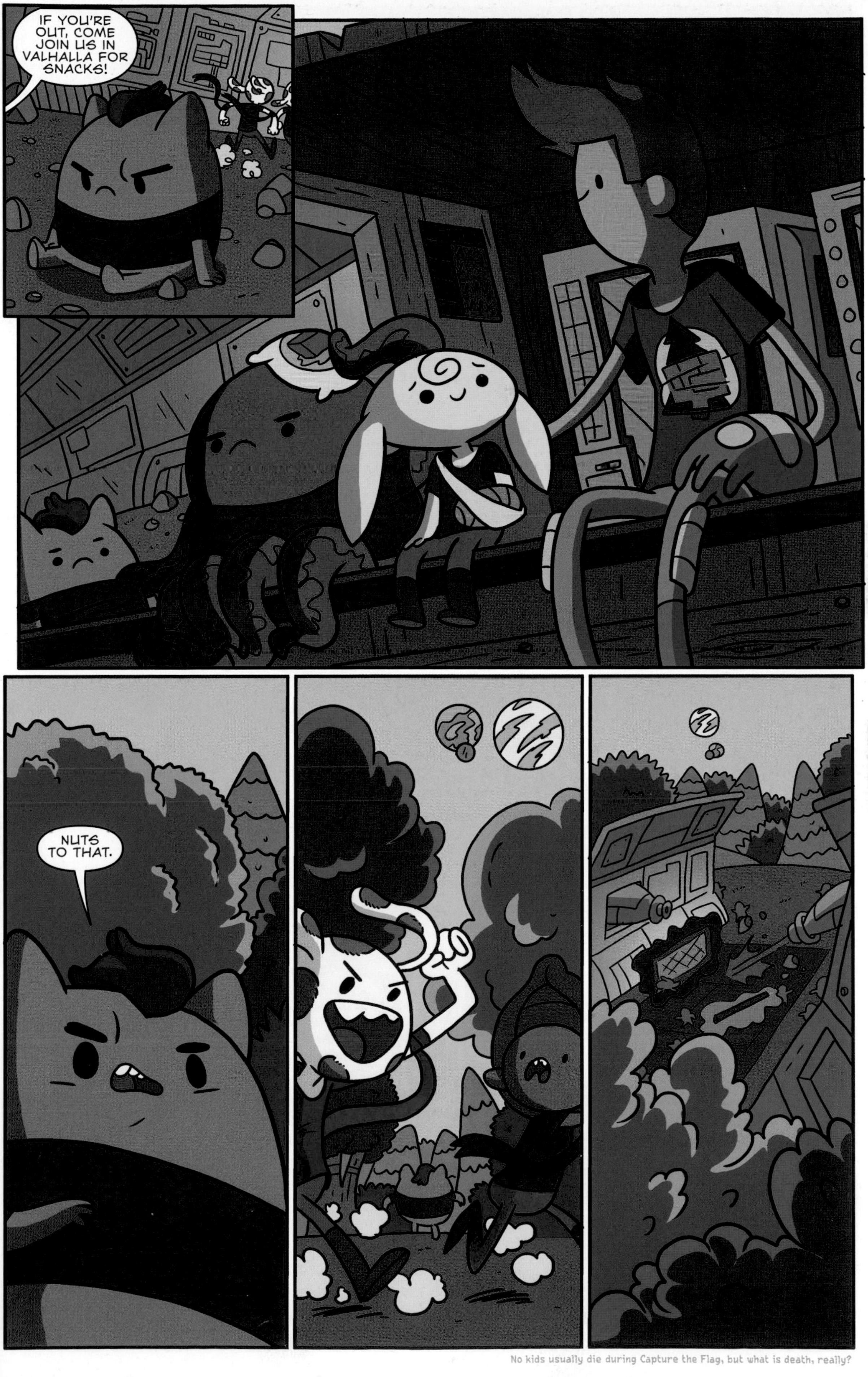
IF YOU'RE OUT, COME JOIN US IN VALHALLA FOR SNACKS!
NUTS TO THAT.

No kids usually die during Capture the Flag, but what is death, really?

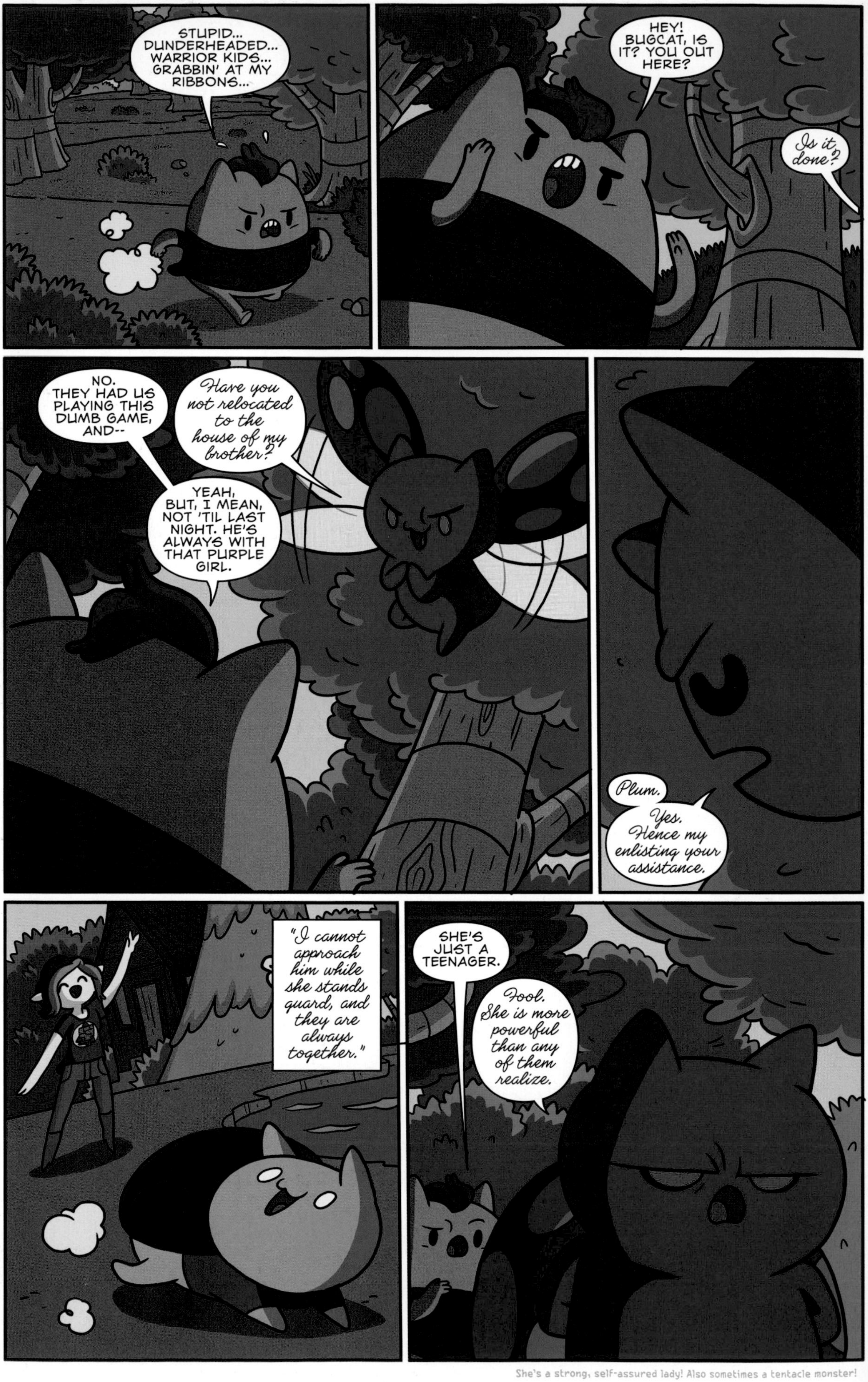
STUPID... DUNDERHEADED... WARRIOR KIDS... GRABBIN' AT MY RIBBONS...
HEY! BUGCAT, IS IT? YOU OUT HERE?
Is it done?
NO. THEY HAD US PLAYING THIS DUMB GAME, AND--
Have you not relocated to the house of my brother?
YEAH, BUT, I MEAN, NOT 'TIL LAST NIGHT. HE'S ALWAYS WITH THAT PURPLE GIRL.
Plum.
Yes. Hence my enlisting your assistance.
"I cannot approach him while she stands guard, and they are always together."
SHE'S JUST A TEENAGER.
Fool. She is more powerful than any of them realize.

She's a strong, self-assured lady! Also sometimes a tentacle monster!

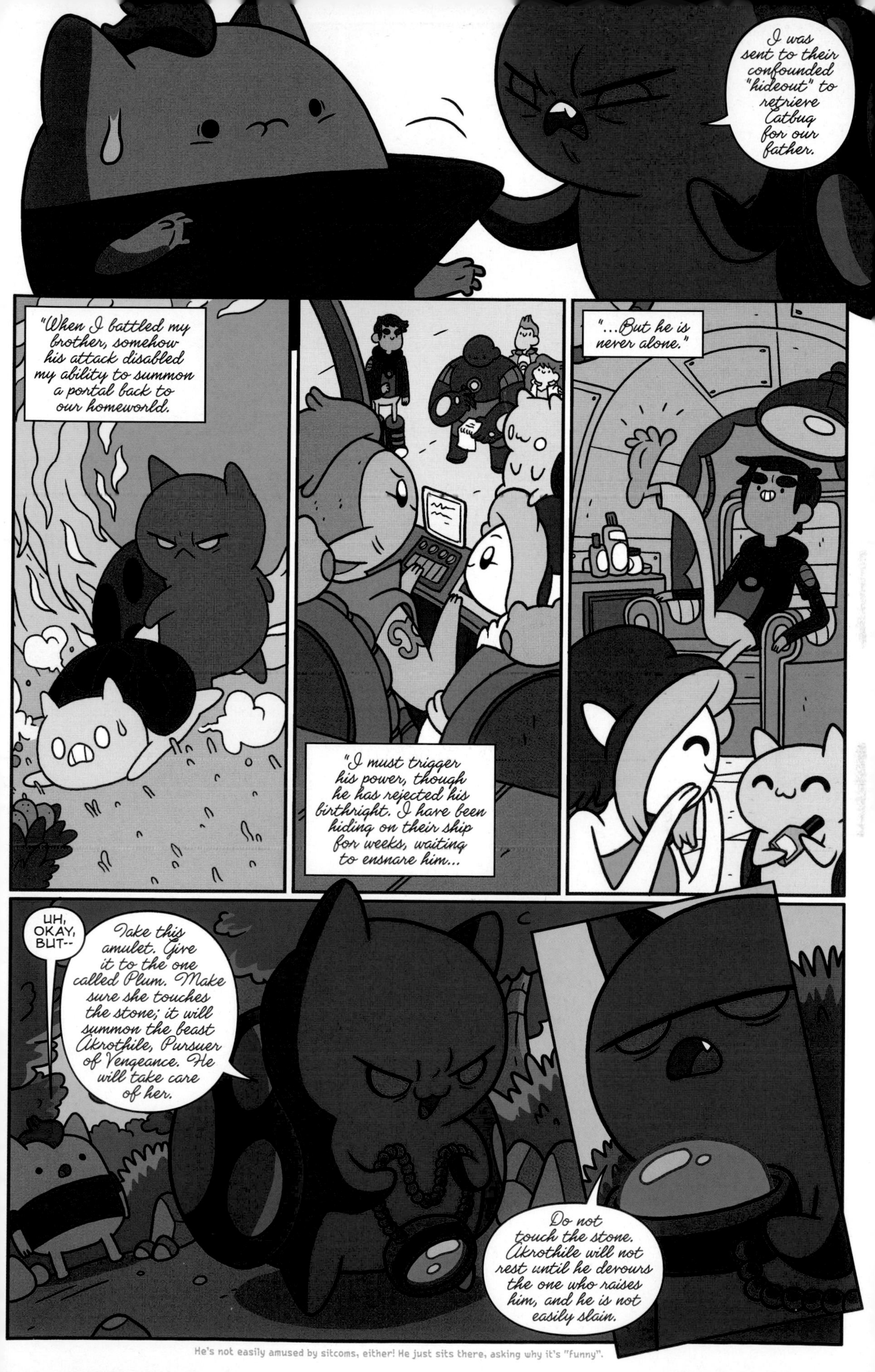
I was sent to their confounded "hideout" to retrieve Catbug for our father.
"When I battled my brother, somehow his attack disabled my ability to summon a portal back to our homeworld.
"I must trigger his power, though he has rejected his birthright. I have been hiding on their ship for weeks, waiting to ensnare him...
"...But he is never alone."
UH, OKAY, BUT--
Take this amulet. Give it to the one called Plum. Make sure she touches the stone; it will summon the beast Akrothile, Pursuer of Vengeance. He will take care of her.
Do not touch the stone. Akrothile will not rest until he devours the one who raises him, and he is not easily slain.

He's not easily amused by sitcoms, either! He just sits there, asking why it's "funny".

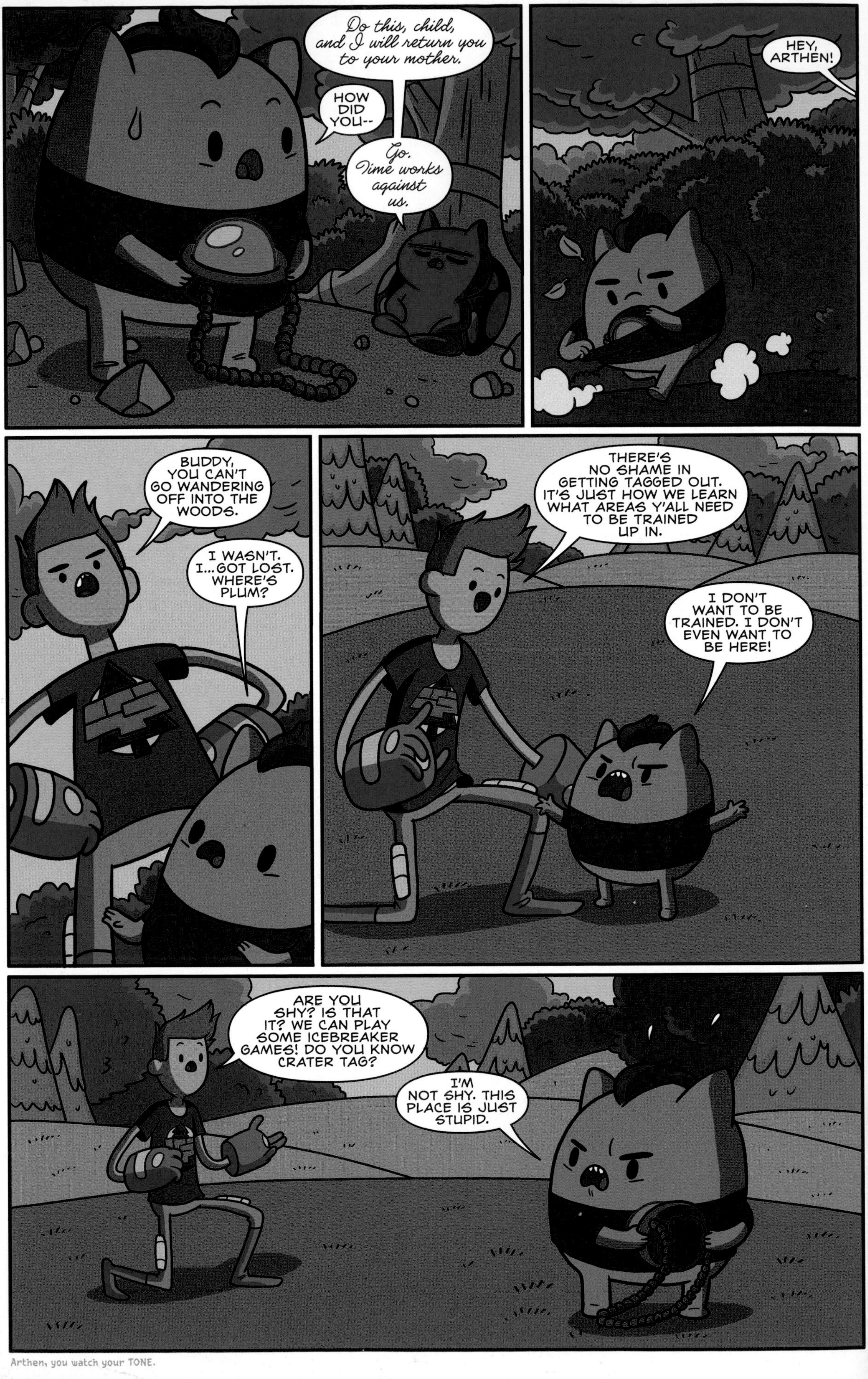
Do this, child, and I will return you to your mother.
HOW DID YOU--
Go. Time works against us.
HEY, ARTHEN!
BUDDY, YOU CAN'T GO WANDERING OFF INTO THE WOODS.
I WASN'T. I...GOT LOST. WHERE'S PLUM?
THERE'S NO SHAME IN GETTING TAGGED OUT. IT'S JUST HOW WE LEARN WHAT AREAS Y'ALL NEED TO BE TRAINED UP IN.
I DON'T WANT TO BE TRAINED. I DON'T EVEN WANT TO BE HERE!
ARE YOU SHY? IS THAT IT? WE CAN PLAY SOME ICEBREAKER GAMES! DO YOU KNOW CRATER TAG?
I'M NOT SHY. THIS PLACE IS JUST STUPID.

Arthen, you watch your TONE.

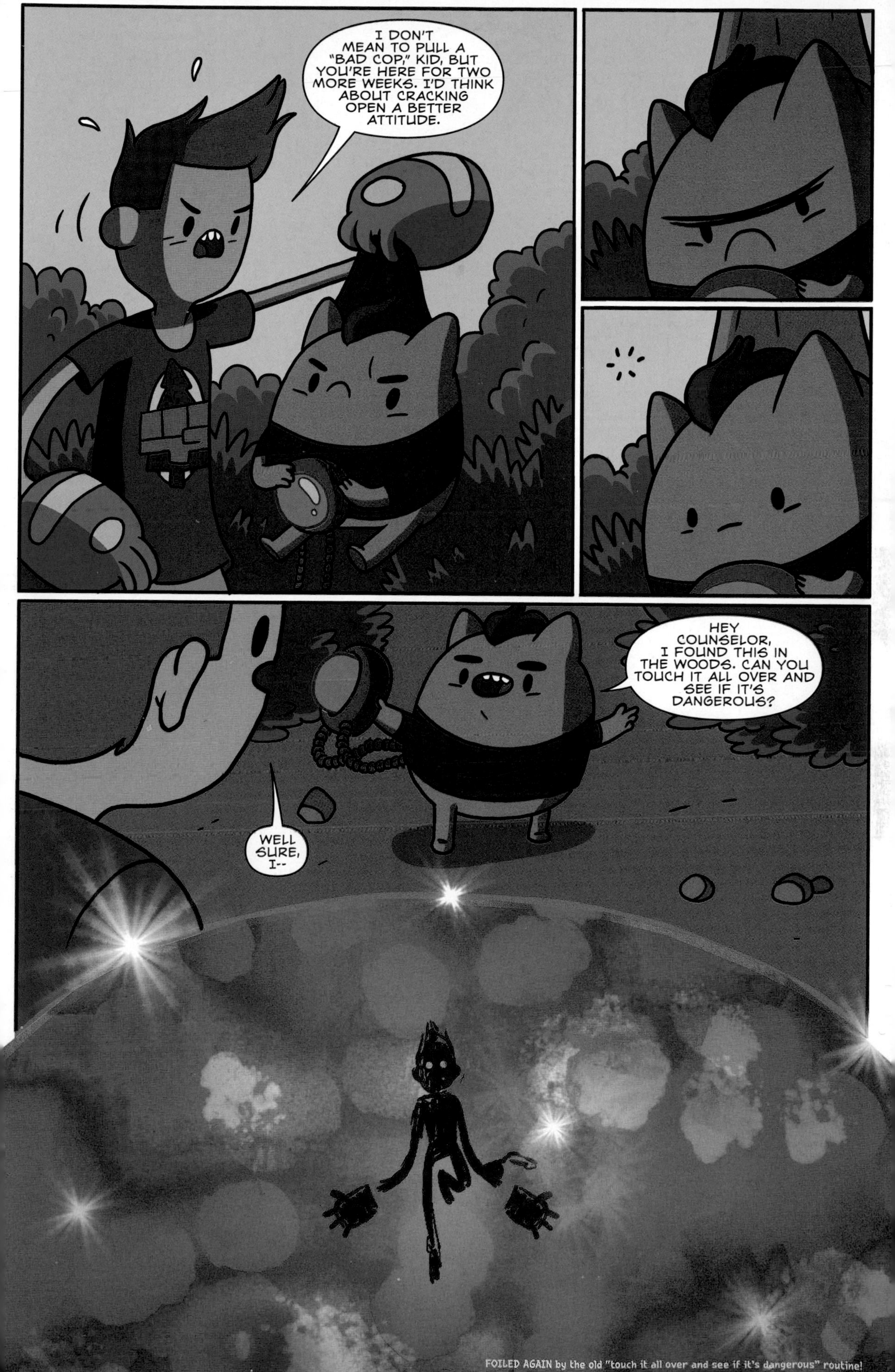
I DON'T MEAN TO PULL A "BAD COP," KID, BUT YOU'RE HERE FOR TWO MORE WEEKS. I'D THINK ABOUT CRACKING OPEN A BETTER ATTITUDE.
HEY COUNSELOR, I FOUND THIS IN THE WOODS. CAN YOU TOUCH IT ALL OVER AND SEE IF IT'S DANGEROUS?
WELL SURE, I--

FOILED AGAIN by the old "touch it all over and see if it's dangerous" routine!

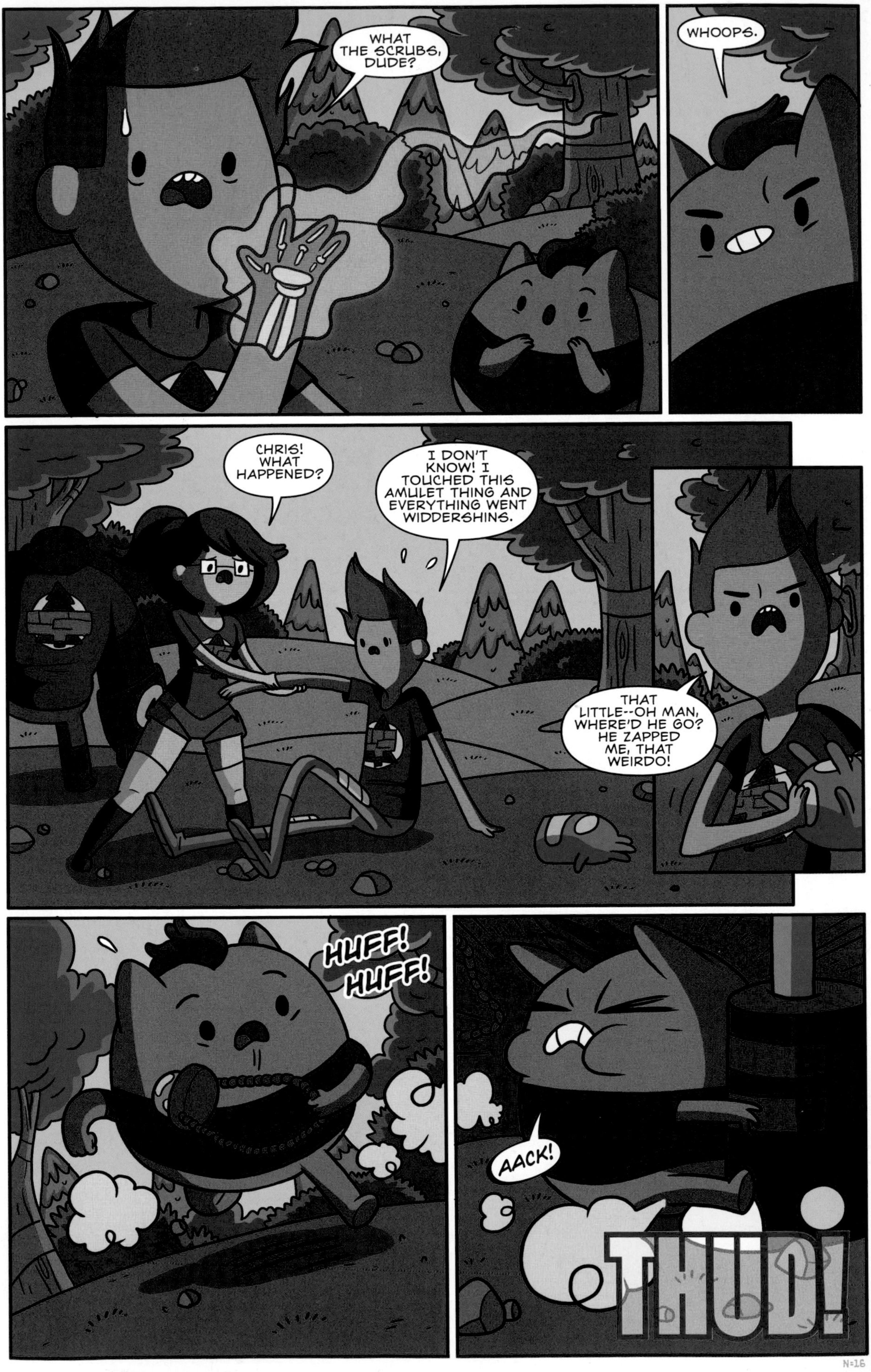
WHAT THE SCRUBS, DUDE?
WHOOPS.
CHRIS! WHAT HAPPENED?
I DON'T KNOW! I TOUCHED THIS AMULET THING AND EVERYTHING WENT WIDDERSHINS.
THAT LITTLE--OH MAN, WHERE'D HE GO? HE ZAPPED ME, THAT WEIRDO!
HUFF! HUFF!
AACK!
THUD!

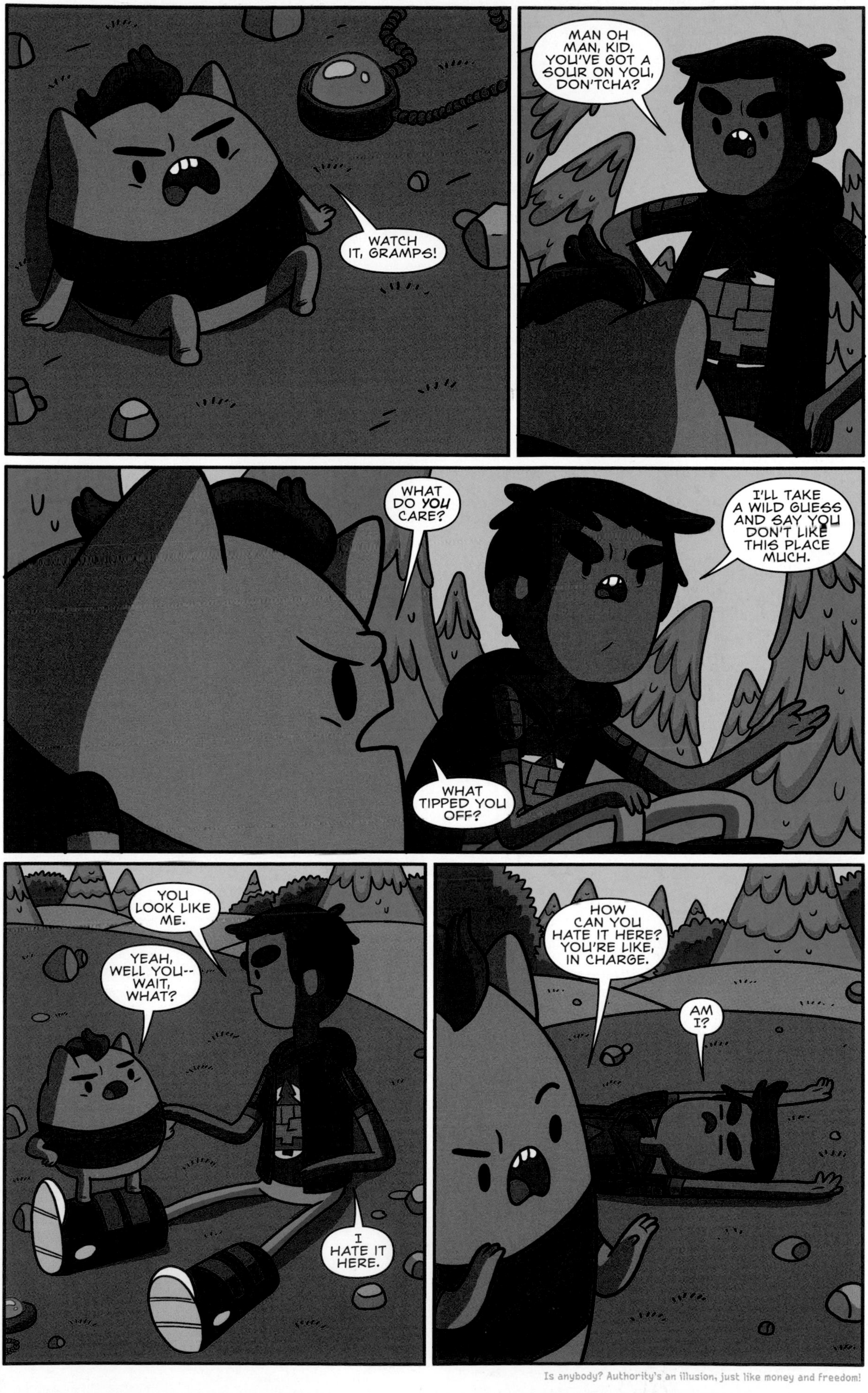
WATCH IT, GRAMPS!
MAN OH MAN, KID, YOU'VE GOT A SOUR ON YOU, DON'TCHA?
WHAT DO YOU CARE?
I'LL TAKE A WILD GUESS AND SAY YOU DON'T LIKE THIS PLACE MUCH.
WHAT TIPPED YOU OFF?
YOU LOOK LIKE ME.
YEAH, WELL YOU-- WAIT, WHAT?
I HATE IT HERE.
HOW CAN YOU HATE IT HERE? YOU'RE LIKE, IN CHARGE.
AM I?

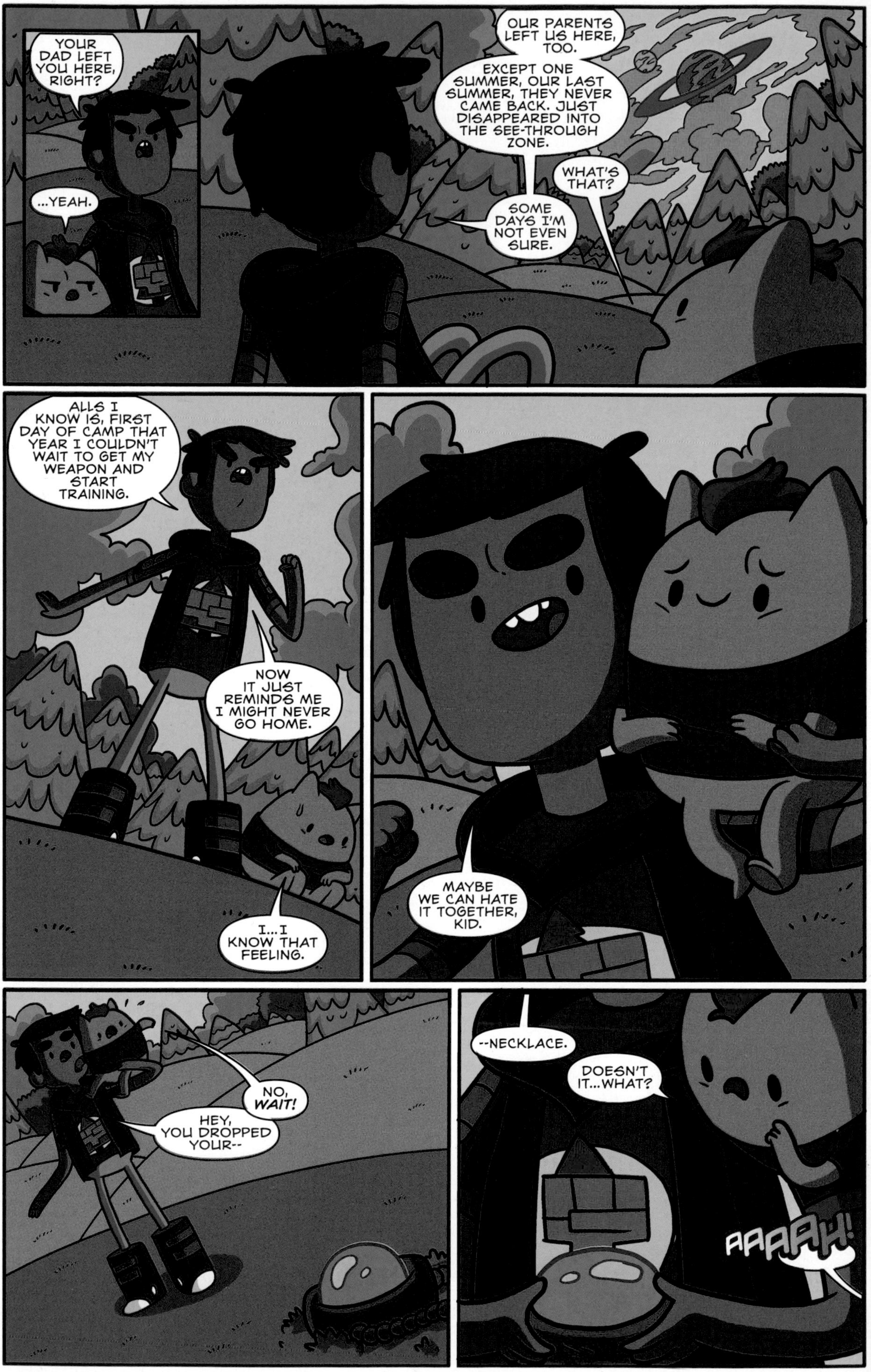
YOUR DAD LEFT YOU HERE, RIGHT?
...YEAH.
OUR PARENTS LEFT US HERE, TOO.
EXCEPT ONE SUMMER, OUR LAST SUMMER, THEY NEVER CAME BACK. JUST DISAPPEARED INTO THE SEE-THROUGH ZONE.
WHAT'S THAT?
SOME DAYS I'M NOT EVEN SURE.
ALLS I KNOW IS, FIRST DAY OF CAMP THAT YEAR I COULDN'T WAIT TO GET MY WEAPON AND START TRAINING.
NOW IT JUST REMINDS ME I MIGHT NEVER GO HOME.
I...I KNOW THAT FEELING.
MAYBE WE CAN HATE IT TOGETHER, KID.
HEY, YOU DROPPED YOUR--
NO, *WAIT!*
--NECKLACE.
DOESN'T IT...WHAT?
AAAAH!

Iecu qckbuji edbo xqlu edu kiu yd 'uc, rkj ex reo, MXQJ Q KIU.

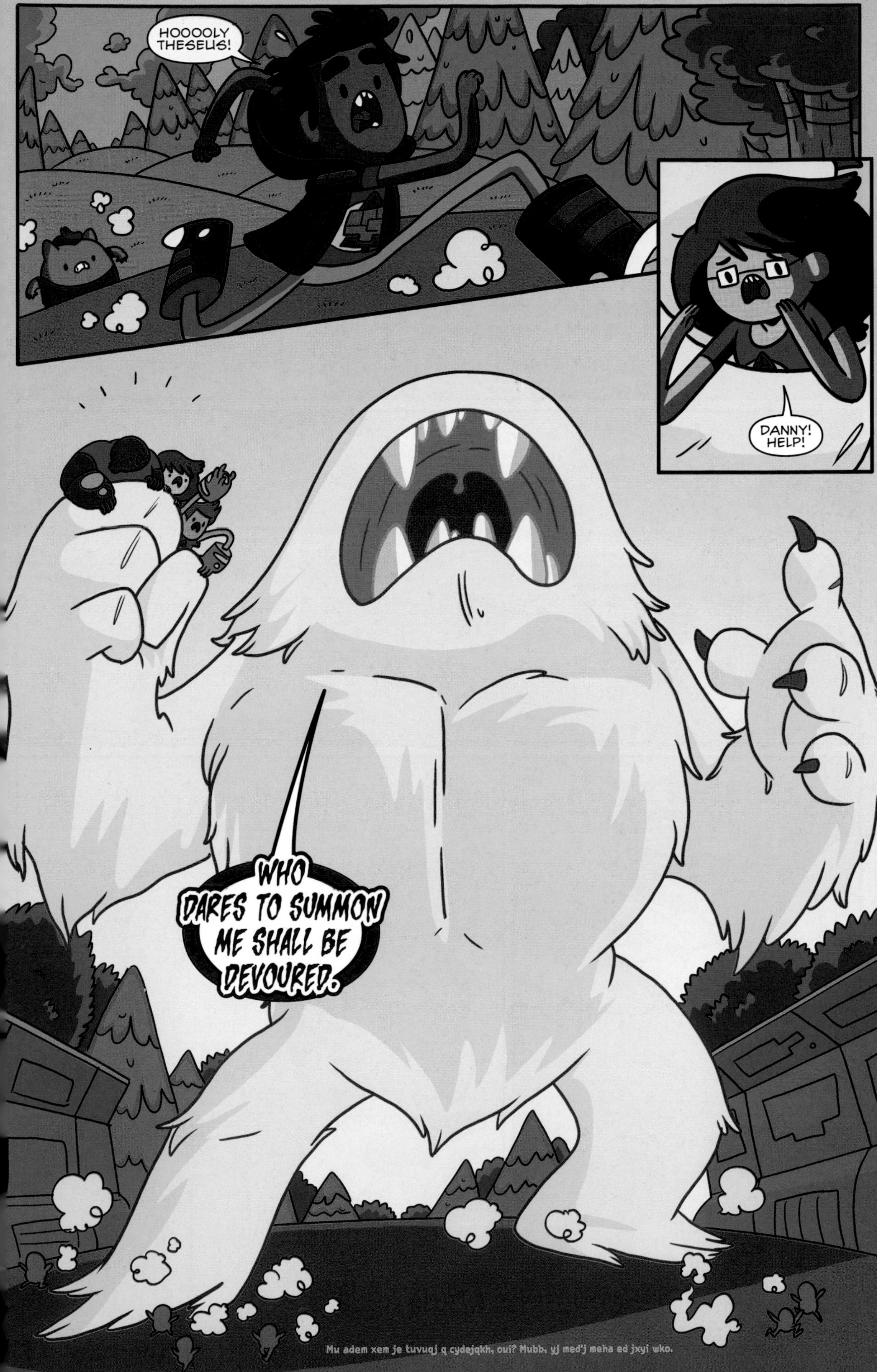
HOOOOLY THESEUS!
DANNY! HELP!
WHO DARES TO SUMMON ME SHALL BE DEVOURED.
Mu adem xem je tuvuqj q cydejqkh, oui? Mubb, yj med'j meha ed jxyi wko.

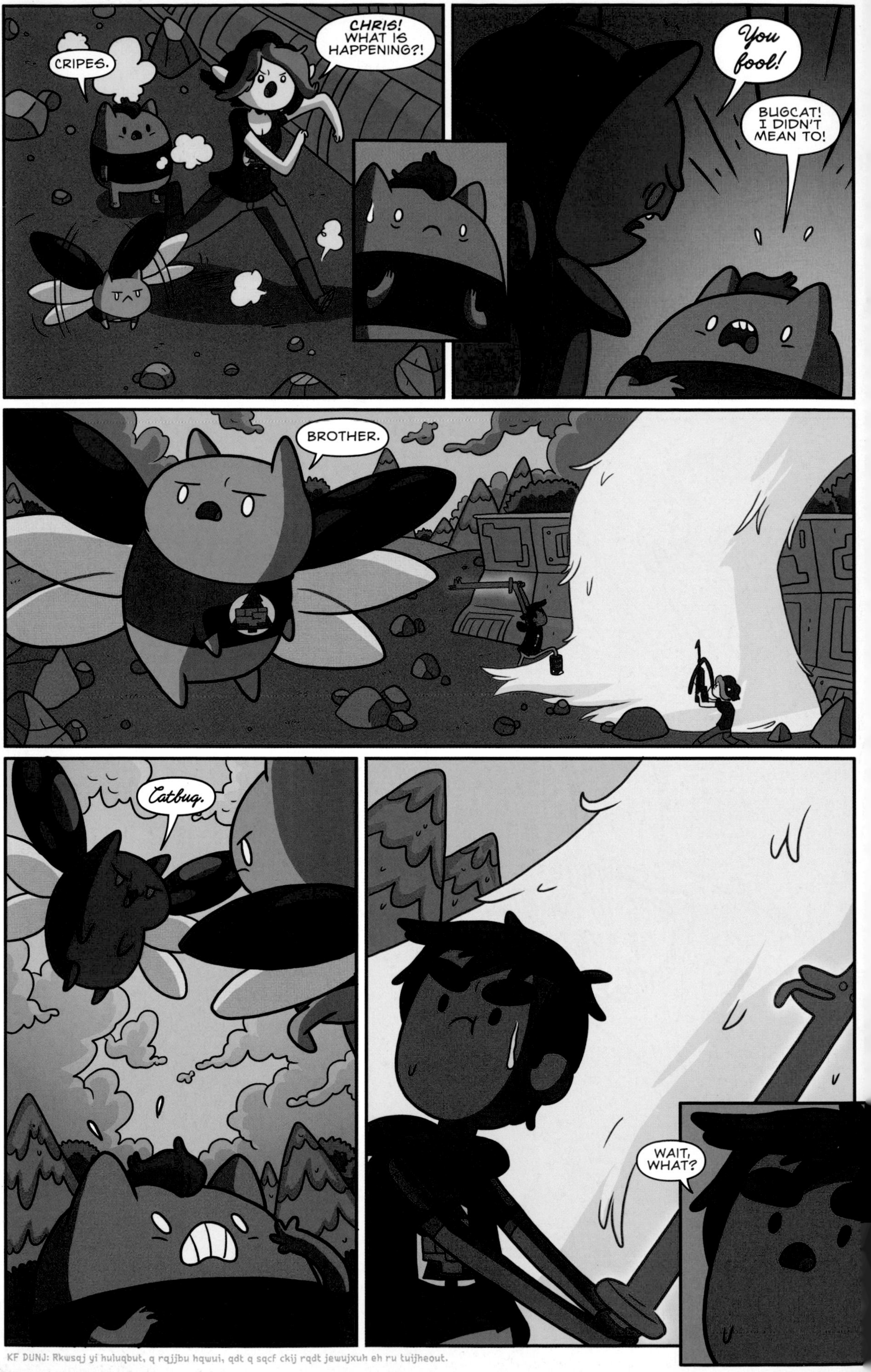
CRIPES.
CHRIS! WHAT IS HAPPENING?!
You fool!
BUGCAT! I DIDN'T MEAN TO!
BROTHER.
Catbug.
WAIT, WHAT?

KF DUNJ: Rkwsqj yi huluqbut, q rqjjbu hqwui, qdt q sqcf ckij rqdt jewujxuh eh ru tuijheout.

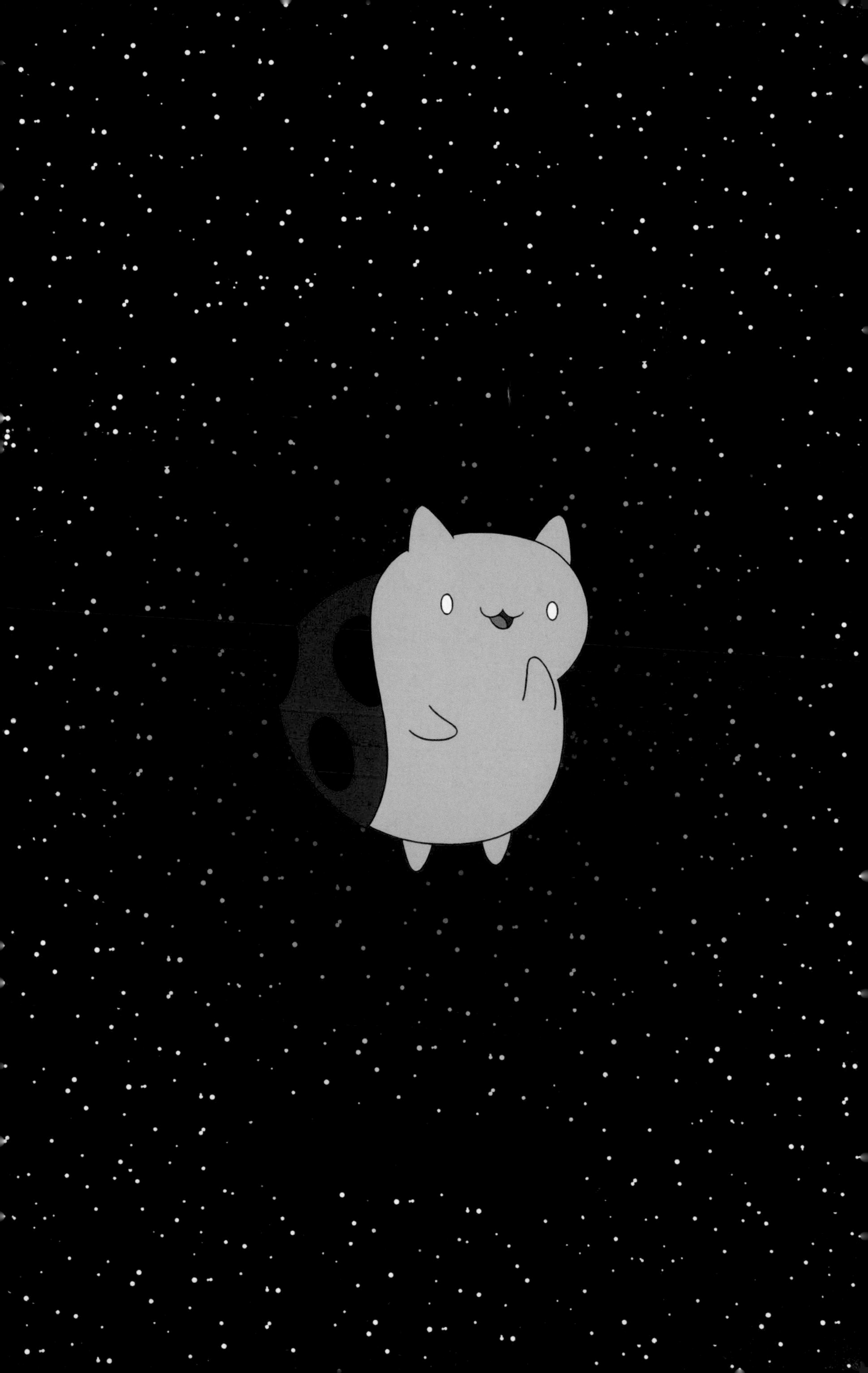

CHAPTER
32

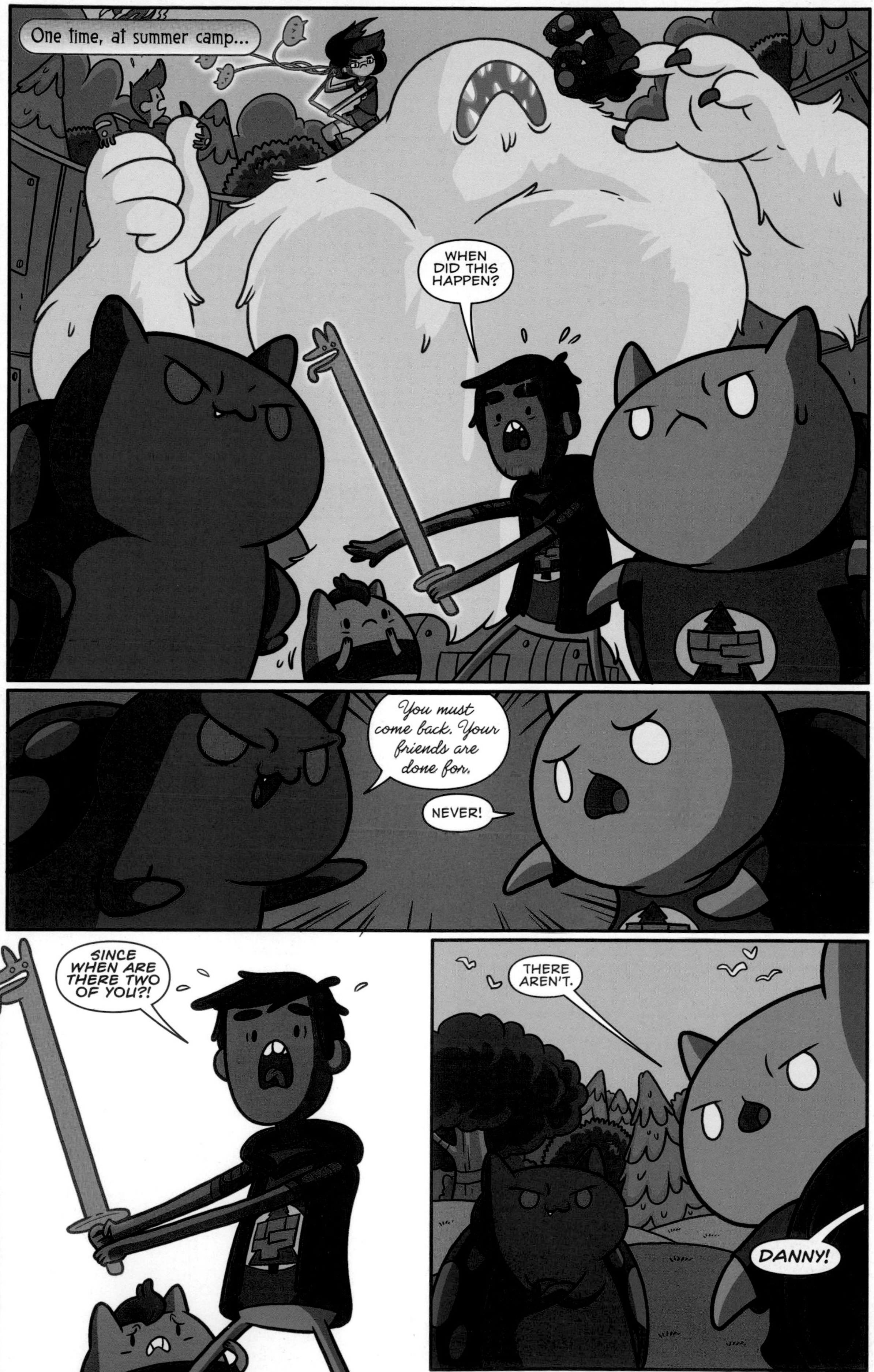
One time, at summer camp...
WHEN DID THIS HAPPEN?
You must come back. Your friends are done for.
NEVER!
SINCE WHEN ARE THERE TWO OF YOU?!
THERE AREN'T.
DANNY!

Last time, on Bravest Warriors: STUFF WENT DOWN, okay?!

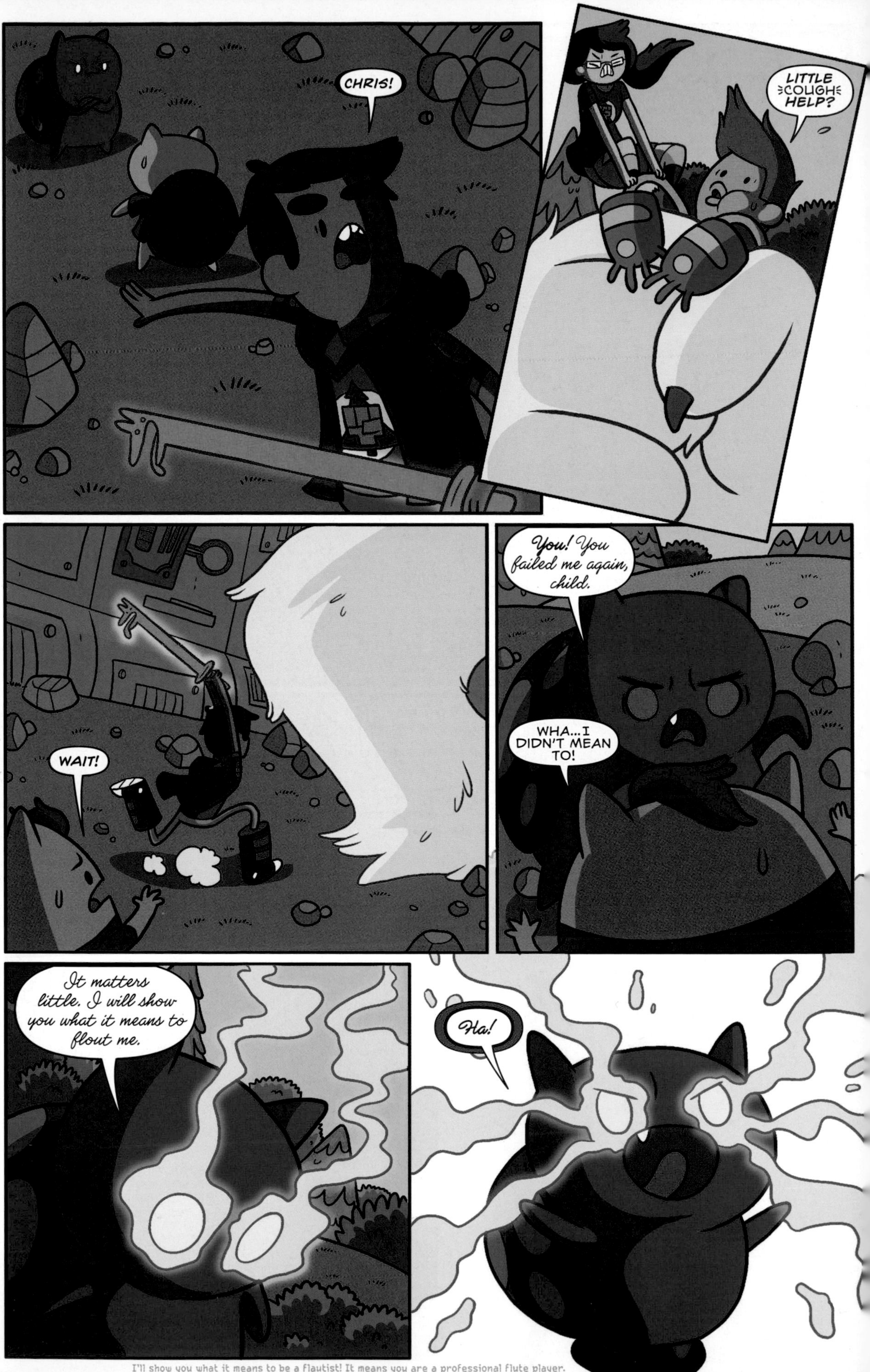
CHRIS!
LITTLE COUGH HELP?
WAIT!
You! You failed me again, child.
WHA...I DIDN'T MEAN TO!
It matters little. I will show you what it means to flout me.
Ha!

I'll show you what it means to be a flautist! It means you are a professional flute player.

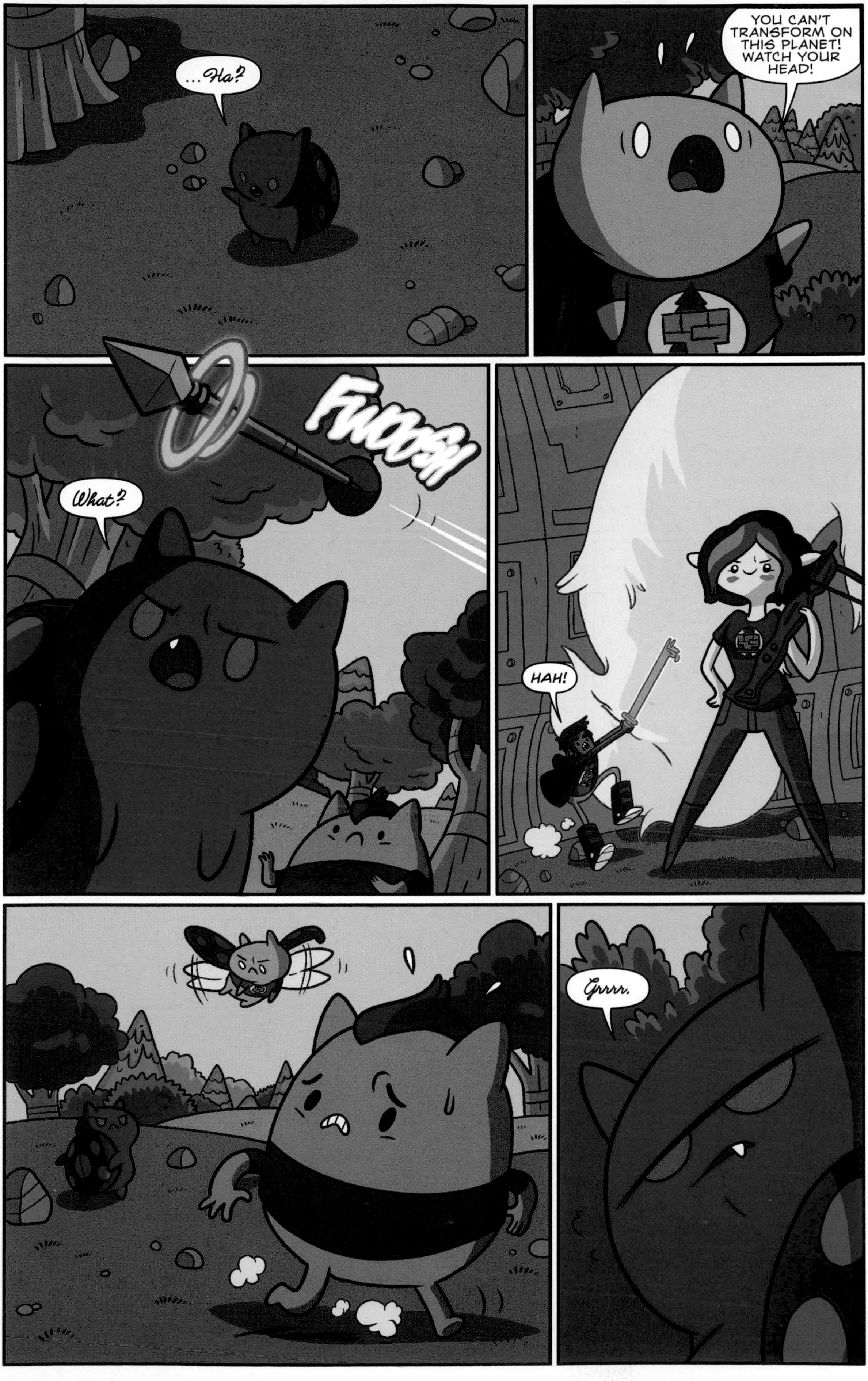
...Ha?
YOU CAN'T TRANSFORM ON THIS PLANET! WATCH YOUR HEAD!
FWOOSH
What?
HAH!
Grrrr.

It's not a good day to be Bugcat! I don't think any day is a good day to be Bugcat. Maybe Sunday.

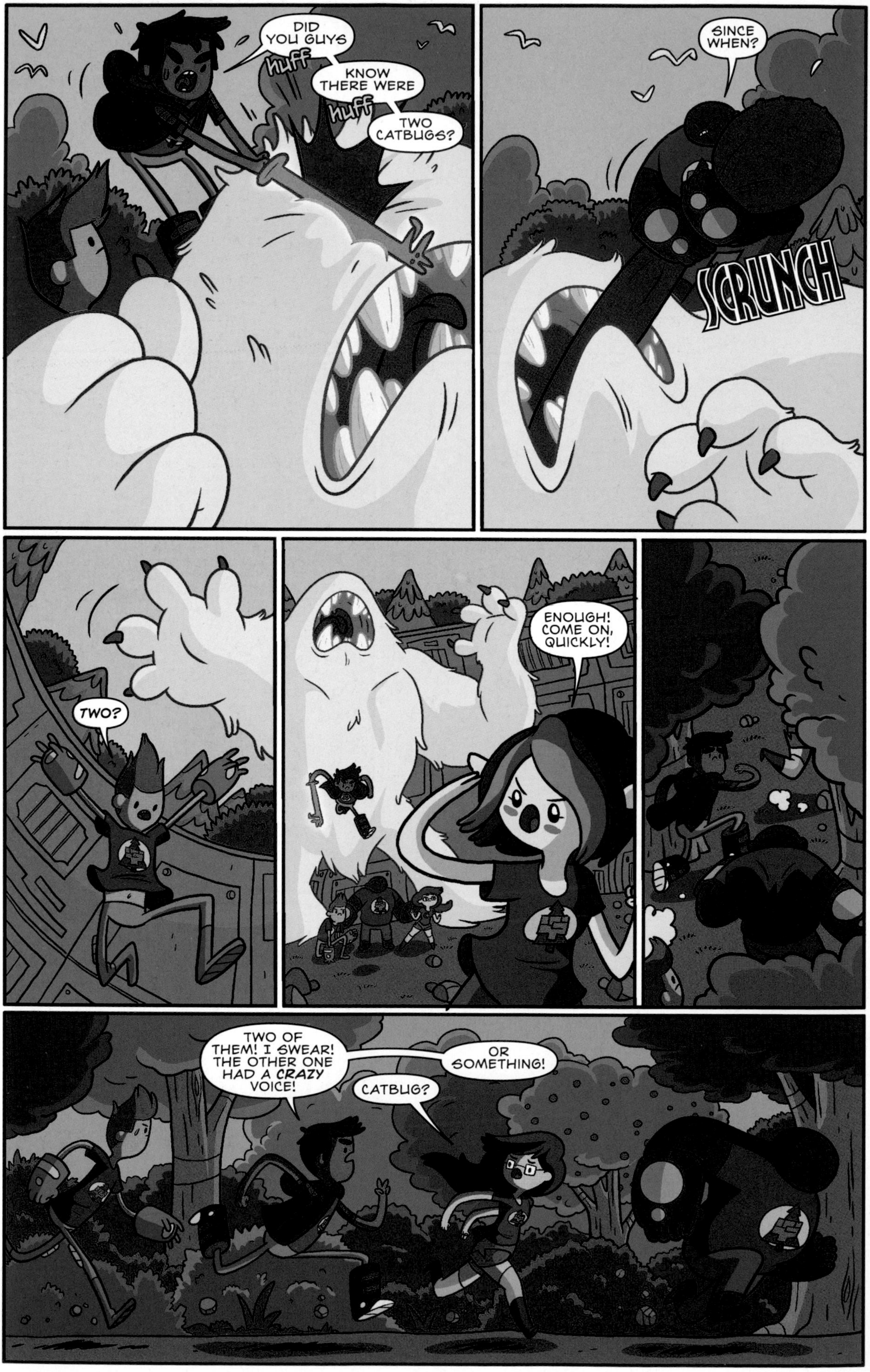
DID YOU GUYS
huff
KNOW THERE WERE
huff
TWO CATBUGS?
SINCE WHEN?
SCRUNCH
TWO?
ENOUGH! COME ON, QUICKLY!
TWO OF THEM! I SWEAR! THE OTHER ONE HAD A CRAZY VOICE!
OR SOMETHING!
CATBUG?

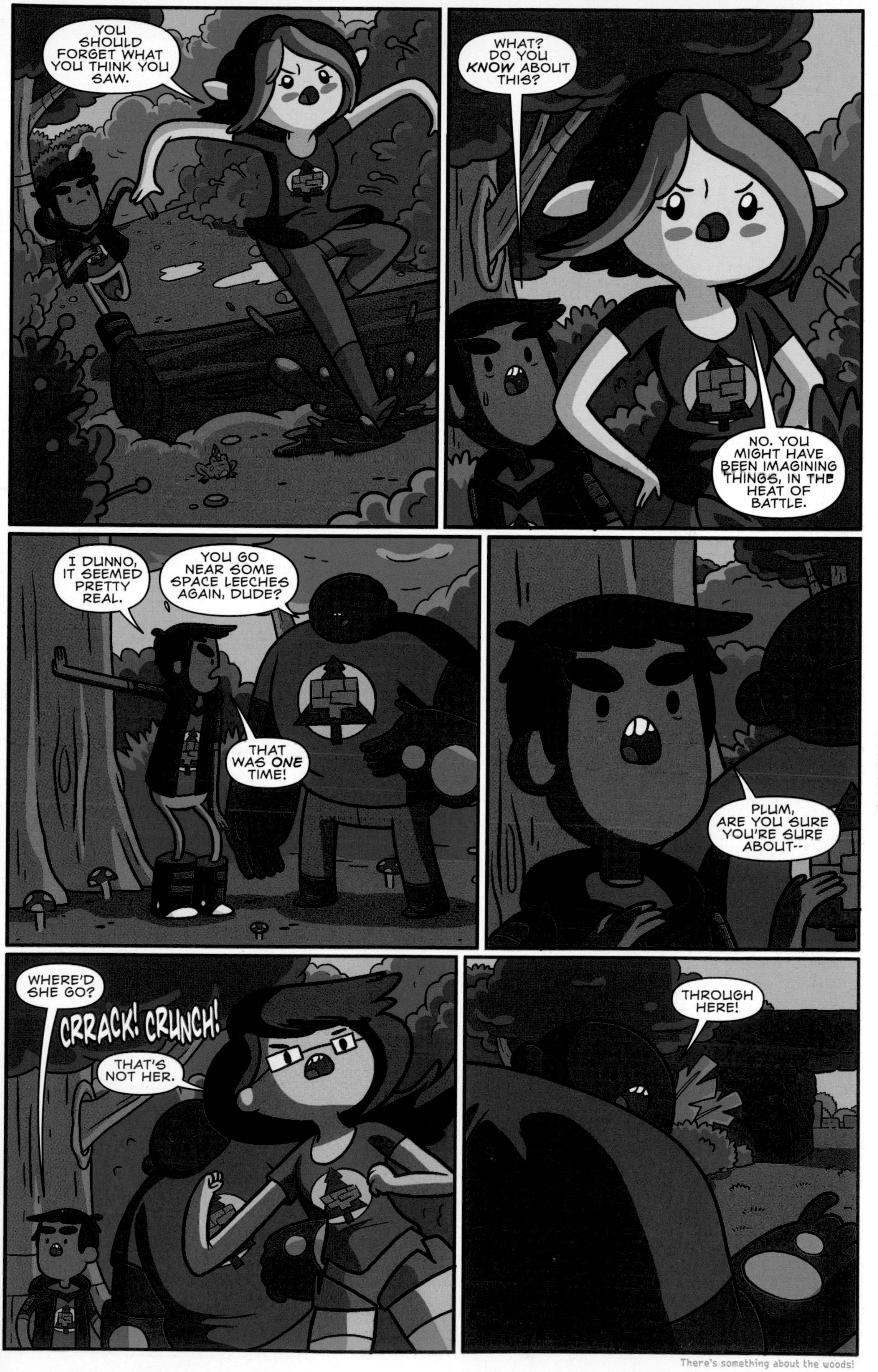
YOU SHOULD FORGET WHAT YOU THINK YOU SAW.
WHAT? DO YOU KNOW ABOUT THIS?
NO. YOU MIGHT HAVE BEEN IMAGINING THINGS, IN THE HEAT OF BATTLE.
I DUNNO, IT SEEMED PRETTY REAL.
YOU GO NEAR SOME SPACE LEECHES AGAIN, DUDE?
THAT WAS ONE TIME!
PLUM, ARE YOU SURE YOU'RE SURE ABOUT--
WHERE'D SHE GO?
CRRACK! CRUNCH!
THAT'S NOT HER.
THROUGH HERE!

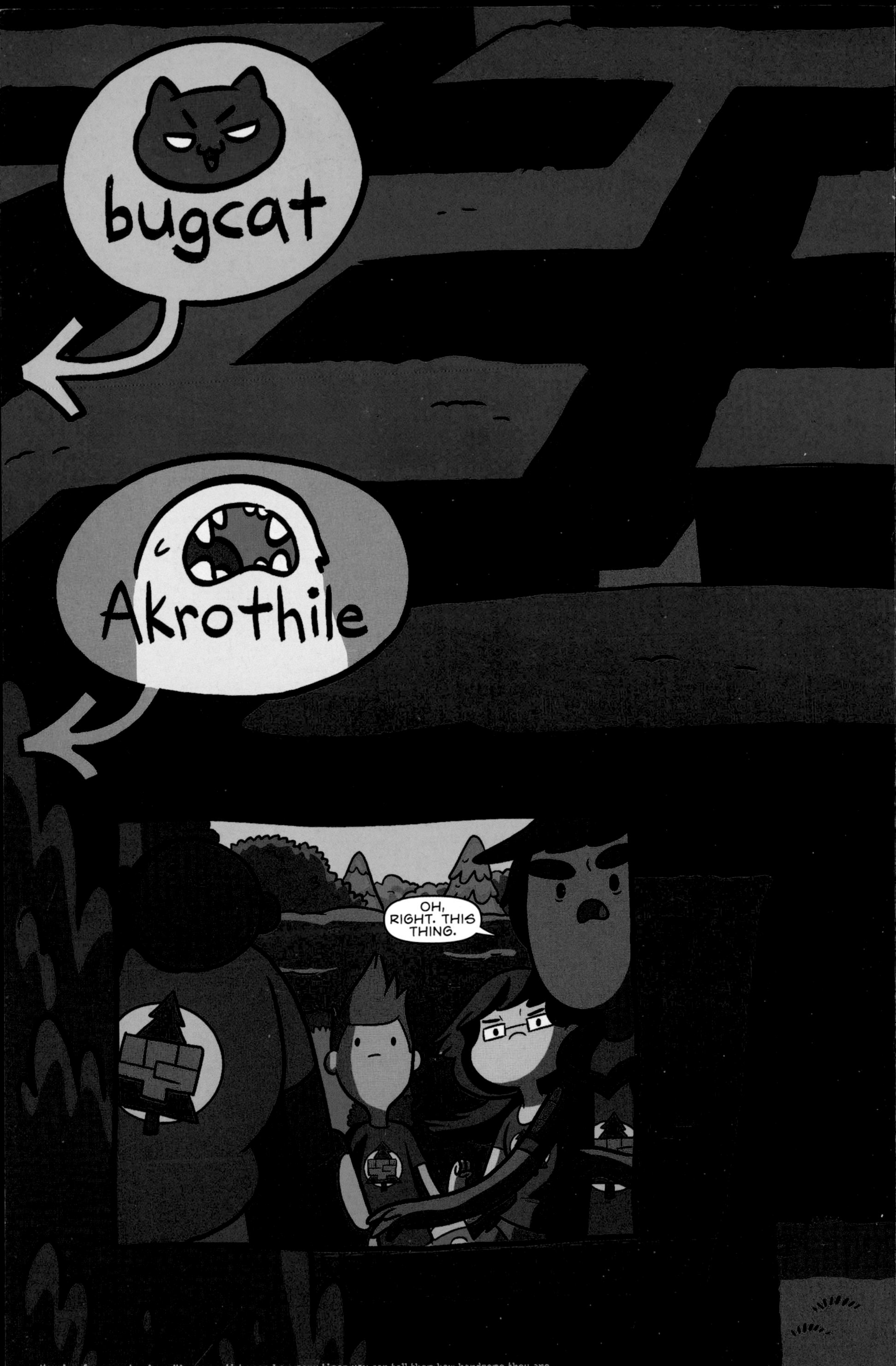
bugcat
Akrothile
OH, RIGHT. THIS THING.

Here's a fun game to play with your artist--see how many times you can tell them how handsome they are.

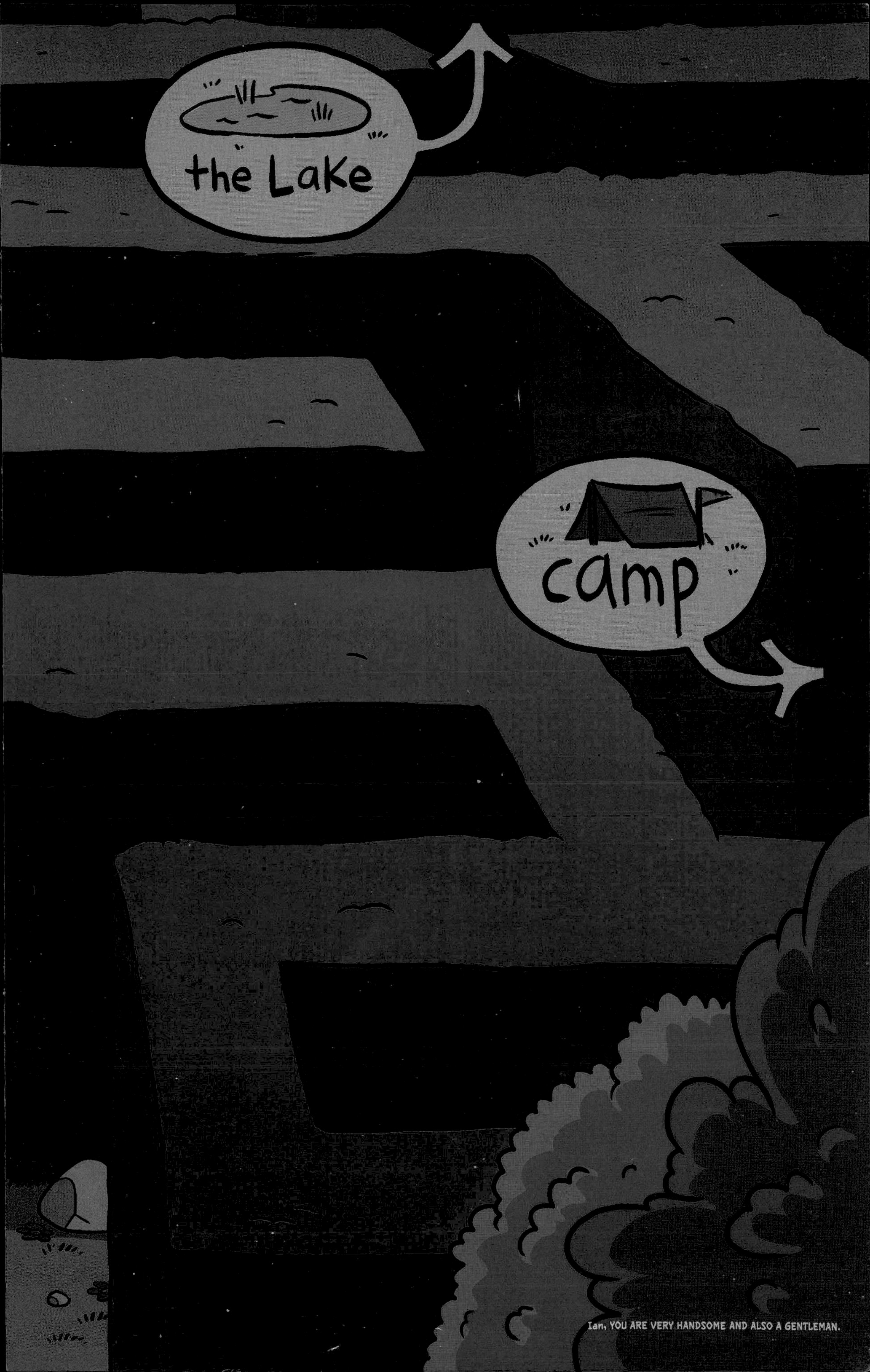
the Lake
camp
Ian, YOU ARE VERY HANDSOME AND ALSO A GENTLEMAN.

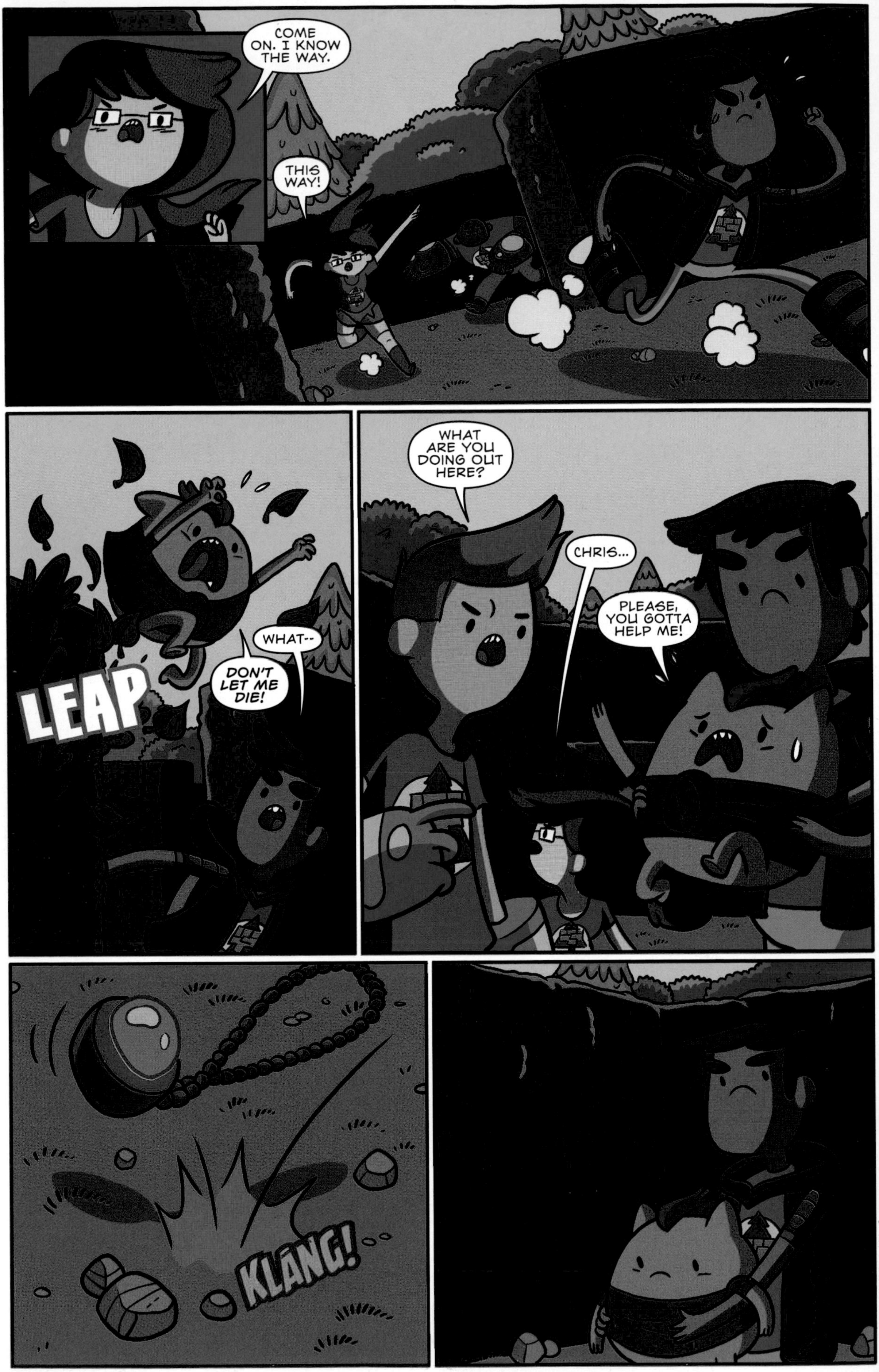
COME ON. I KNOW THE WAY.
THIS WAY!
LEAP
DON'T LET ME DIE!
WHAT--
WHAT ARE YOU DOING OUT HERE?
CHRIS...
PLEASE, YOU GOTTA HELP ME!
KLANG!

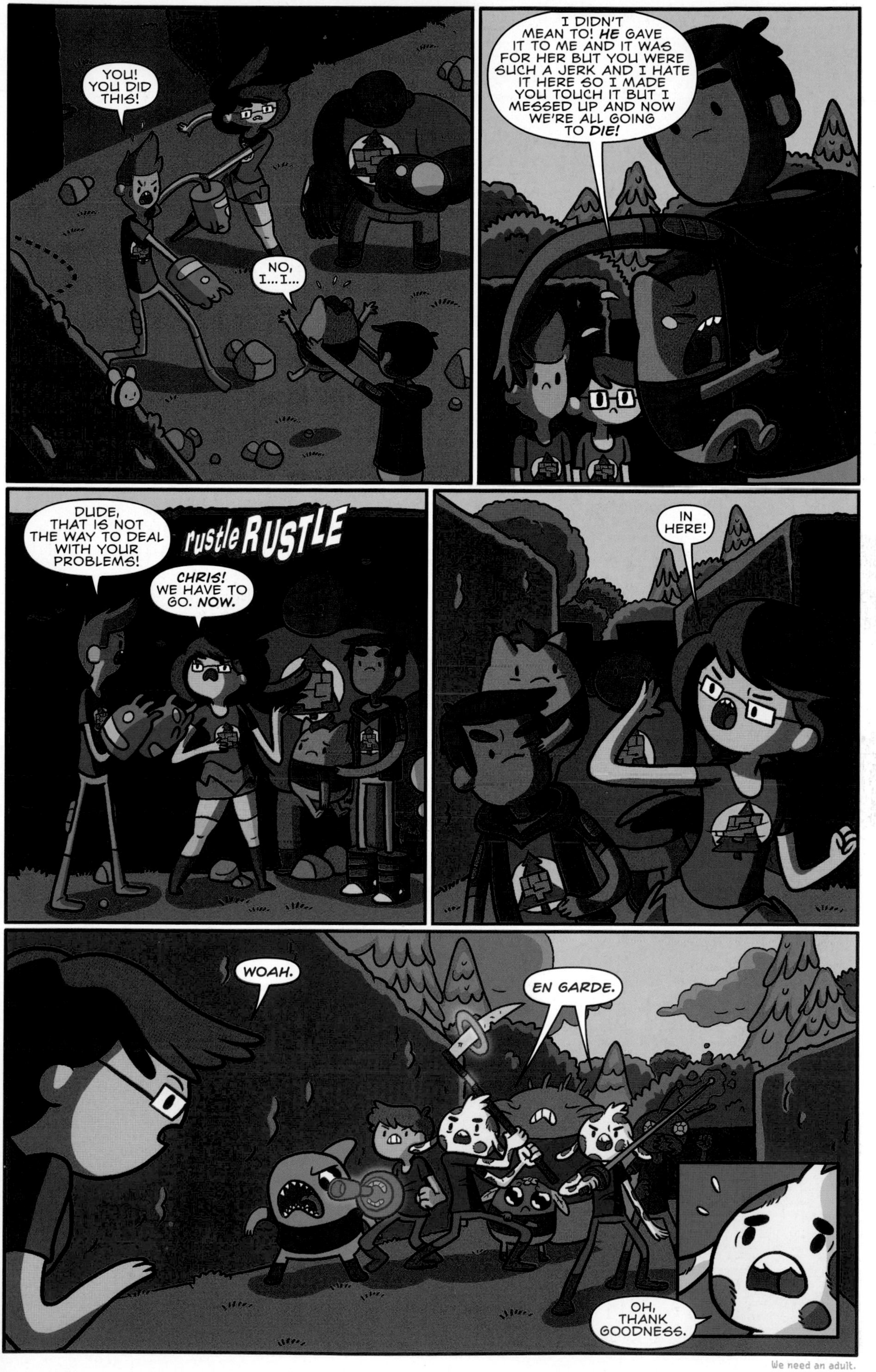
YOU! YOU DID THIS!
NO, I... I...
I DIDN'T MEAN TO! HE GAVE IT TO ME AND IT WAS FOR HER BUT YOU WERE SUCH A JERK AND I HATE IT HERE SO I MADE YOU TOUCH IT BUT I MESSED UP AND NOW WE'RE ALL GOING TO DIE!
DUDE, THAT IS NOT THE WAY TO DEAL WITH YOUR PROBLEMS!
rustle RUSTLE
CHRIS! WE HAVE TO GO. NOW.
IN HERE!
WOAH.
EN GARDE.
OH, THANK GOODNESS.

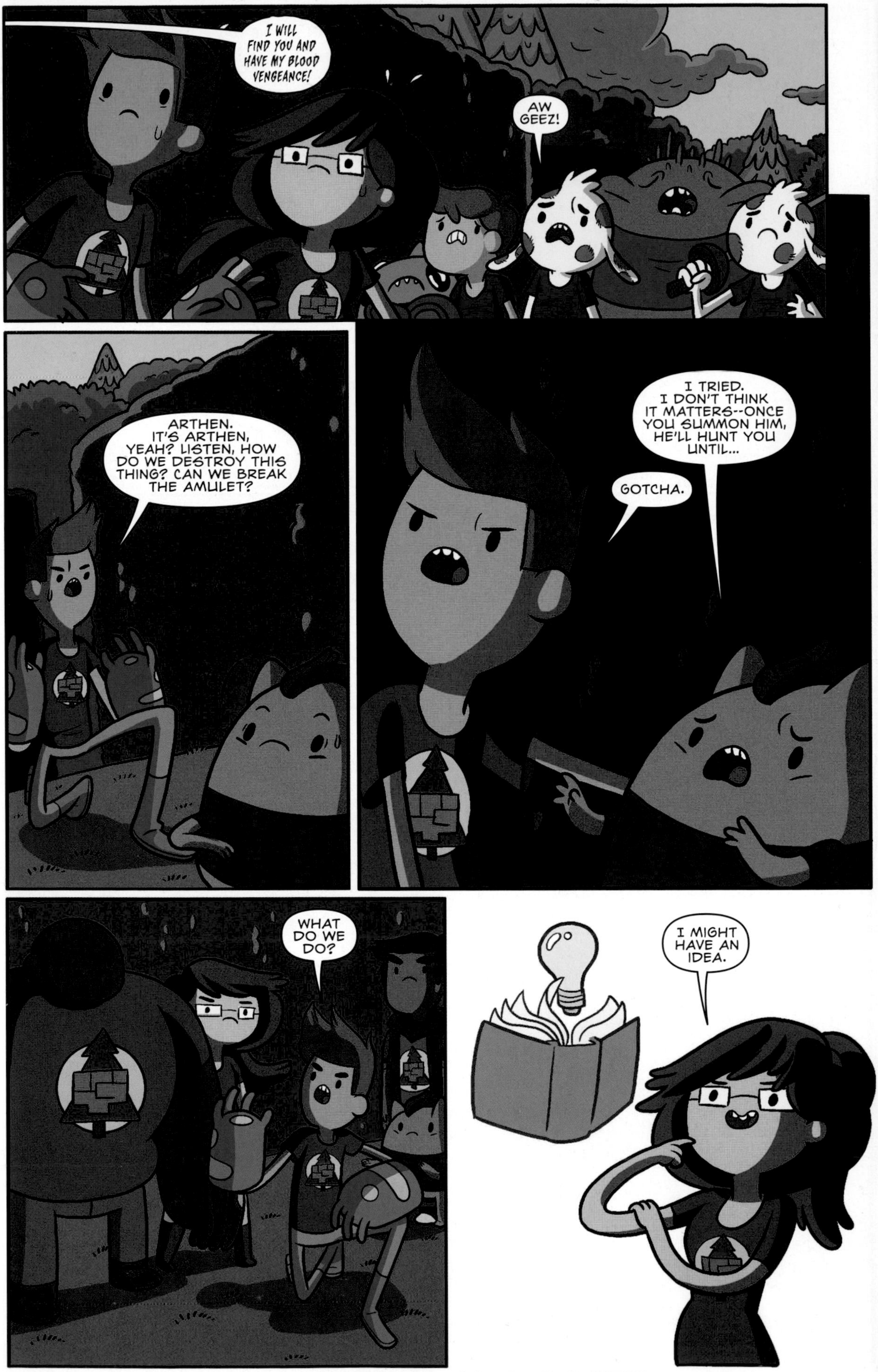
I WILL FIND YOU AND HAVE MY BLOOD VENGEANCE!
AW GEEZ!
ARTHEN. IT'S ARTHEN, YEAH? LISTEN, HOW DO WE DESTROY THIS THING? CAN WE BREAK THE AMULET?
I TRIED. I DON'T THINK IT MATTERS--ONCE YOU SUMMON HIM, HE'LL HUNT YOU UNTIL...
GOTCHA.
WHAT DO WE DO?
I MIGHT HAVE AN IDEA.

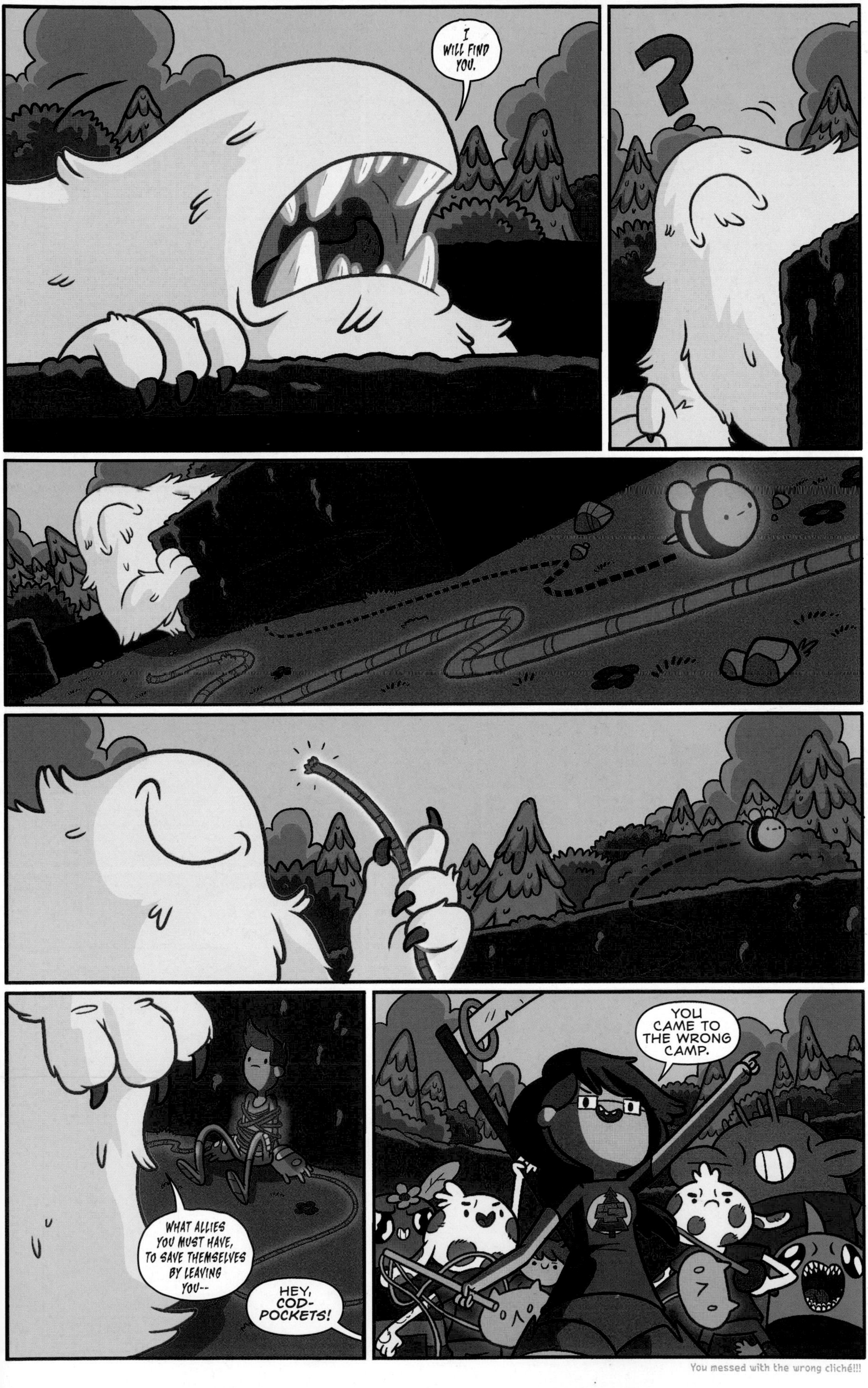
I WILL FIND YOU.
?
WHAT ALLIES YOU MUST HAVE, TO SAVE THEMSELVES BY LEAVING YOU--
HEY, COD-POCKETS!
YOU CAME TO THE WRONG CAMP.

You messed with the wrong cliché!!!

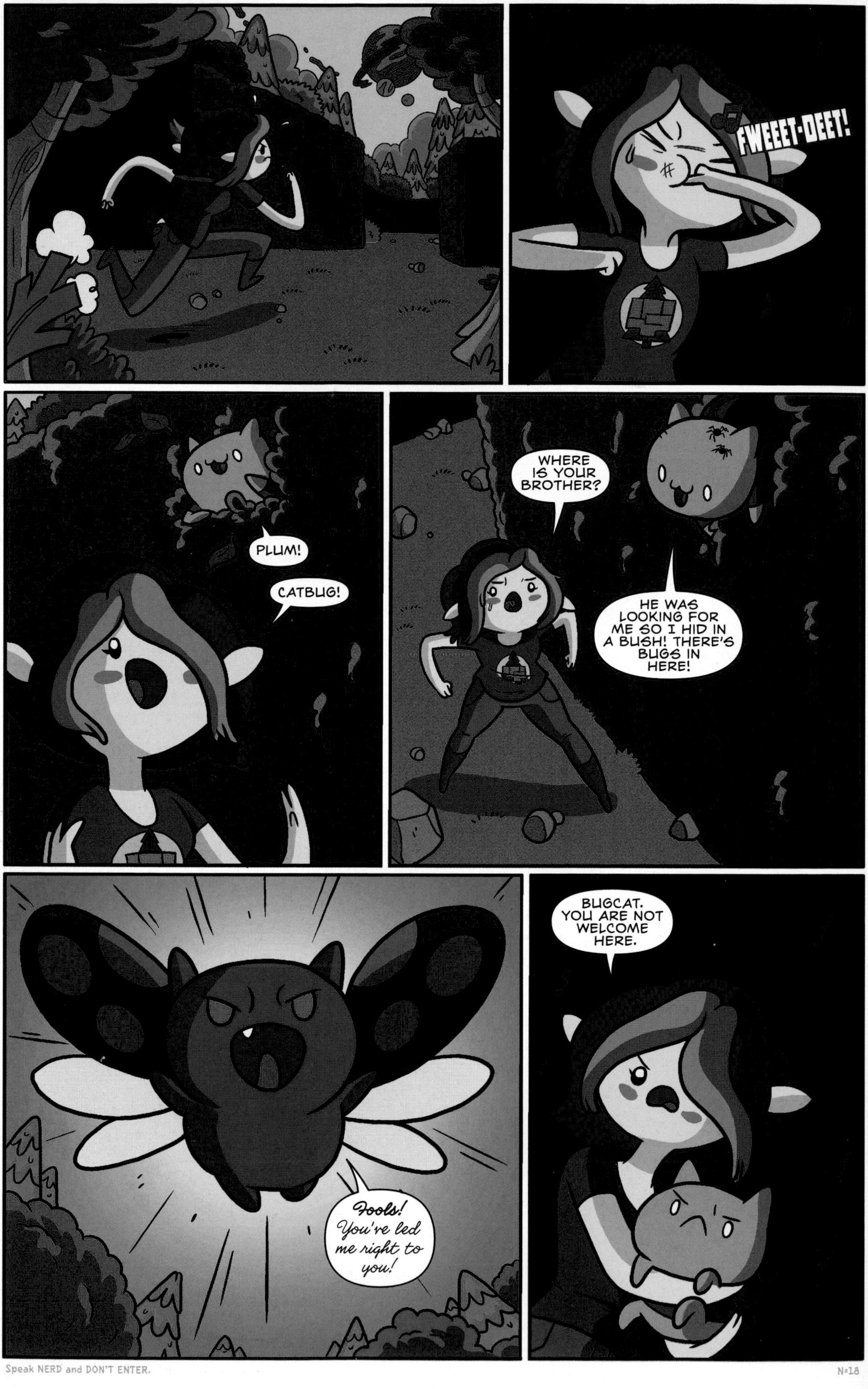

FWEEET-DEET!
PLUM!
CATBUG!
WHERE IS YOUR BROTHER?
HE WAS LOOKING FOR ME SO I HID IN A BUSH! THERE'S BUGS IN HERE!
Fools! You've led me right to you!
BUGCAT. YOU ARE NOT WELCOME HERE.

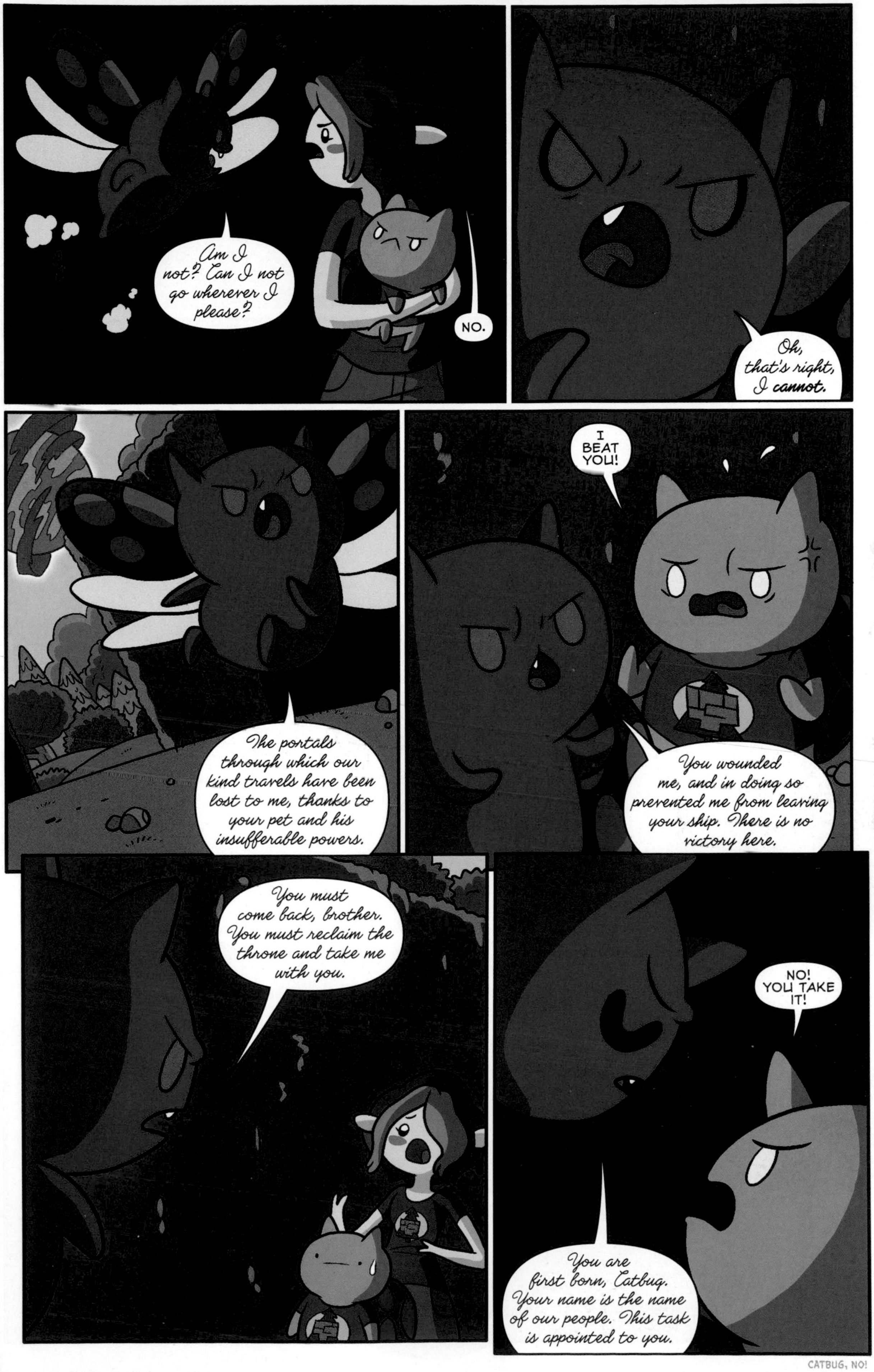
Am I not? Can I not go wherever I please?
NO.
Oh, that's right, I **cannot.**
The portals through which our kind travels have been lost to me, thanks to your pet and his insufferable powers.
I BEAT YOU!
You wounded me, and in doing so prevented me from leaving your ship. There is no victory here.
You must come back, brother. You must reclaim the throne and take me with you.
NO! YOU TAKE IT!
You are first born, Catbug. Your name is the name of our people. This task is appointed to you.

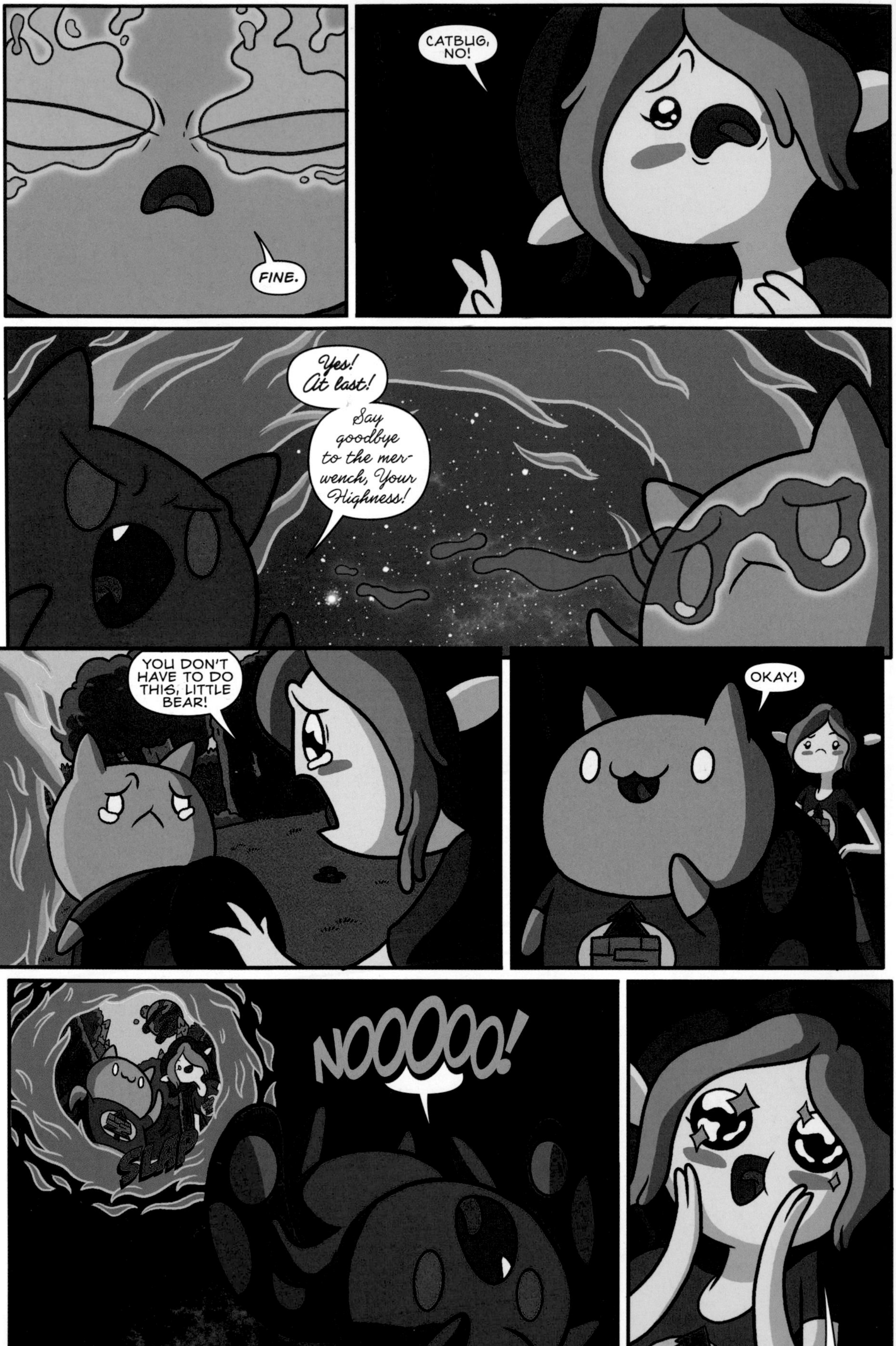
FINE.
CATBUG, NO!
Yes! At last!
Say goodbye to the mer-wench, Your Highness!
YOU DON'T HAVE TO DO THIS, LITTLE BEAR!
OKAY!
SLAP
NOOOOO!
CATBUG!

CATBUG, YES!!!

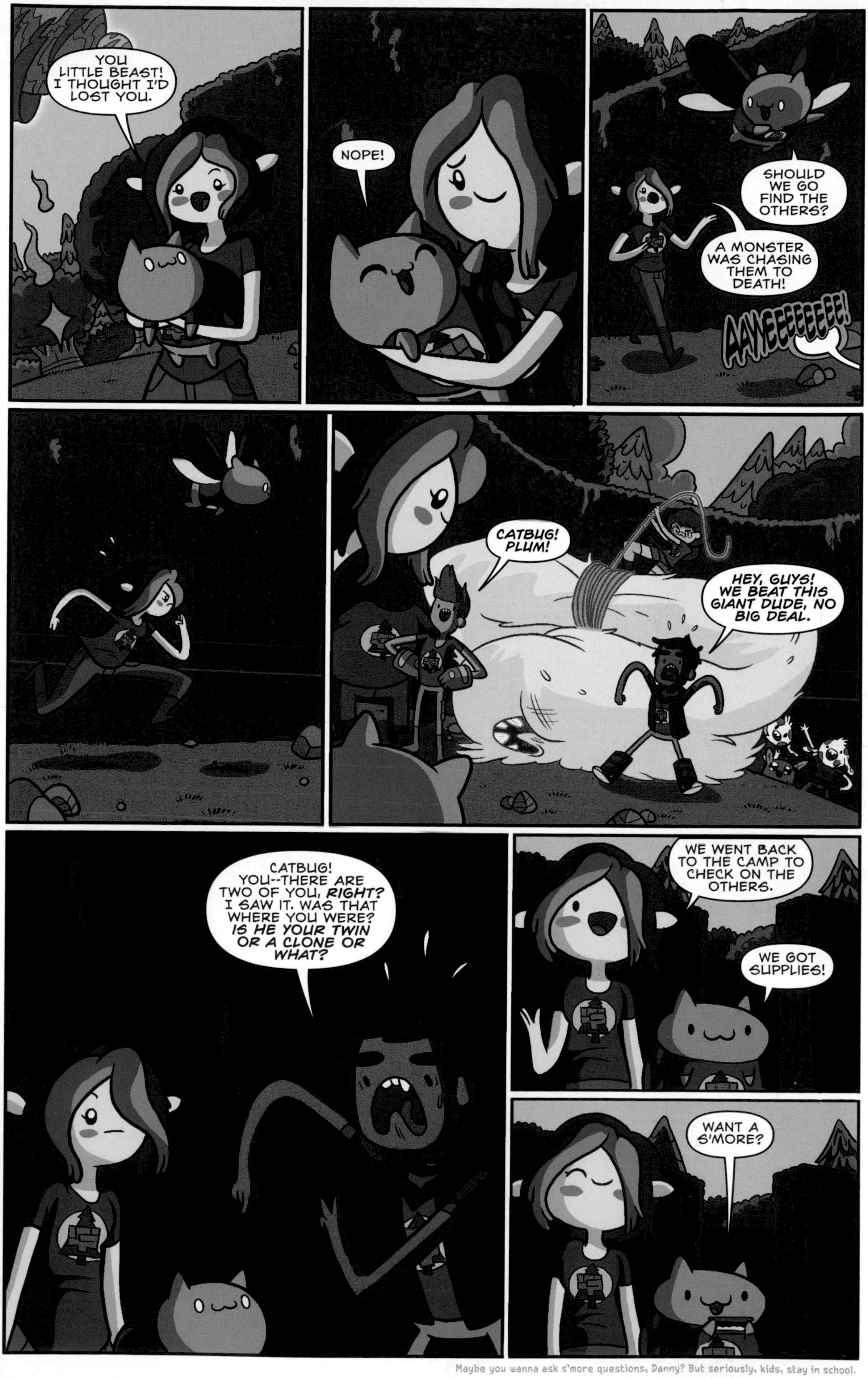
YOU LITTLE BEAST! I THOUGHT I'D LOST YOU.
NOPE!
SHOULD WE GO FIND THE OTHERS?
A MONSTER WAS CHASING THEM TO DEATH!
AAYEEEEEEEE!
CATBUG! PLUM!
HEY, GUYS! WE BEAT THIS GIANT DUDE, NO BIG DEAL.
CATBUG! YOU--THERE ARE TWO OF YOU, RIGHT? I SAW IT. WAS THAT WHERE YOU WERE? IS HE YOUR TWIN OR A CLONE OR WHAT?
WE WENT BACK TO THE CAMP TO CHECK ON THE OTHERS.
WE GOT SUPPLIES!
WANT A S'MORE?

Maybe you wanna ask s'more questions, Danny? But seriously, kids, stay in school.

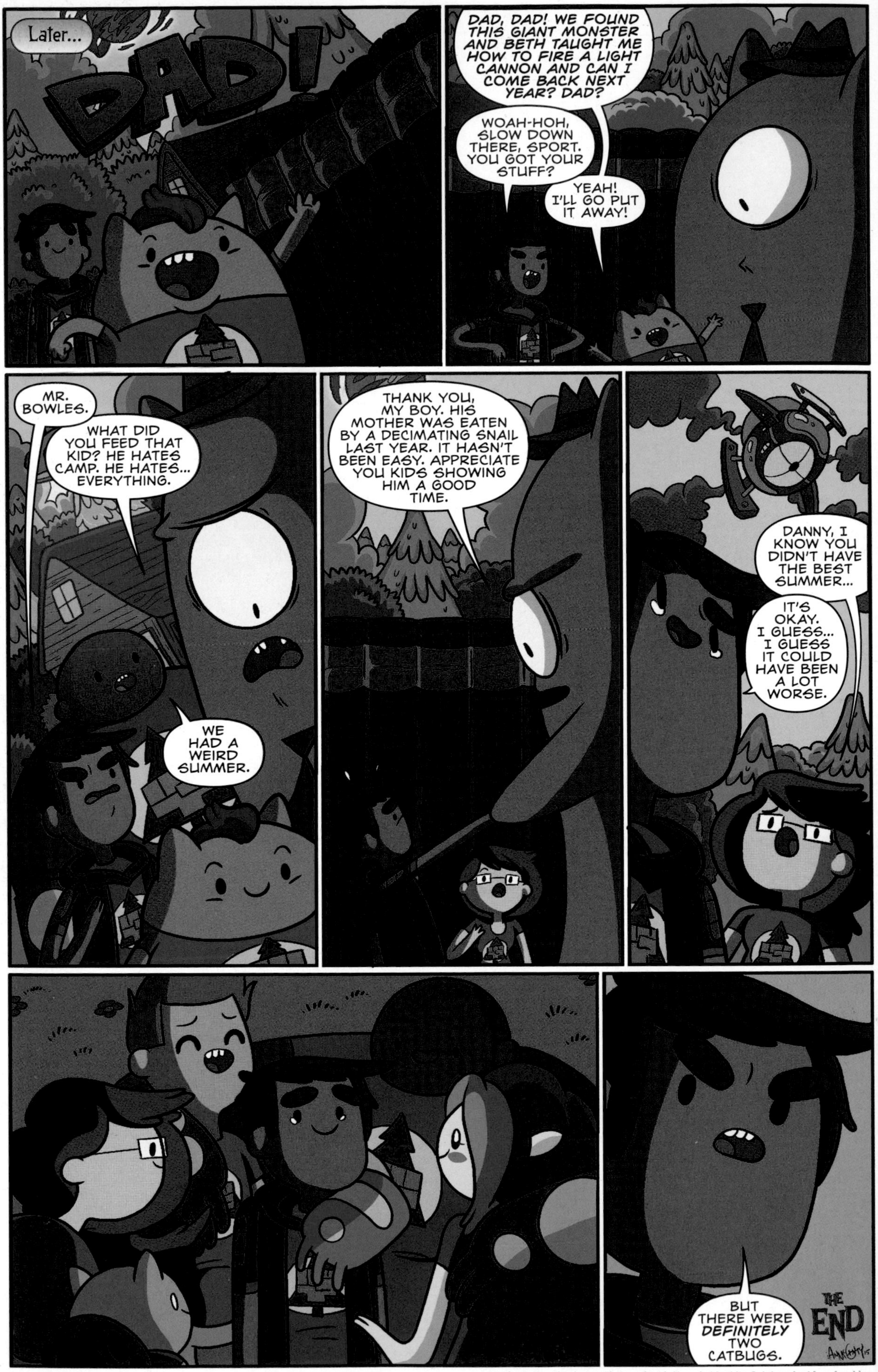
Later...
DAD!
DAD, DAD! WE FOUND THIS GIANT MONSTER AND BETH TAUGHT ME HOW TO FIRE A LIGHT CANNON AND CAN I COME BACK NEXT YEAR? DAD?
WOAH-HOH, SLOW DOWN THERE, SPORT. YOU GOT YOUR STUFF?
YEAH! I'LL GO PUT IT AWAY!
MR. BOWLES.
WHAT DID YOU FEED THAT KID? HE HATES CAMP. HE HATES... EVERYTHING.
WE HAD A WEIRD SUMMER.
THANK YOU, MY BOY. HIS MOTHER WAS EATEN BY A DECIMATING SNAIL LAST YEAR. IT HASN'T BEEN EASY. APPRECIATE YOU KIDS SHOWING HIM A GOOD TIME.
DANNY, I KNOW YOU DIDN'T HAVE THE BEST SUMMER...
IT'S OKAY. I GUESS... I GUESS IT COULD HAVE BEEN A LOT WORSE.
BUT THERE WERE *DEFINITELY* TWO CATBUGS.
THE END

Mh fwpl: S emjvwj, s eqklwjq, s lgskl. Kwnwjsd lgsklk. S dgl gx lgskl, sulmsddq.

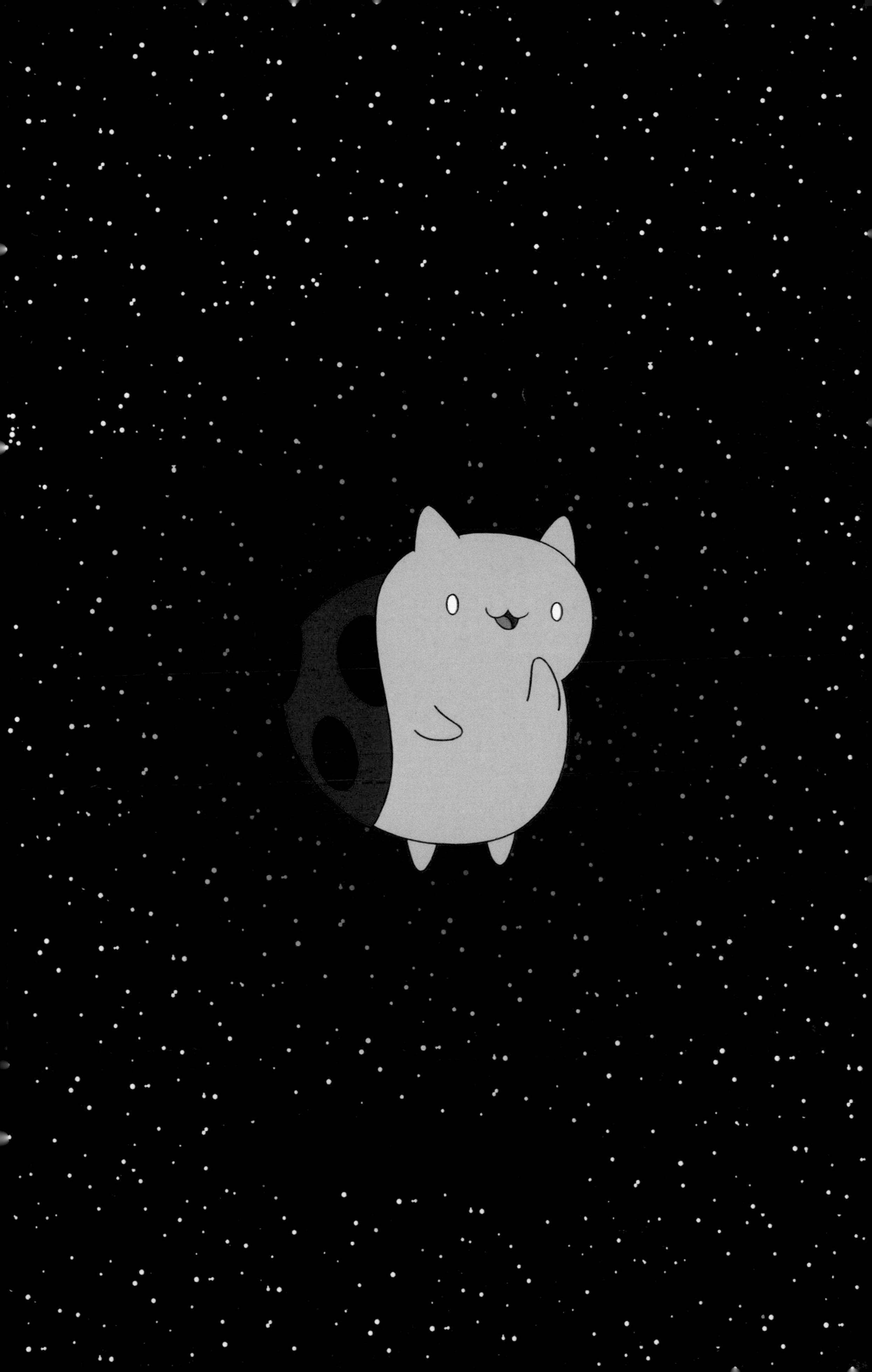

SHORT MISSIONS

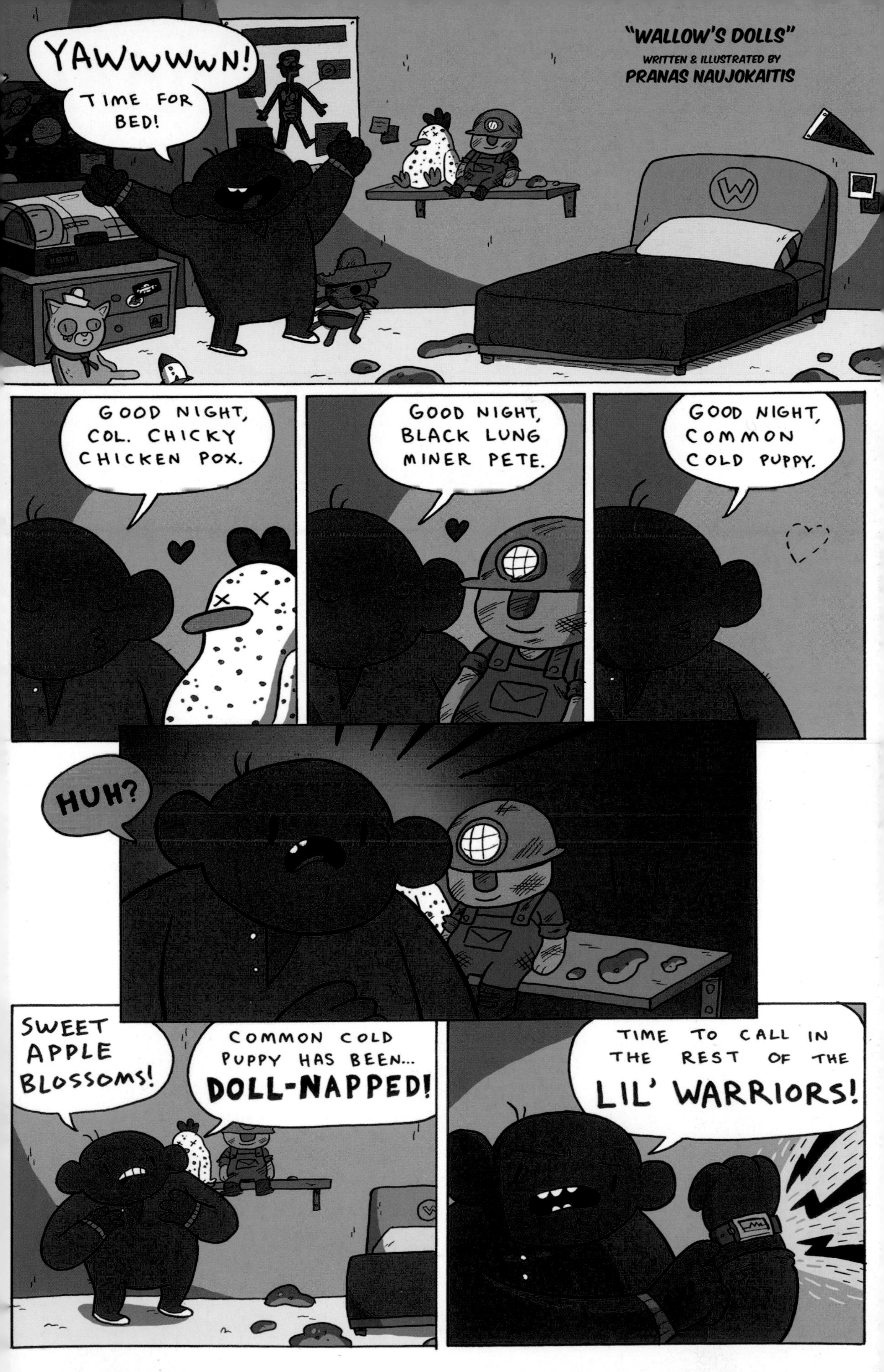
"WALLOW'S DOLLS"
WRITTEN & ILLUSTRATED BY
PRANAS NAUJOKAITIS
YAWWWWN!
TIME FOR BED!
GOOD NIGHT, COL. CHICKY CHICKEN POX.
GOOD NIGHT, BLACK LUNG MINER PETE.
GOOD NIGHT, COMMON COLD PUPPY.
HUH?
SWEET APPLE BLOSSOMS!
COMMON COLD PUPPY HAS BEEN... DOLL-NAPPED!
TIME TO CALL IN THE REST OF THE LIL' WARRIORS!

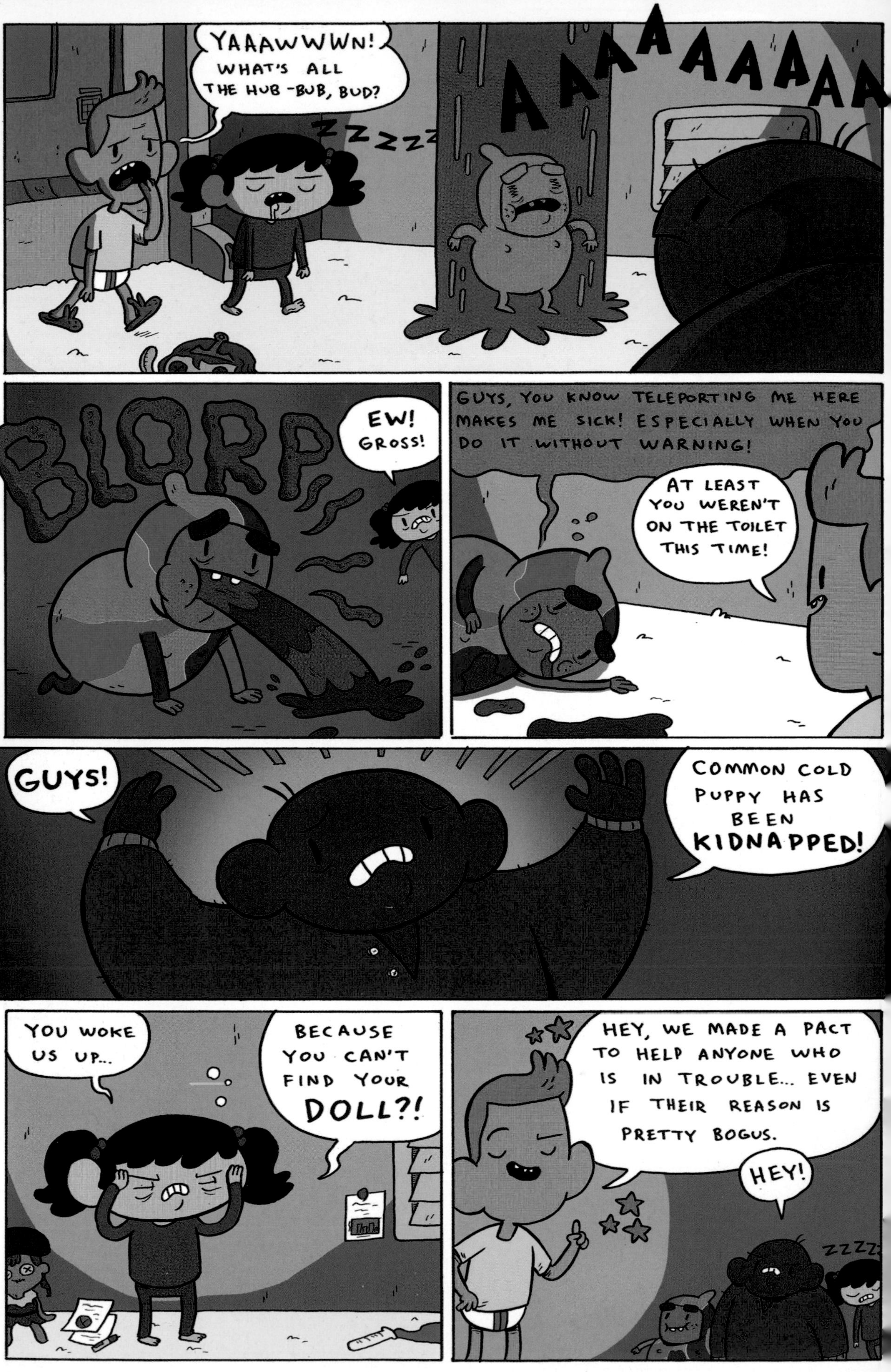
YAAAWWWN! WHAT'S ALL THE HUB-BUB, BUD?
ZZZZZ
AAAAAAAAA
BLORP
EW! GROSS!
GUYS, YOU KNOW TELEPORTING ME HERE MAKES ME SICK! ESPECIALLY WHEN YOU DO IT WITHOUT WARNING!
AT LEAST YOU WEREN'T ON THE TOILET THIS TIME!
GUYS!
COMMON COLD PUPPY HAS BEEN KIDNAPPED!
YOU WOKE US UP...
BECAUSE YOU CAN'T FIND YOUR DOLL?!
HEY, WE MADE A PACT TO HELP ANYONE WHO IS IN TROUBLE... EVEN IF THEIR REASON IS PRETTY BOGUS.
HEY!
ZZZZZ

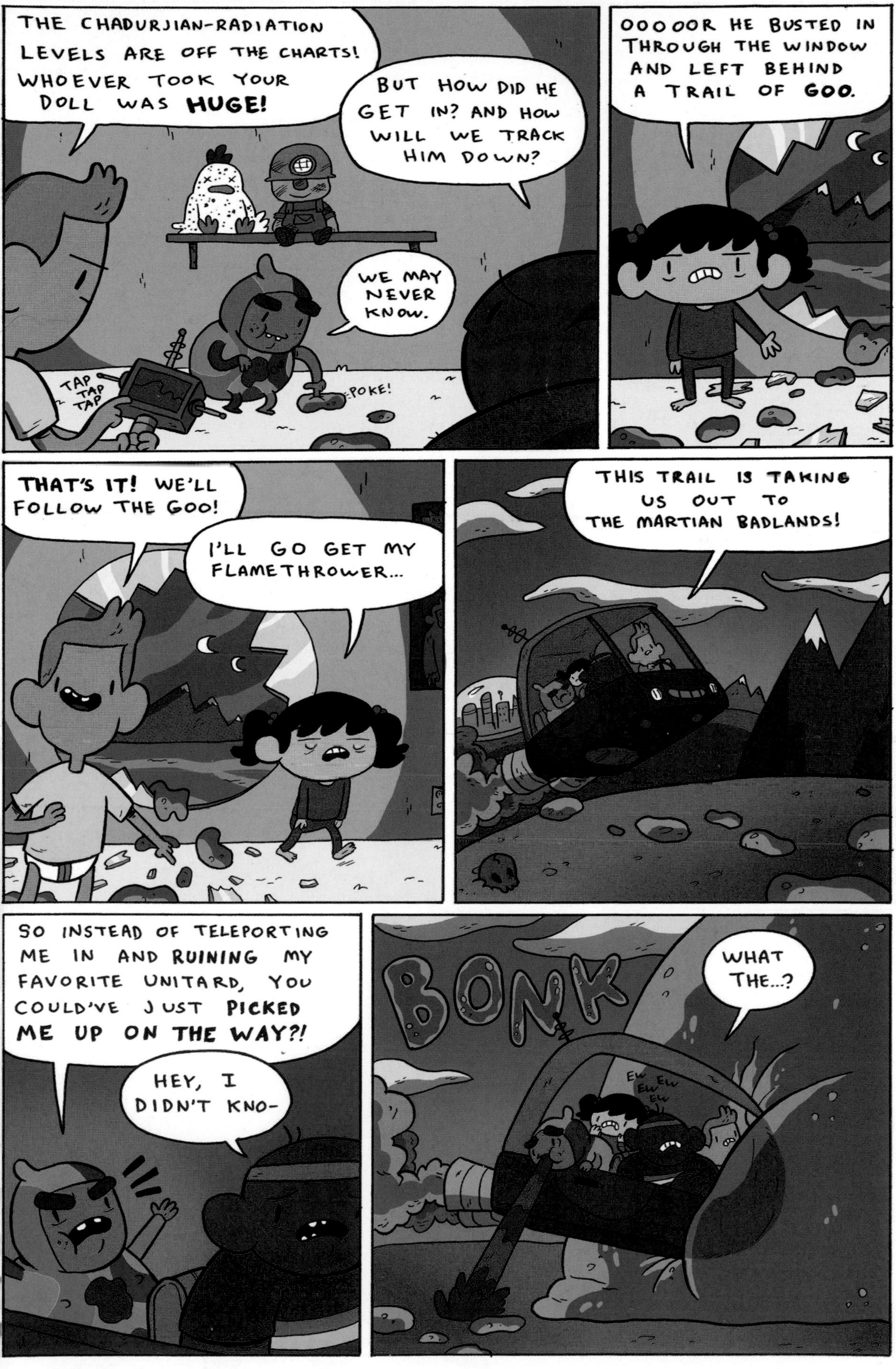
THE CHADURJIAN-RADIATION LEVELS ARE OFF THE CHARTS! WHOEVER TOOK YOUR DOLL WAS **HUGE!**
BUT HOW DID HE GET IN? AND HOW WILL WE TRACK HIM DOWN?
WE MAY NEVER KNOW.
TAP TAP TAP
POKE!
OOOOOR HE BUSTED IN THROUGH THE WINDOW AND LEFT BEHIND A TRAIL OF **GOO.**
THAT'S IT! WE'LL FOLLOW THE GOO!
I'LL GO GET MY FLAMETHROWER...
THIS TRAIL IS TAKING US OUT TO THE MARTIAN BADLANDS!
SO INSTEAD OF TELEPORTING ME IN AND **RUINING** MY FAVORITE UNITARD, YOU COULD'VE JUST **PICKED ME UP ON THE WAY?!**
HEY, I DIDN'T KNO-
BONK
WHAT THE...?
EW EW EW EW

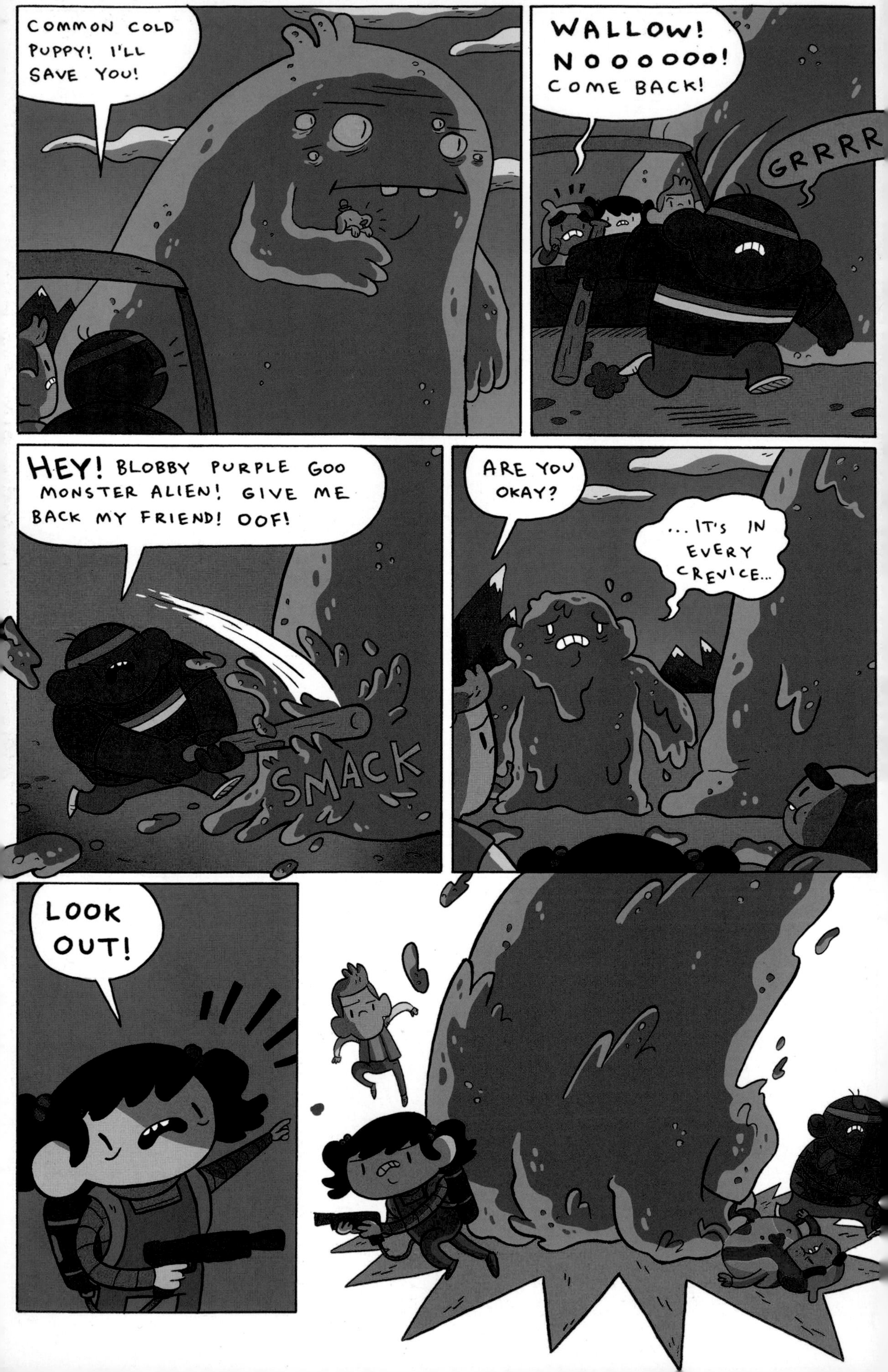
COMMON COLD PUPPY! I'LL SAVE YOU!
WALLOW! NOOOOOOO! COME BACK!
GRRRR
HEY! BLOBBY PURPLE GOO MONSTER ALIEN! GIVE ME BACK MY FRIEND! OOF!
SMACK
ARE YOU OKAY?
...IT'S IN EVERY CREVICE...
LOOK OUT!

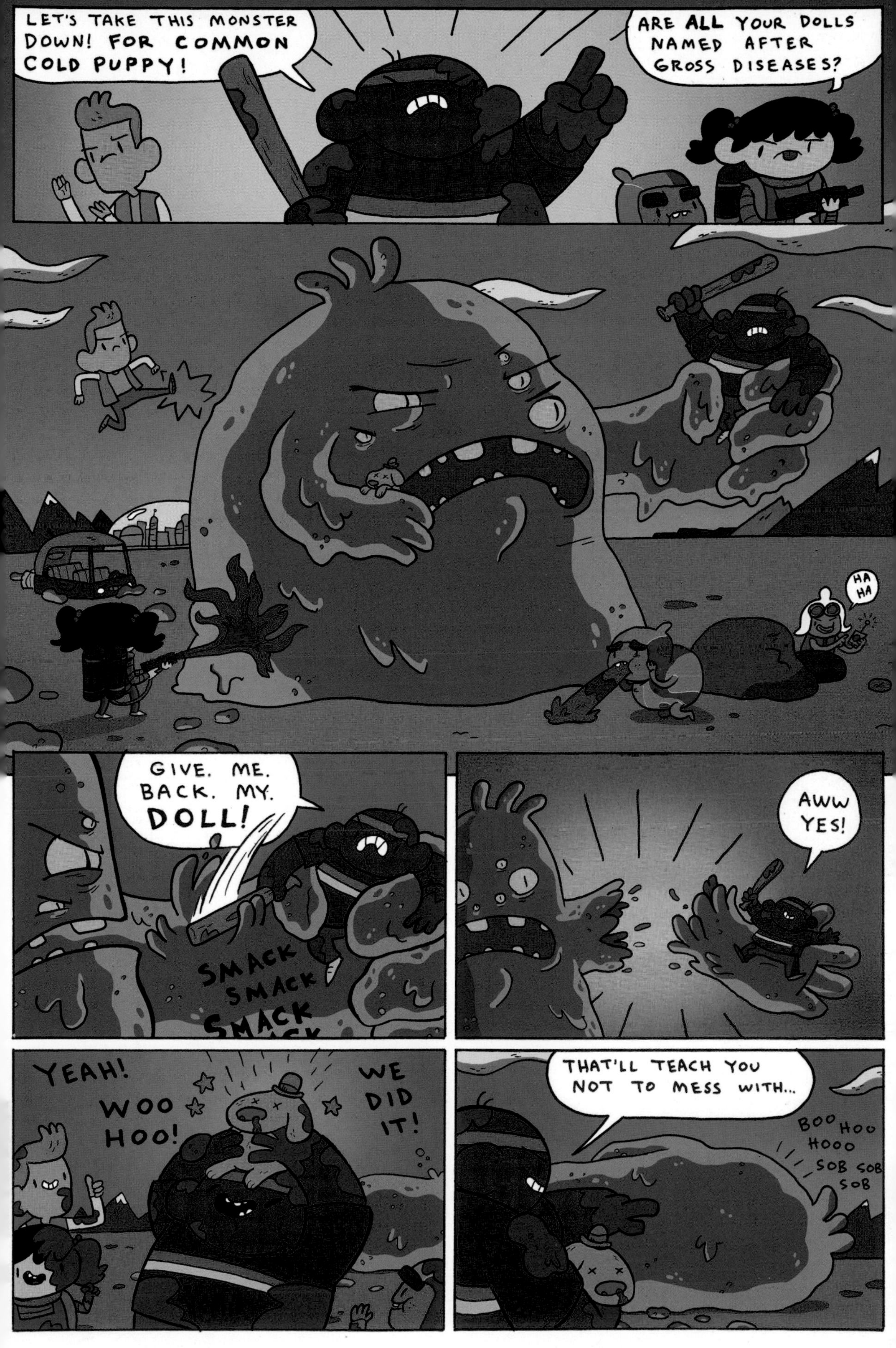
LET'S TAKE THIS MONSTER DOWN! FOR COMMON COLD PUPPY!
ARE ALL YOUR DOLLS NAMED AFTER GROSS DISEASES?
HA HA
GIVE. ME. BACK. MY. DOLL!
SMACK
SMACK
SMACK
AWW YES!
YEAH!
WOO HOO!
WE DID IT!
THAT'LL TEACH YOU NOT TO MESS WITH...
BOO HOO HOOO
SOB SOB SOB

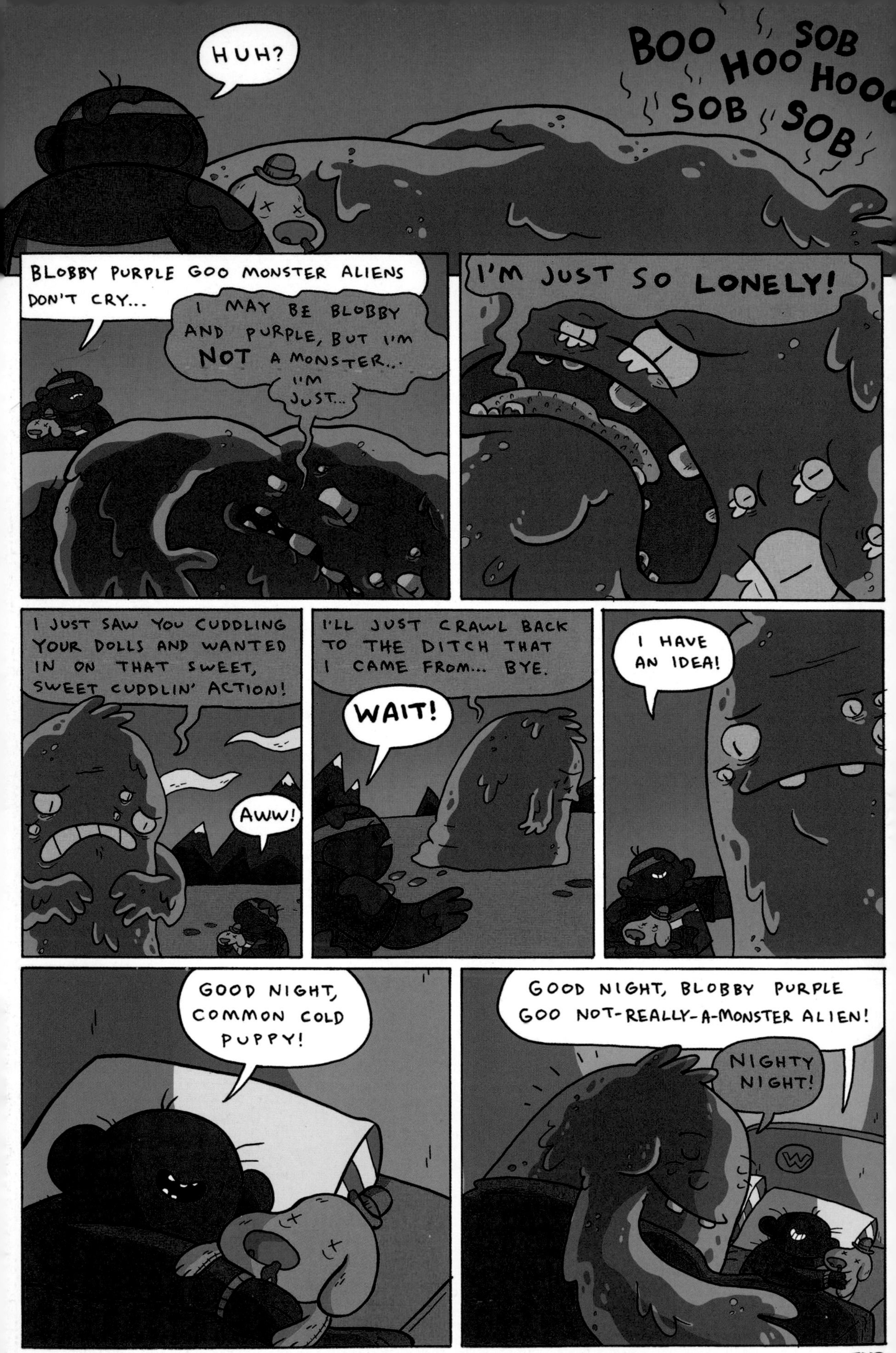
HUH?
BOO HOO SOB HOO SOB HOOO SOB
BLOBBY PURPLE GOO MONSTER ALIENS DON'T CRY...
I MAY BE BLOBBY AND PURPLE, BUT I'M NOT A MONSTER... I'M JUST...
I'M JUST SO LONELY!
I JUST SAW YOU CUDDLING YOUR DOLLS AND WANTED IN ON THAT SWEET, SWEET CUDDLIN' ACTION!
AWW!
I'LL JUST CRAWL BACK TO THE DITCH THAT I CAME FROM... BYE.
WAIT!
I HAVE AN IDEA!
GOOD NIGHT, COMMON COLD PUPPY!
GOOD NIGHT, BLOBBY PURPLE GOO NOT-REALLY-A-MONSTER ALIEN!
NIGHTY NIGHT!
END

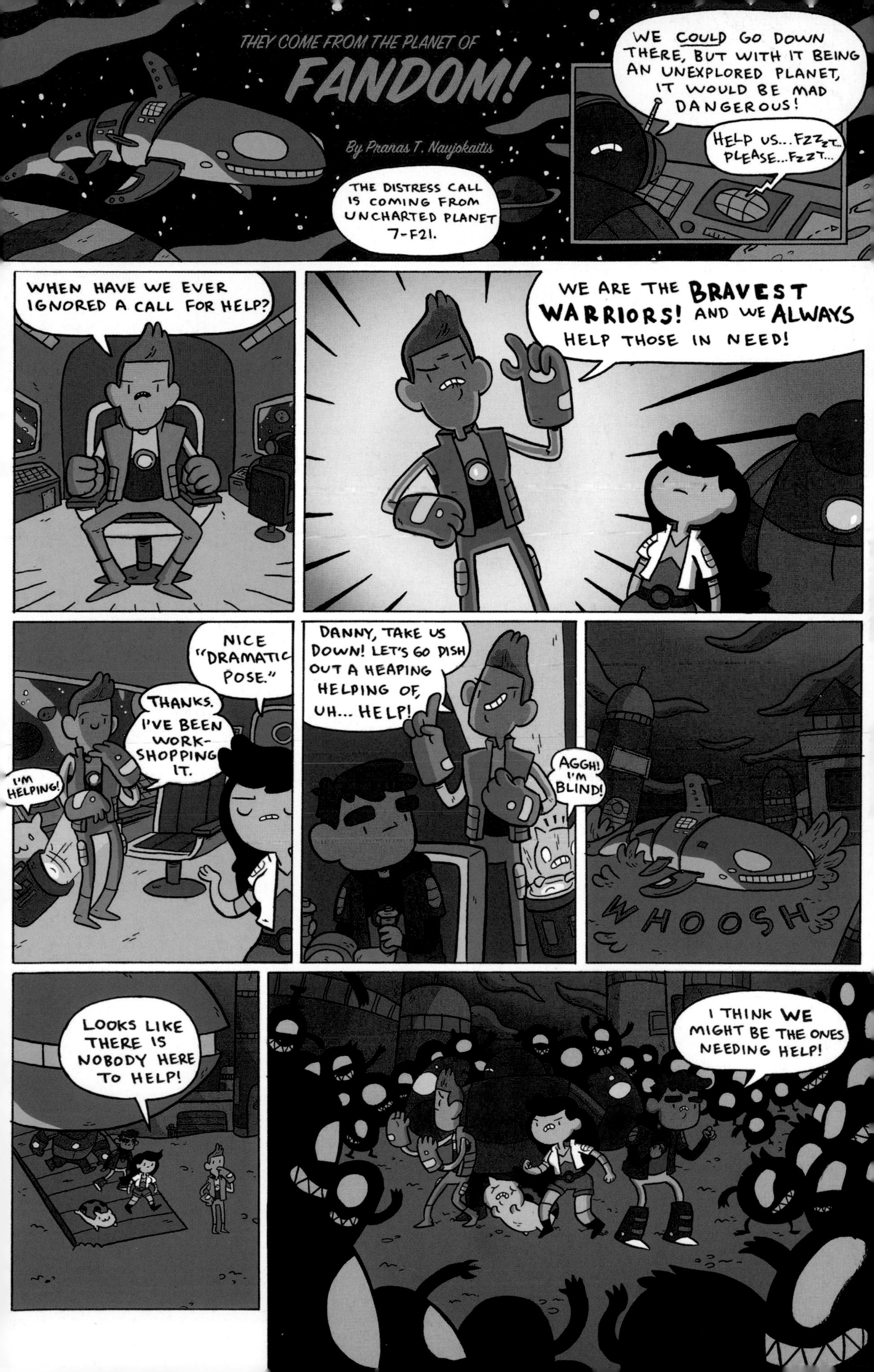

THEY COME FROM THE PLANET OF
FANDOM!
By Pranas T. Naujokaitis
THE DISTRESS CALL IS COMING FROM UNCHARTED PLANET 7-F21.
WE COULD GO DOWN THERE, BUT WITH IT BEING AN UNEXPLORED PLANET, IT WOULD BE MAD DANGEROUS!
HELP US... FZZZT... PLEASE... FZZT...
WHEN HAVE WE EVER IGNORED A CALL FOR HELP?
WE ARE THE BRAVEST WARRIORS! AND WE ALWAYS HELP THOSE IN NEED!
NICE "DRAMATIC POSE."
THANKS. I'VE BEEN WORK-SHOPPING IT.
I'M HELPING!
DANNY, TAKE US DOWN! LET'S GO DISH OUT A HEAPING HELPING OF, UH... HELP!
AGGH! I'M BLIND!
WHOOSH
LOOKS LIKE THERE IS NOBODY HERE TO HELP!
I THINK WE MIGHT BE THE ONES NEEDING HELP!

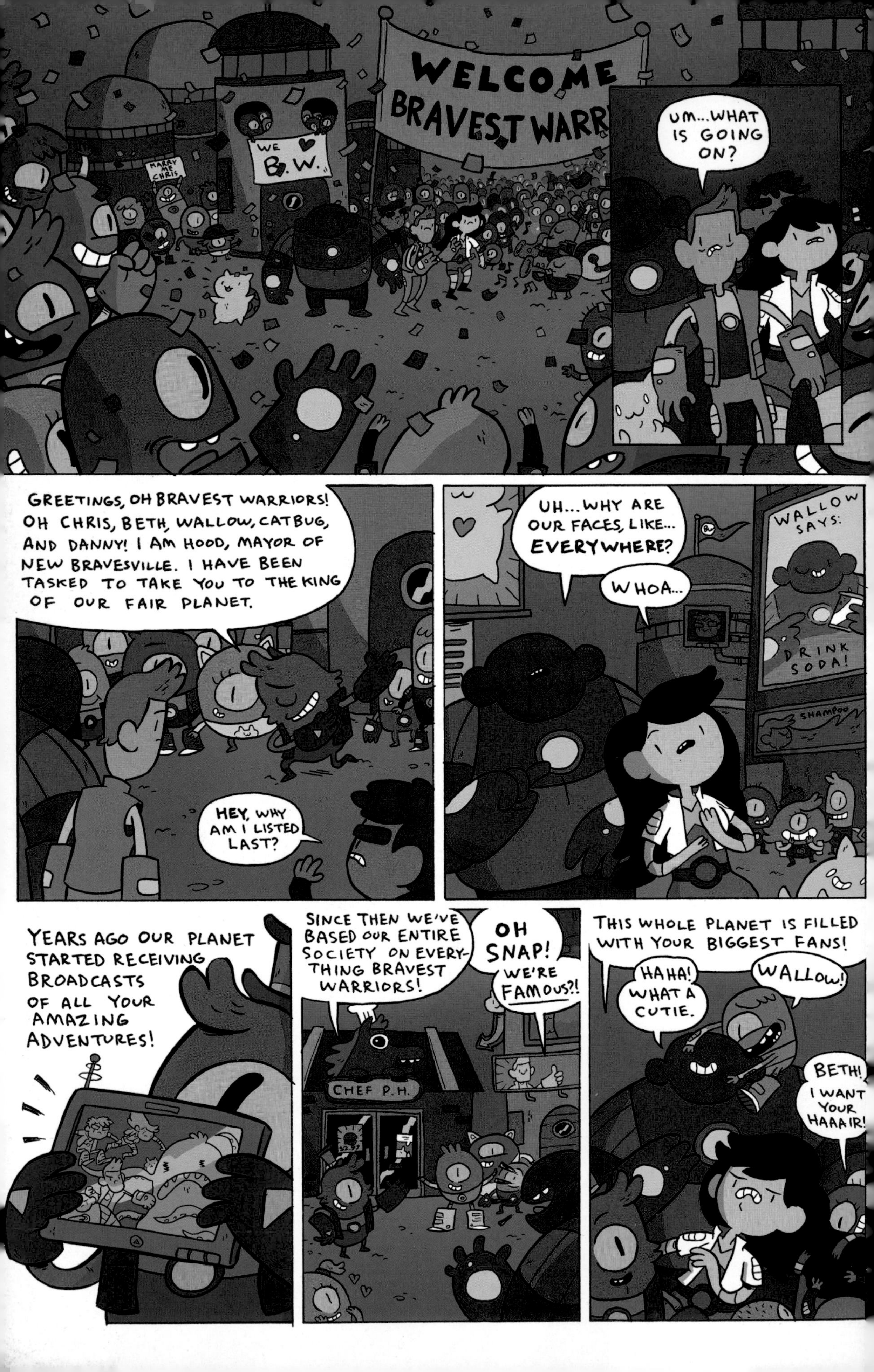
WELCOME BRAVEST WARR
WE ♥ B.W.
MARRY ME CHRIS
UM...WHAT IS GOING ON?
GREETINGS, OH BRAVEST WARRIORS! OH CHRIS, BETH, WALLOW, CATBUG, AND DANNY! I AM HOOD, MAYOR OF NEW BRAVESVILLE. I HAVE BEEN TASKED TO TAKE YOU TO THE KING OF OUR FAIR PLANET.
HEY, WHY AM I LISTED LAST?
UH... WHY ARE OUR FACES, LIKE... EVERYWHERE?
WHOA...
WALLOW SAYS: DRINK SODA!
SHAMPOO
YEARS AGO OUR PLANET STARTED RECEIVING BROADCASTS OF ALL YOUR AMAZING ADVENTURES!
SINCE THEN WE'VE BASED OUR ENTIRE SOCIETY ON EVERYTHING BRAVEST WARRIORS!
OH SNAP! WE'RE FAMOUS?!
CHEF P.H.
THIS WHOLE PLANET IS FILLED WITH YOUR BIGGEST FANS!
HAHA! WHAT A CUTIE.
WALLOW!
BETH! I WANT YOUR HAAAIR!

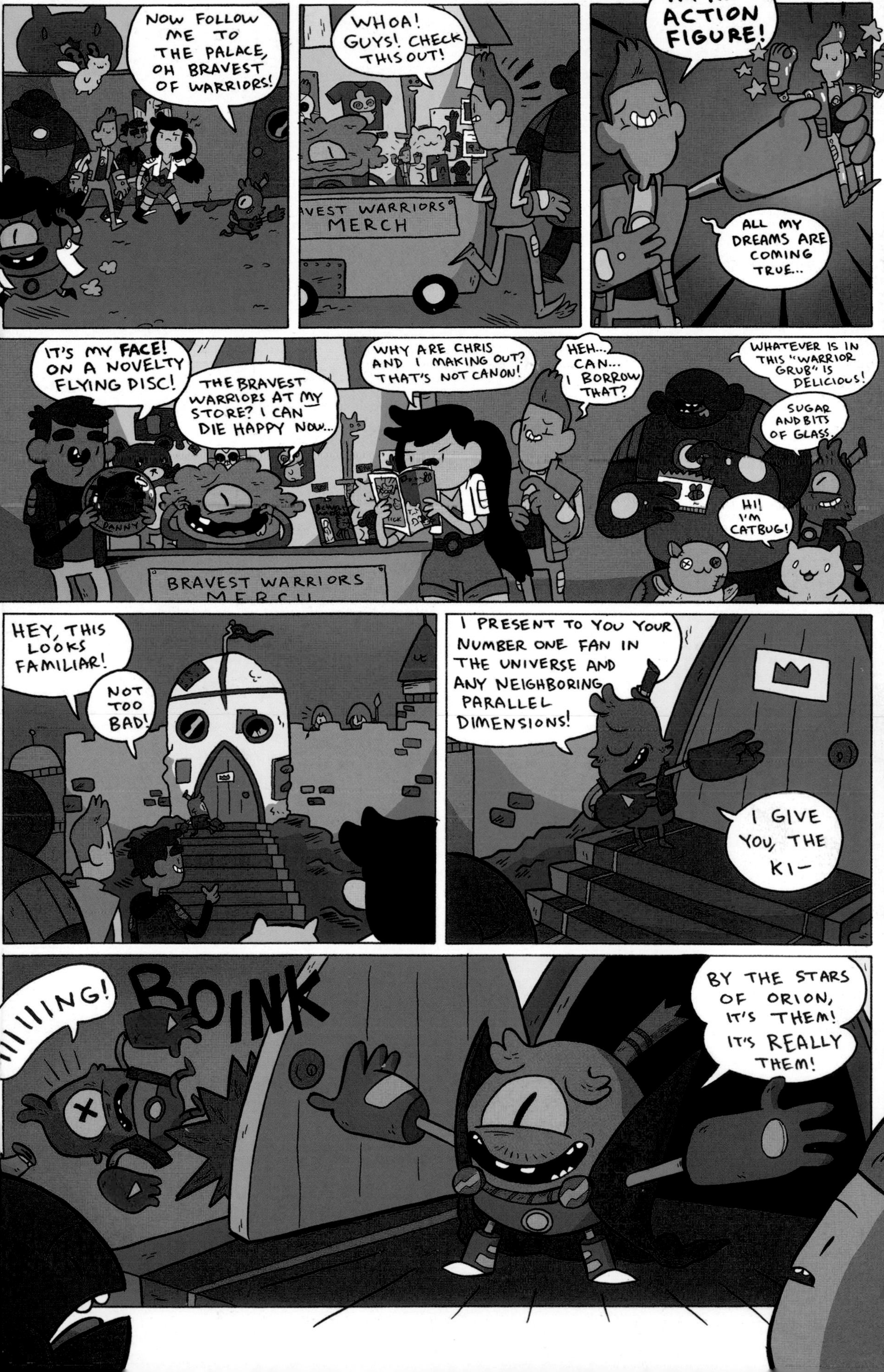
NOW FOLLOW ME TO THE PALACE, OH BRAVEST OF WARRIORS!
WHOA! GUYS! CHECK THIS OUT!
BRAVEST WARRIORS MERCH
I'M AN ACTION FIGURE!
ALL MY DREAMS ARE COMING TRUE...
IT'S MY FACE! ON A NOVELTY FLYING DISC!
THE BRAVEST WARRIORS AT MY STORE? I CAN DIE HAPPY NOW...
DANNY
WHY ARE CHRIS AND I MAKING OUT? THAT'S NOT CANON!
HEH... CAN... I BORROW THAT?
WHATEVER IS IN THIS "WARRIOR GRUB" IS DELICIOUS!
SUGAR AND BITS OF GLASS.
HI! I'M CATBUG!
BRAVEST WARRIORS MERCH
HEY, THIS LOOKS FAMILIAR!
NOT TOO BAD!
I PRESENT TO YOU YOUR NUMBER ONE FAN IN THE UNIVERSE AND ANY NEIGHBORING PARALLEL DIMENSIONS!
I GIVE YOU, THE KI—
IIIIIING!
BOINK
BY THE STARS OF ORION, IT'S THEM! IT'S REALLY THEM!

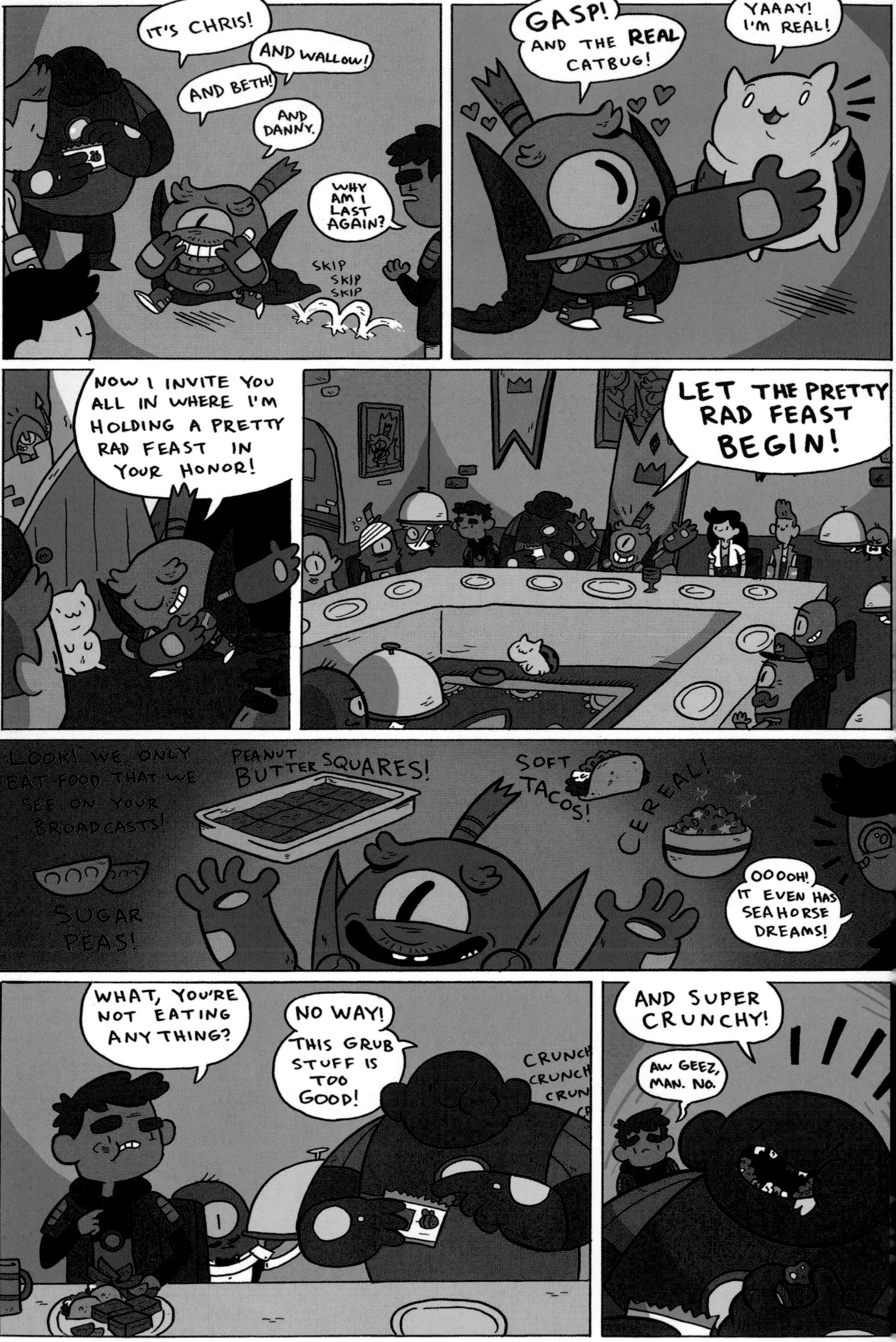

IT'S CHRIS!
AND WALLOW!
AND BETH!
AND DANNY.
WHY AM I LAST AGAIN?
SKIP SKIP SKIP
GASP! AND THE REAL CATBUG!
YAAAY! I'M REAL!
NOW I INVITE YOU ALL IN WHERE I'M HOLDING A PRETTY RAD FEAST IN YOUR HONOR!
LET THE PRETTY RAD FEAST BEGIN!
LOOK! WE ONLY EAT FOOD THAT WE SEE ON YOUR BROADCASTS!
PEANUT BUTTER SQUARES!
SOFT TACOS!
CEREAL!
SUGAR PEAS!
OOOOH! IT EVEN HAS SEA HORSE DREAMS!
WHAT, YOU'RE NOT EATING ANY THING?
NO WAY!
THIS GRUB STUFF IS TOO GOOD!
CRUNCH CRUNCH CRUN
AND SUPER CRUNCHY!
AW GEEZ, MAN. NO.

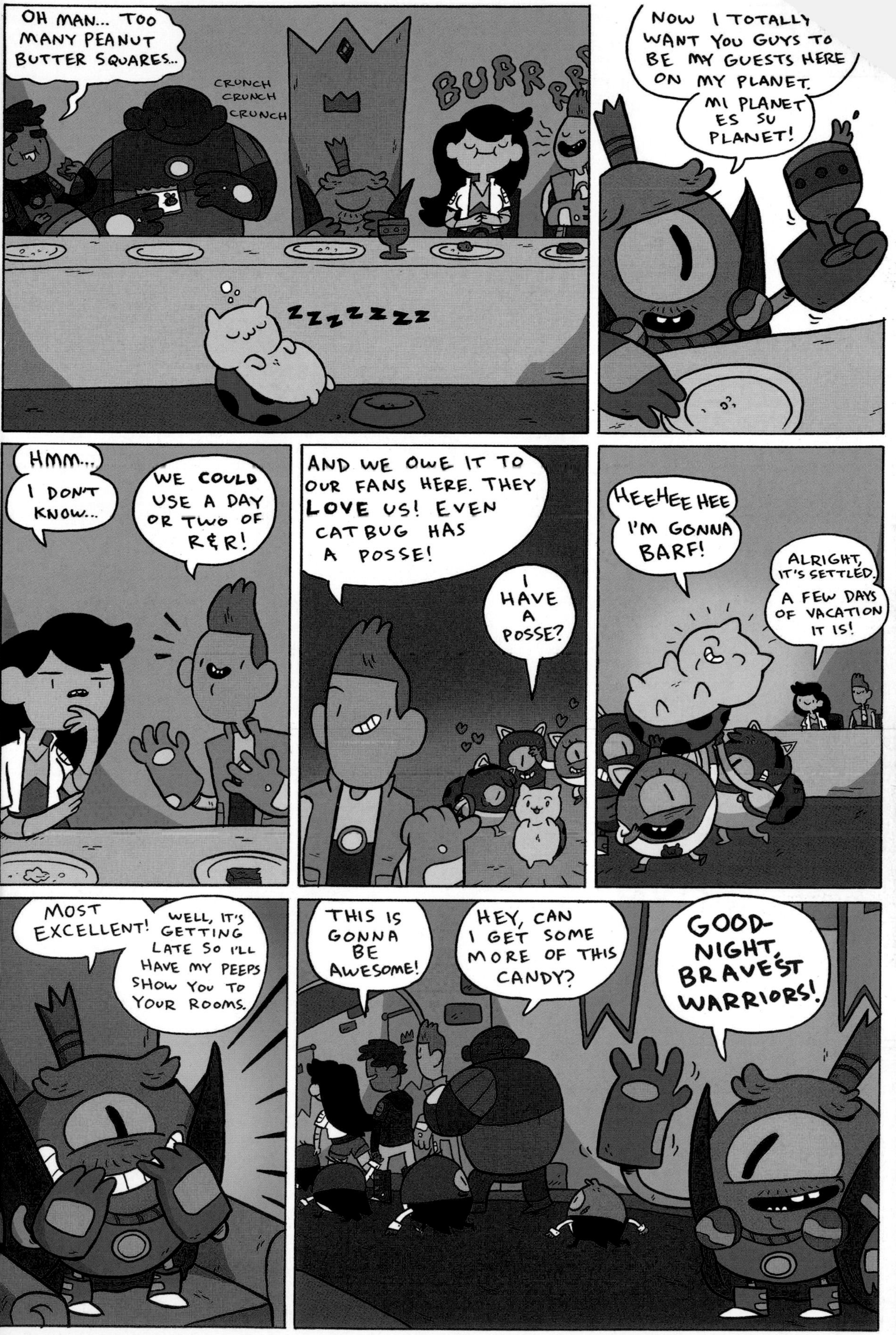
OH MAN... TOO MANY PEANUT BUTTER SQUARES...
CRUNCH CRUNCH CRUNCH
BURRRP
ZZZZZZZ
NOW I TOTALLY WANT YOU GUYS TO BE MY GUESTS HERE ON MY PLANET.
MI PLANET ES SU PLANET!
HMM...
I DON'T KNOW...
WE COULD USE A DAY OR TWO OF R&R!
AND WE OWE IT TO OUR FANS HERE. THEY LOVE US! EVEN CATBUG HAS A POSSE!
I HAVE A POSSE?
HEEHEE HEE
I'M GONNA BARF!
ALRIGHT, IT'S SETTLED. A FEW DAYS OF VACATION IT IS!
MOST EXCELLENT!
WELL, IT'S GETTING LATE SO I'LL HAVE MY PEEPS SHOW YOU TO YOUR ROOMS.
THIS IS GONNA BE AWESOME!
HEY, CAN I GET SOME MORE OF THIS CANDY?
GOOD-NIGHT, BRAVEST WARRIORS!

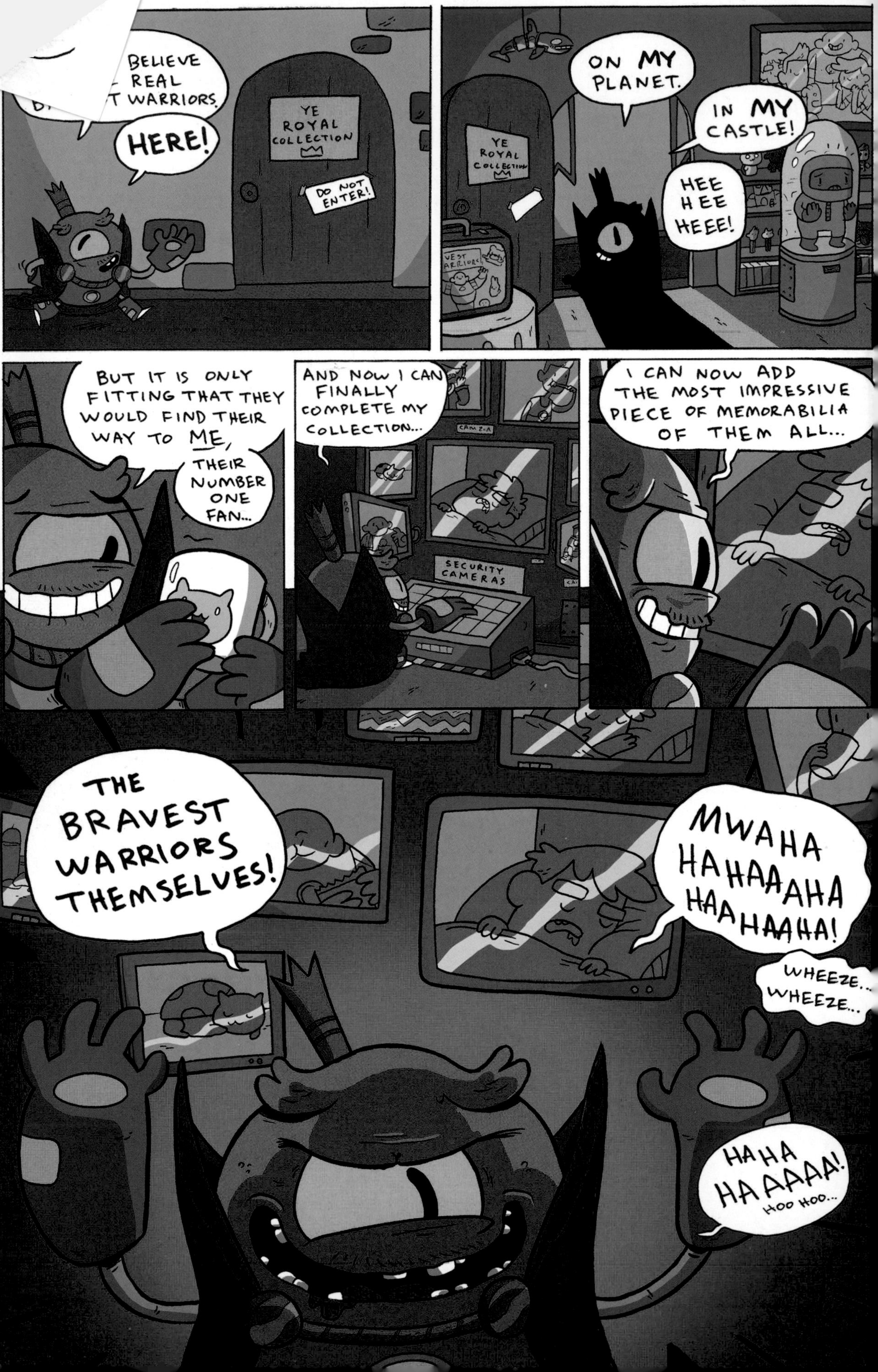
BELIEVE REAL WARRIORS.
HERE!
YE ROYAL COLLECTION
DO NOT ENTER!
ON MY PLANET.
IN MY CASTLE!
HEE HEE HEEE!
YE ROYAL COLLECTION
BUT IT IS ONLY FITTING THAT THEY WOULD FIND THEIR WAY TO ME,
THEIR NUMBER ONE FAN...
AND NOW I CAN FINALLY COMPLETE MY COLLECTION...
SECURITY CAMERAS
I CAN NOW ADD THE MOST IMPRESSIVE PIECE OF MEMORABILIA OF THEM ALL...
THE BRAVEST WARRIORS THEMSELVES!
MWAHA HAHAAAAHA HAAHAAAHA!
WHEEZE... WHEEZE...
HAHA HAAAAA!
HOO HOO...

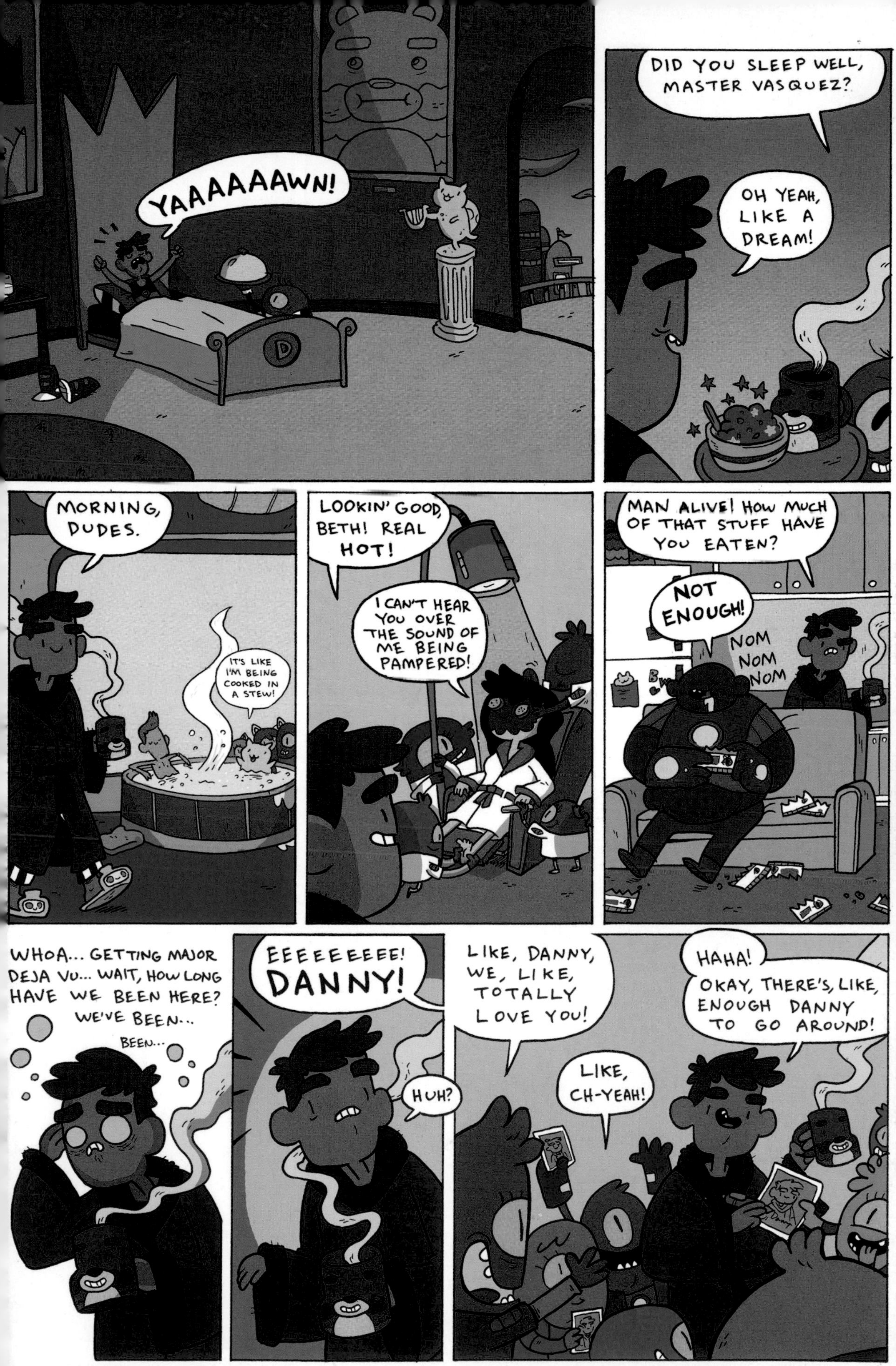

YAAAAAAWN!
DID YOU SLEEP WELL, MASTER VASQUEZ?
OH YEAH, LIKE A DREAM!
MORNING, DUDES.
IT'S LIKE I'M BEING COOKED IN A STEW!
LOOKIN' GOOD, BETH! REAL HOT!
I CAN'T HEAR YOU OVER THE SOUND OF ME BEING PAMPERED!
MAN ALIVE! HOW MUCH OF THAT STUFF HAVE YOU EATEN?
NOT ENOUGH!
NOM NOM NOM
WHOA... GETTING MAJOR DEJA VU... WAIT, HOW LONG HAVE WE BEEN HERE? WE'VE BEEN...
BEEN...
EEEEEEEEE! DANNY!
HUH?
LIKE, DANNY, WE, LIKE, TOTALLY LOVE YOU!
LIKE, CH-YEAH!
HAHA! OKAY, THERE'S, LIKE, ENOUGH DANNY TO GO AROUND!

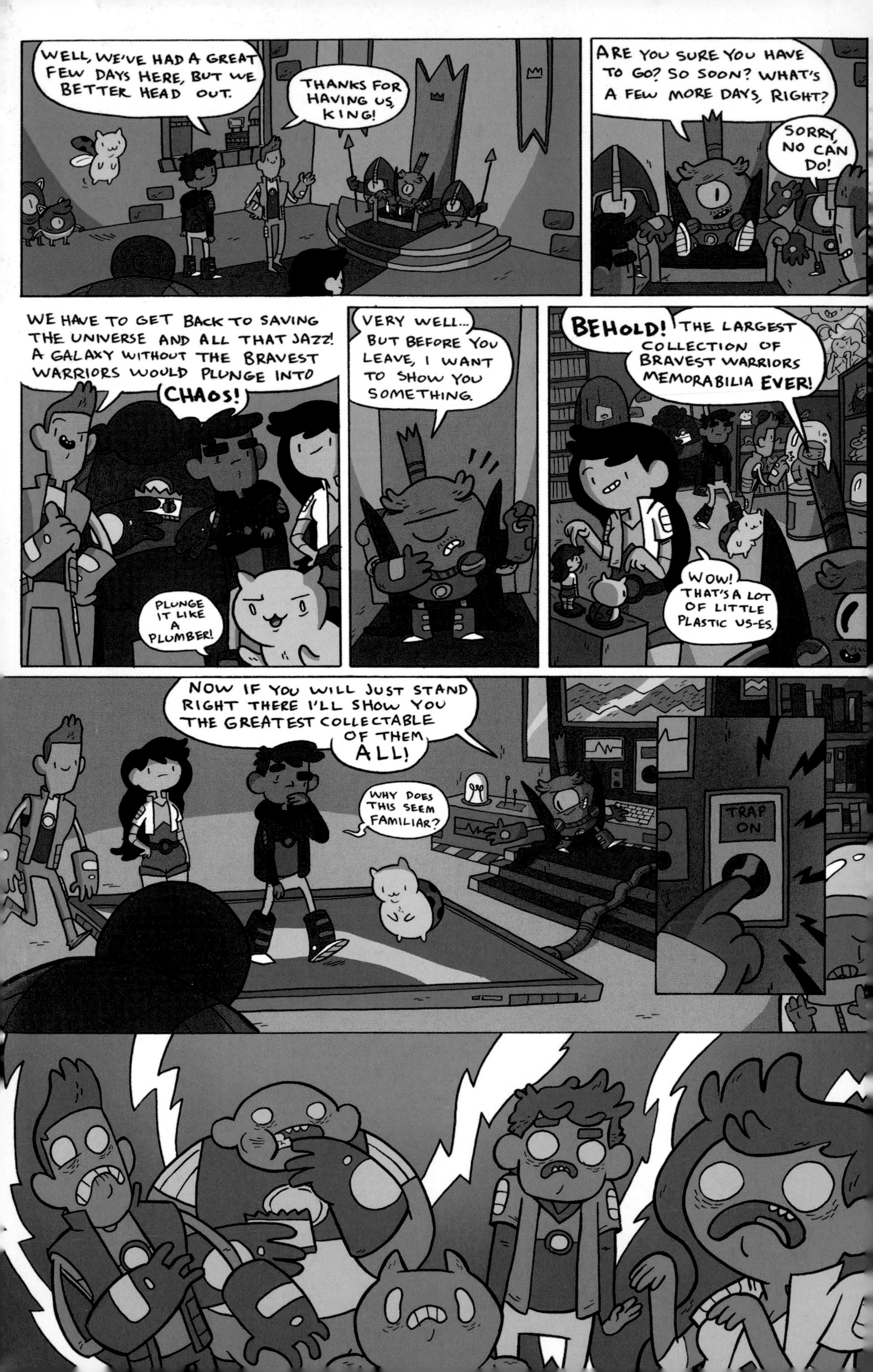
WELL, WE'VE HAD A GREAT FEW DAYS HERE, BUT WE BETTER HEAD OUT.
THANKS FOR HAVING US, KING!
ARE YOU SURE YOU HAVE TO GO? SO SOON? WHAT'S A FEW MORE DAYS, RIGHT?
SORRY, NO CAN DO!
WE HAVE TO GET BACK TO SAVING THE UNIVERSE AND ALL THAT JAZZ! A GALAXY WITHOUT THE BRAVEST WARRIORS WOULD PLUNGE INTO CHAOS!
PLUNGE IT LIKE A PLUMBER!
VERY WELL... BUT BEFORE YOU LEAVE, I WANT TO SHOW YOU SOMETHING.
BEHOLD! THE LARGEST COLLECTION OF BRAVEST WARRIORS MEMORABILIA EVER!
WOW! THAT'S A LOT OF LITTLE PLASTIC US-ES.
NOW IF YOU WILL JUST STAND RIGHT THERE I'LL SHOW YOU THE GREATEST COLLECTABLE OF THEM ALL!
WHY DOES THIS SEEM FAMILIAR?
TRAP ON

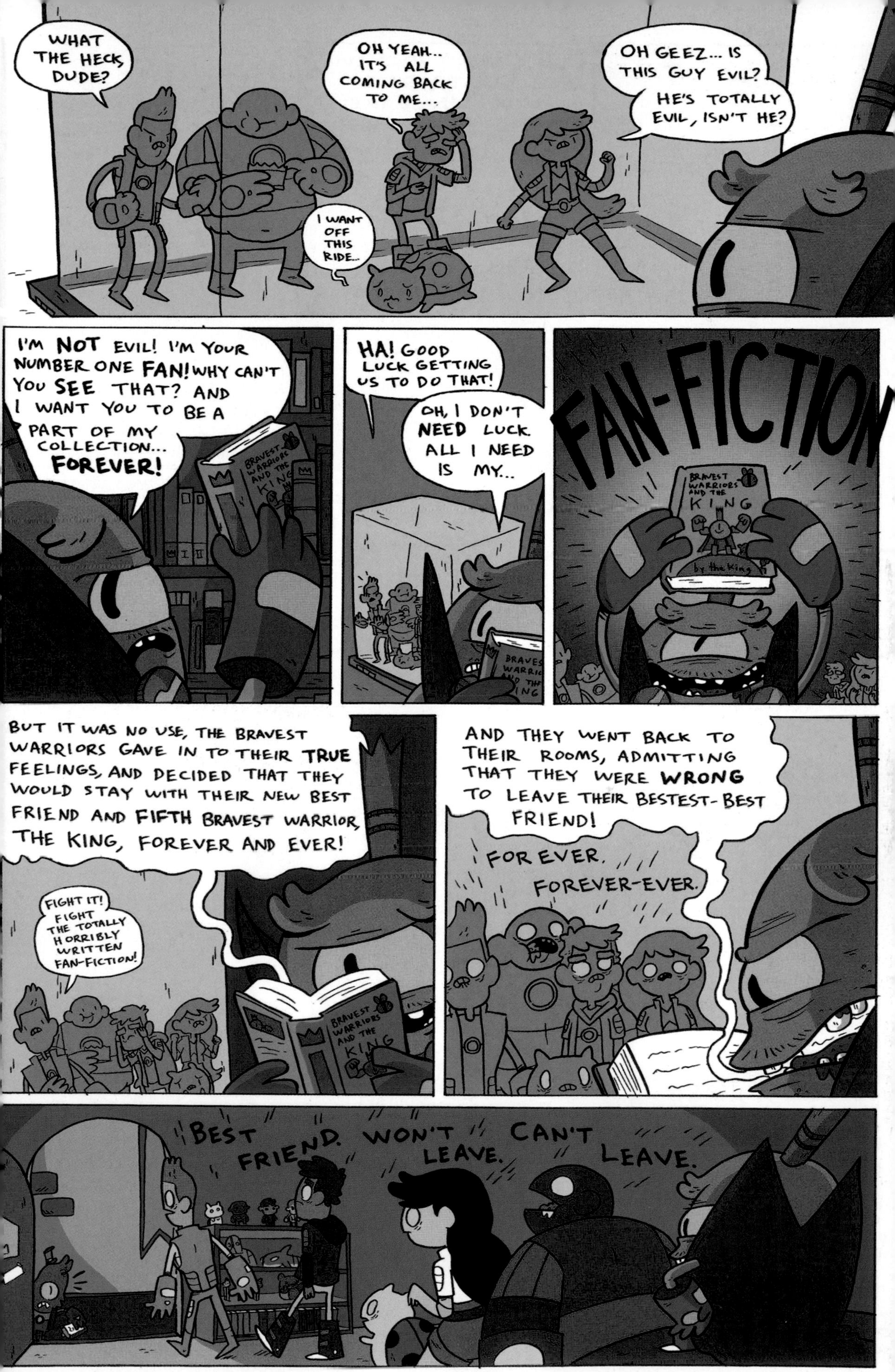
WHAT THE HECK DUDE?
OH YEAH... IT'S ALL COMING BACK TO ME...
OH GEEZ... IS THIS GUY EVIL?
HE'S TOTALLY EVIL, ISN'T HE?
I WANT OFF THIS RIDE...
I'M NOT EVIL! I'M YOUR NUMBER ONE FAN! WHY CAN'T YOU SEE THAT? AND I WANT YOU TO BE A PART OF MY COLLECTION... FOREVER!
BRAVEST WARRIORS AND THE KING
HA! GOOD LUCK GETTING US TO DO THAT!
OH, I DON'T NEED LUCK. ALL I NEED IS MY...
FAN-FICTION
BRAVEST WARRIORS AND THE KING
by the King
BUT IT WAS NO USE, THE BRAVEST WARRIORS GAVE IN TO THEIR TRUE FEELINGS, AND DECIDED THAT THEY WOULD STAY WITH THEIR NEW BEST FRIEND AND FIFTH BRAVEST WARRIOR, THE KING, FOREVER AND EVER!
FIGHT IT! FIGHT THE TOTALLY HORRIBLY WRITTEN FAN-FICTION!
BRAVEST WARRIORS AND THE KING
AND THEY WENT BACK TO THEIR ROOMS, ADMITTING THAT THEY WERE WRONG TO LEAVE THEIR BESTEST-BEST FRIEND!
FOREVER.
FOREVER-EVER.
BEST FRIEND.
WON'T LEAVE.
CAN'T LEAVE.

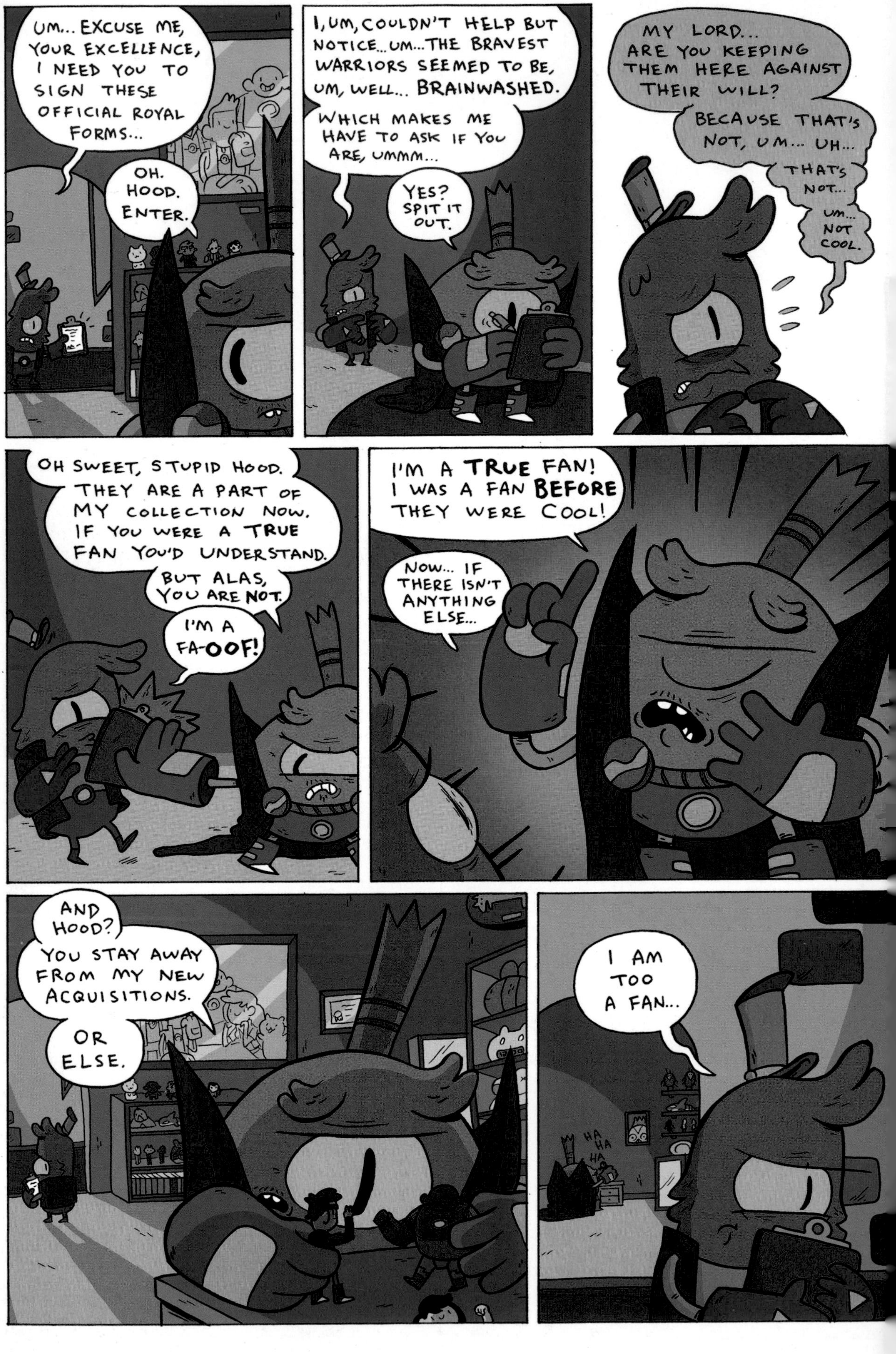
UM... EXCUSE ME, YOUR EXCELLENCE, I NEED YOU TO SIGN THESE OFFICIAL ROYAL FORMS...
OH. HOOD. ENTER.
I, UM, COULDN'T HELP BUT NOTICE... UM... THE BRAVEST WARRIORS SEEMED TO BE, UM, WELL... BRAINWASHED.
WHICH MAKES ME HAVE TO ASK IF YOU ARE, UMMM...
YES? SPIT IT OUT.
MY LORD... ARE YOU KEEPING THEM HERE AGAINST THEIR WILL?
BECAUSE THAT'S NOT, UM... UH...
THAT'S NOT...
UM... NOT COOL.
OH SWEET, STUPID HOOD. THEY ARE A PART OF MY COLLECTION NOW. IF YOU WERE A TRUE FAN YOU'D UNDERSTAND.
BUT ALAS, YOU ARE NOT.
I'M A FA-OOF!
I'M A TRUE FAN! I WAS A FAN BEFORE THEY WERE COOL!
NOW... IF THERE ISN'T ANYTHING ELSE...
AND HOOD?
YOU STAY AWAY FROM MY NEW ACQUISITIONS.
OR ELSE.
HA HA HA
I AM TOO A FAN...

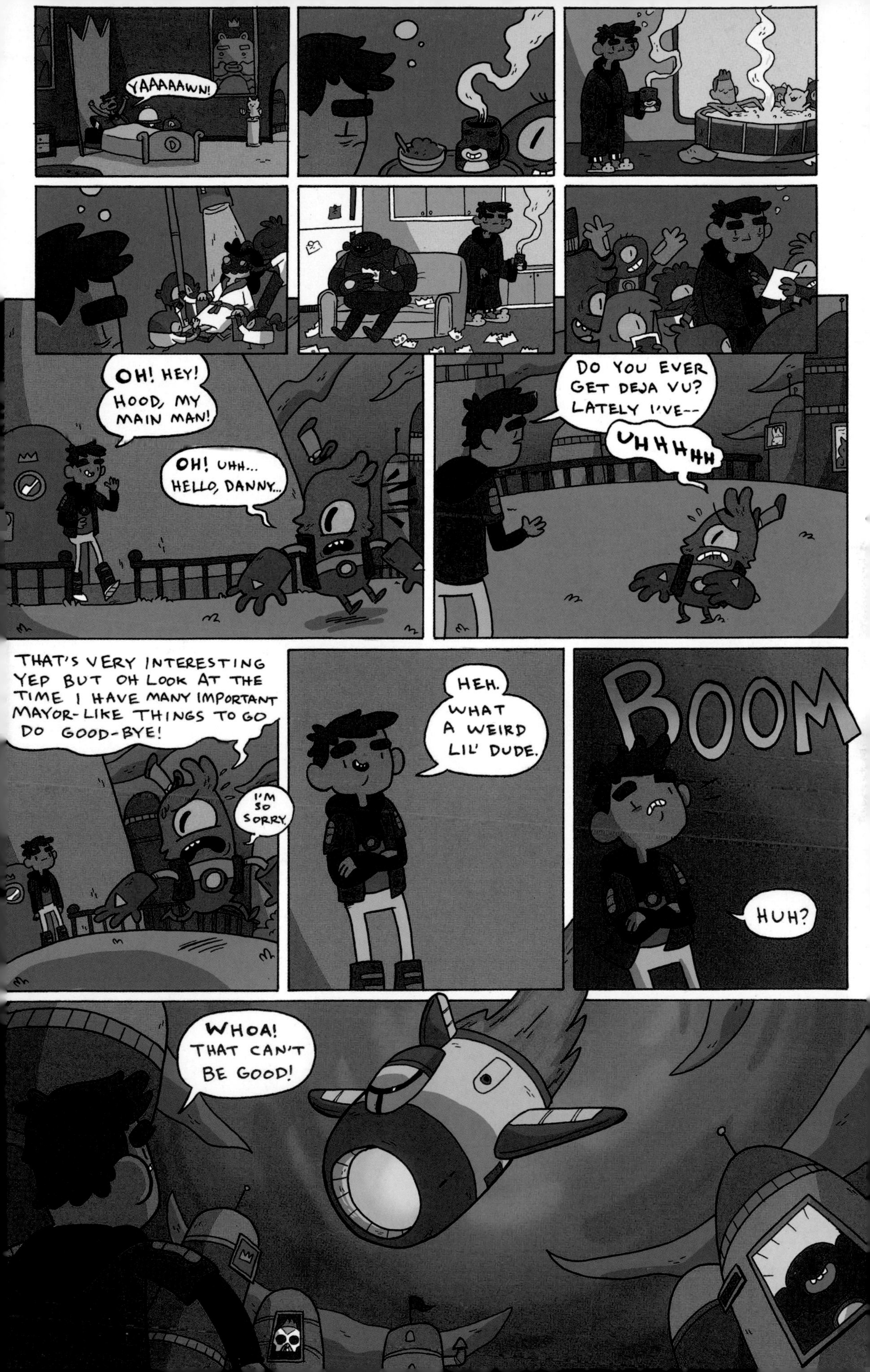
YAAAAAWN!
OH! HEY! HOOD, MY MAIN MAN!
OH! UHH... HELLO, DANNY...
DO YOU EVER GET DEJA VU? LATELY I'VE--
UHHHHH
THAT'S VERY INTERESTING YEP BUT OH LOOK AT THE TIME I HAVE MANY IMPORTANT MAYOR-LIKE THINGS TO GO DO GOOD-BYE!
I'M SO SORRY.
HEH. WHAT A WEIRD LIL' DUDE.
BOOM
HUH?
WHOA! THAT CAN'T BE GOOD!

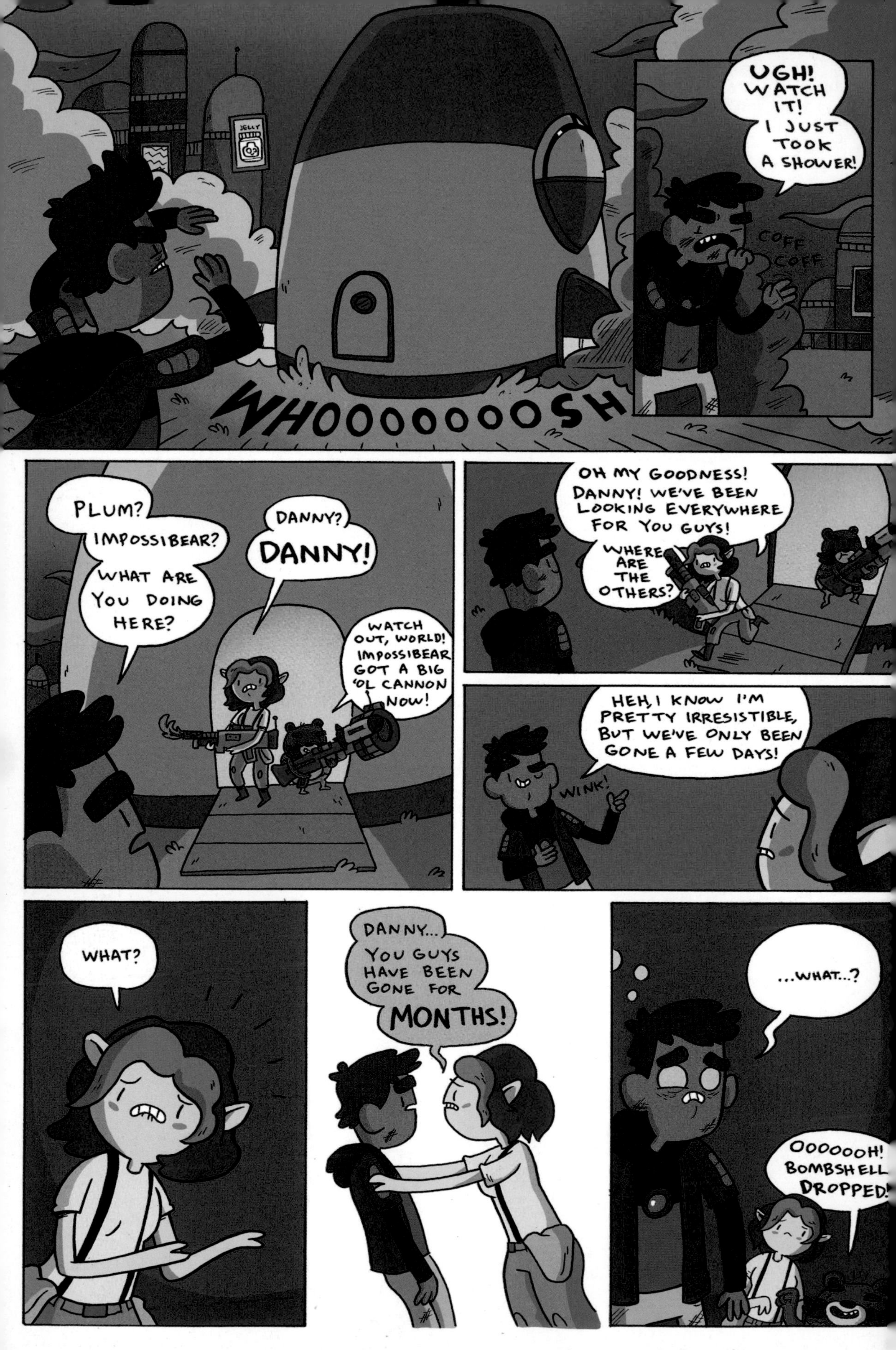
JELLY
WHOOOOOOOOSH
UGH! WATCH IT! I JUST TOOK A SHOWER!
COFF COFF
PLUM? IMPOSSIBEAR?
WHAT ARE YOU DOING HERE?
DANNY? DANNY!
WATCH OUT, WORLD! IMPOSSIBEAR GOT A BIG 'OL CANNON NOW!
OH MY GOODNESS! DANNY! WE'VE BEEN LOOKING EVERYWHERE FOR YOU GUYS!
WHERE ARE THE OTHERS?
HEH, I KNOW I'M PRETTY IRRESISTIBLE, BUT WE'VE ONLY BEEN GONE A FEW DAYS!
WINK!
WHAT?
DANNY... YOU GUYS HAVE BEEN GONE FOR MONTHS!
...WHAT...?
OOOOOOH! BOMBSHELL DROPPED!

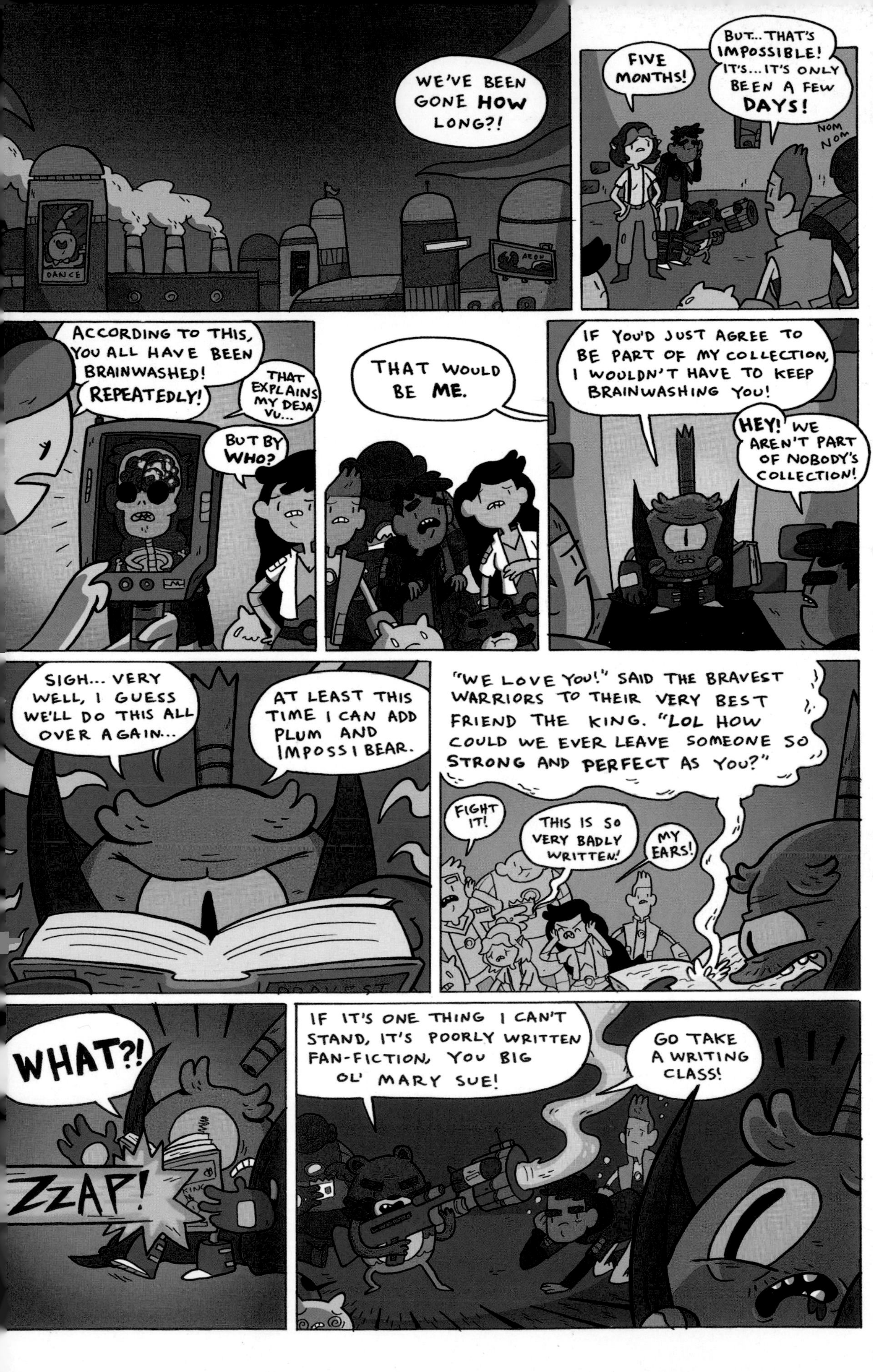
WE'VE BEEN GONE HOW LONG?!
FIVE MONTHS!
BUT... THAT'S IMPOSSIBLE! IT'S... IT'S ONLY BEEN A FEW DAYS!
NOM NOM
ACCORDING TO THIS, YOU ALL HAVE BEEN BRAINWASHED! REPEATEDLY!
THAT EXPLAINS MY DEJA VU...
BUT BY WHO?
THAT WOULD BE ME.
IF YOU'D JUST AGREE TO BE PART OF MY COLLECTION, I WOULDN'T HAVE TO KEEP BRAINWASHING YOU!
HEY! WE AREN'T PART OF NOBODY'S COLLECTION!
SIGH... VERY WELL, I GUESS WE'LL DO THIS ALL OVER AGAIN...
AT LEAST THIS TIME I CAN ADD PLUM AND IMPOSSIBEAR.
"WE LOVE YOU!" SAID THE BRAVEST WARRIORS TO THEIR VERY BEST FRIEND THE KING. "LOL HOW COULD WE EVER LEAVE SOMEONE SO STRONG AND PERFECT AS YOU?"
FIGHT IT!
THIS IS SO VERY BADLY WRITTEN!
MY EARS!
WHAT?!
ZZAP!
IF IT'S ONE THING I CAN'T STAND, IT'S POORLY WRITTEN FAN-FICTION, YOU BIG OL' MARY SUE!
GO TAKE A WRITING CLASS!

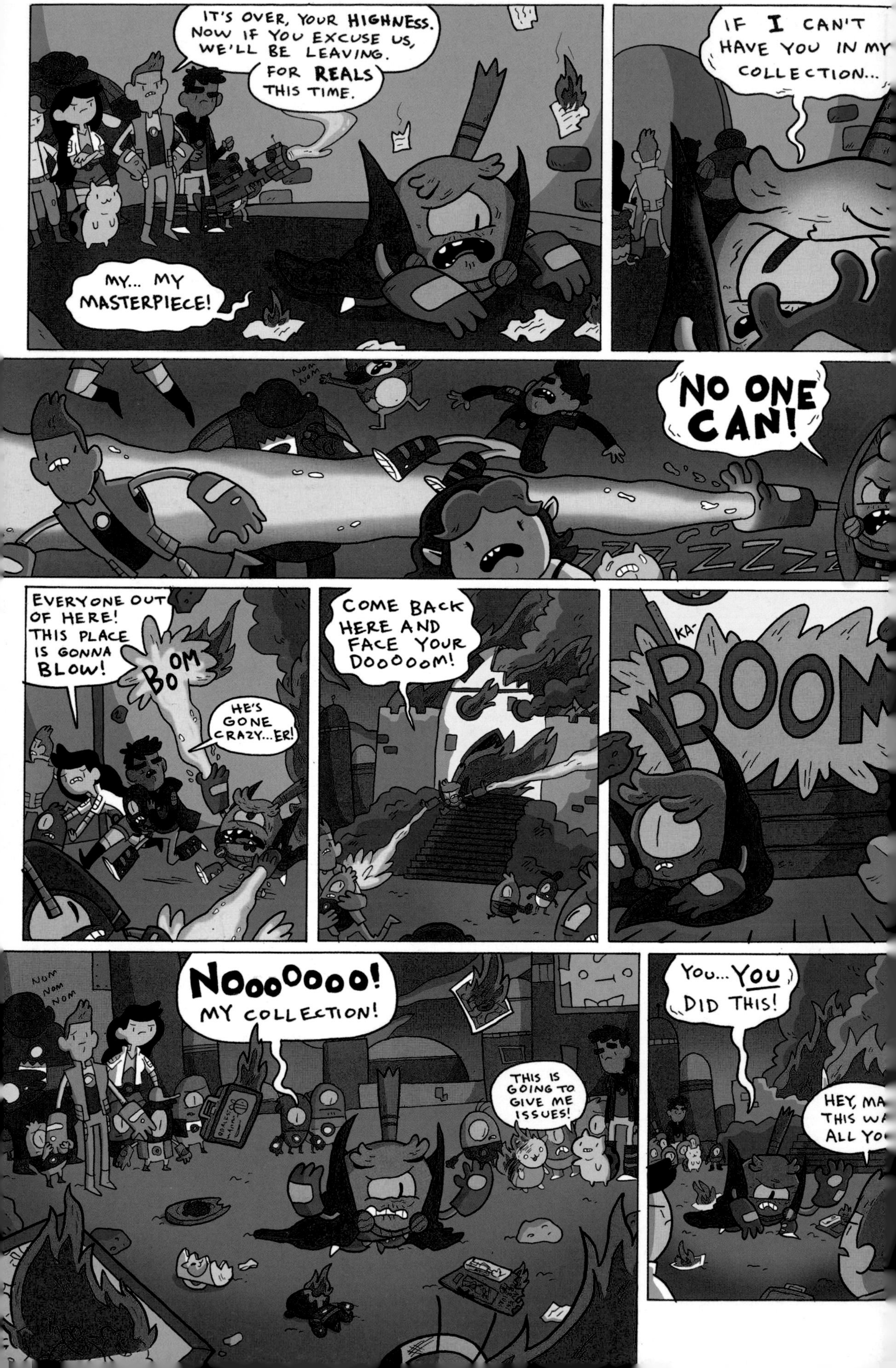
IT'S OVER, YOUR HIGHNESS. NOW IF YOU EXCUSE US, WE'LL BE LEAVING.
FOR REALS THIS TIME.
MY... MY MASTERPIECE!
IF I CAN'T HAVE YOU IN MY COLLECTION...
NOM NOM
NO ONE CAN!
ZZZZZ
EVERYONE OUT OF HERE! THIS PLACE IS GONNA BLOW!
BOOM
HE'S GONE CRAZY...ER!
COME BACK HERE AND FACE YOUR DOOOOOOM!
KA-
BOOM
NOM NOM NOM
NOOOOOOO! MY COLLECTION!
THIS IS GOING TO GIVE ME ISSUES!
YOU... YOU DID THIS!
HEY, MA
THIS WA
ALL YO

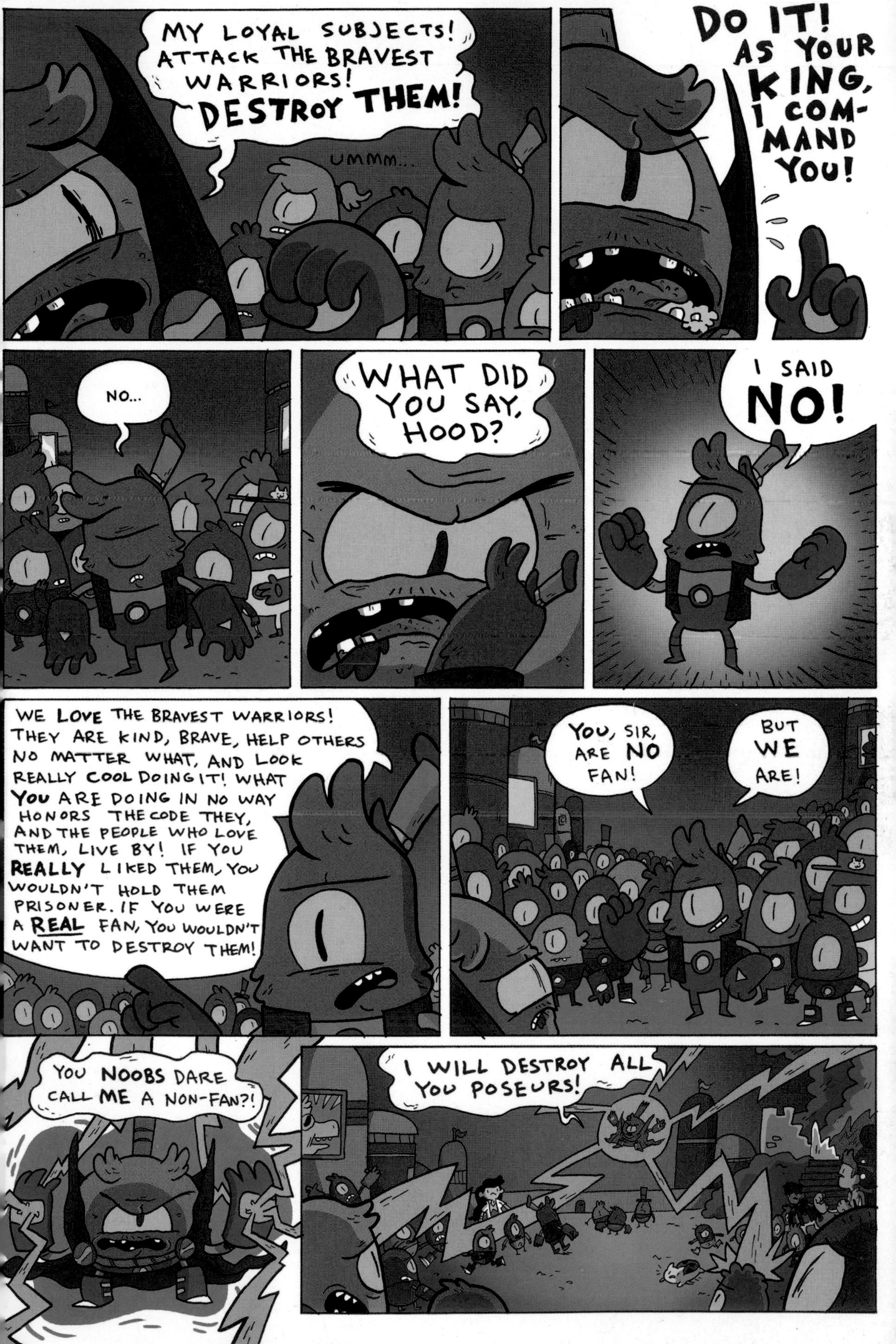
MY LOYAL SUBJECTS! ATTACK THE BRAVEST WARRIORS! DESTROY THEM!
UMMM...
DO IT! AS YOUR KING, I COMMAND YOU!
NO...
WHAT DID YOU SAY, HOOD?
I SAID NO!
WE LOVE THE BRAVEST WARRIORS! THEY ARE KIND, BRAVE, HELP OTHERS NO MATTER WHAT, AND LOOK REALLY COOL DOING IT! WHAT YOU ARE DOING IN NO WAY HONORS THE CODE THEY, AND THE PEOPLE WHO LOVE THEM, LIVE BY! IF YOU REALLY LIKED THEM, YOU WOULDN'T HOLD THEM PRISONER. IF YOU WERE A REAL FAN, YOU WOULDN'T WANT TO DESTROY THEM!
YOU, SIR, ARE NO FAN!
BUT WE ARE!
YOU NOOBS DARE CALL ME A NON-FAN?!
I WILL DESTROY ALL YOU POSEURS!

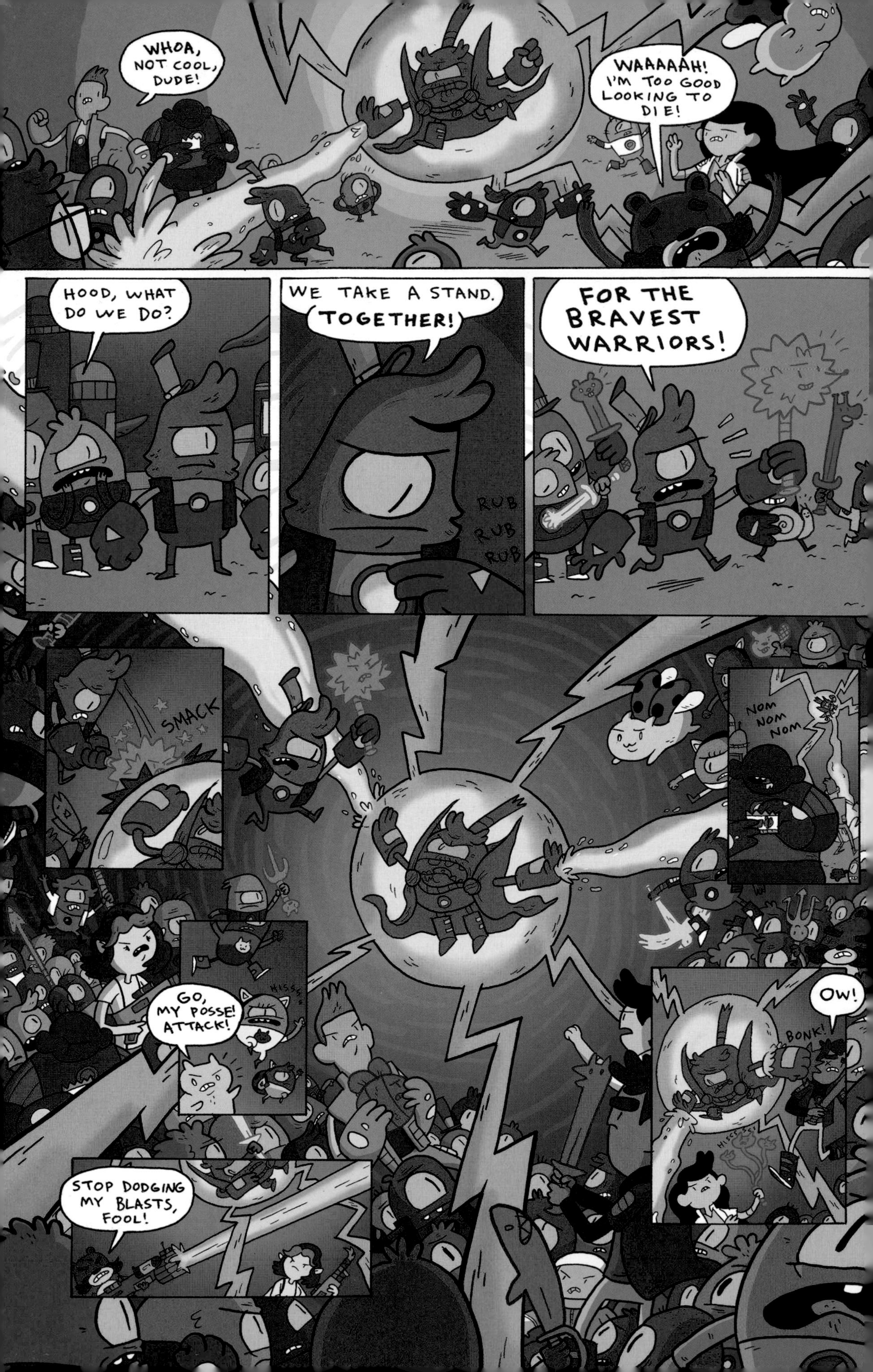
WHOA, NOT COOL, DUDE!
WAAAAAH! I'M TOO GOOD LOOKING TO DIE!
HOOD, WHAT DO WE DO?
WE TAKE A STAND. TOGETHER!
RUB RUB RUB
FOR THE BRAVEST WARRIORS!
SMACK
NOM NOM NOM
GO, MY POSSE! ATTACK!
OW!
BONK!
STOP DODGING MY BLASTS, FOOL!

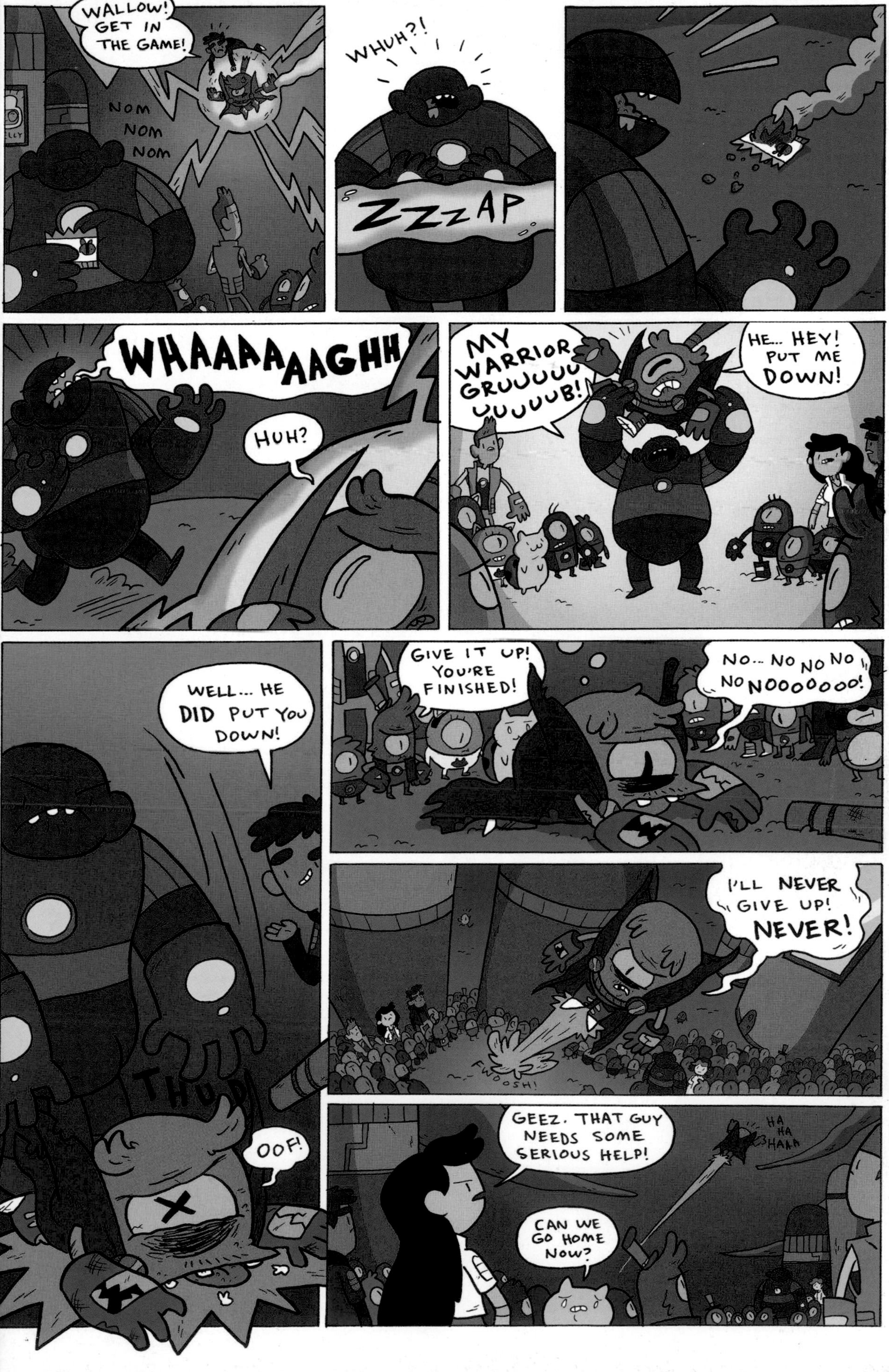
WALLOW! GET IN THE GAME!
NOM NOM NOM
WHUH?!
ZZZAP
WHAAAAAAGHH
HUH?
MY WARRIOR GRUUUUUUUUUUB!
HE... HEY! PUT ME DOWN!
WELL... HE DID PUT YOU DOWN!
THUD
OOF!
GIVE IT UP! YOU'RE FINISHED!
NO... NO NO NO NO NOOOOOOO!
I'LL NEVER GIVE UP! NEVER!
FWOOSH!
GEEZ. THAT GUY NEEDS SOME SERIOUS HELP!
HA HA HAAA
CAN WE GO HOME NOW?

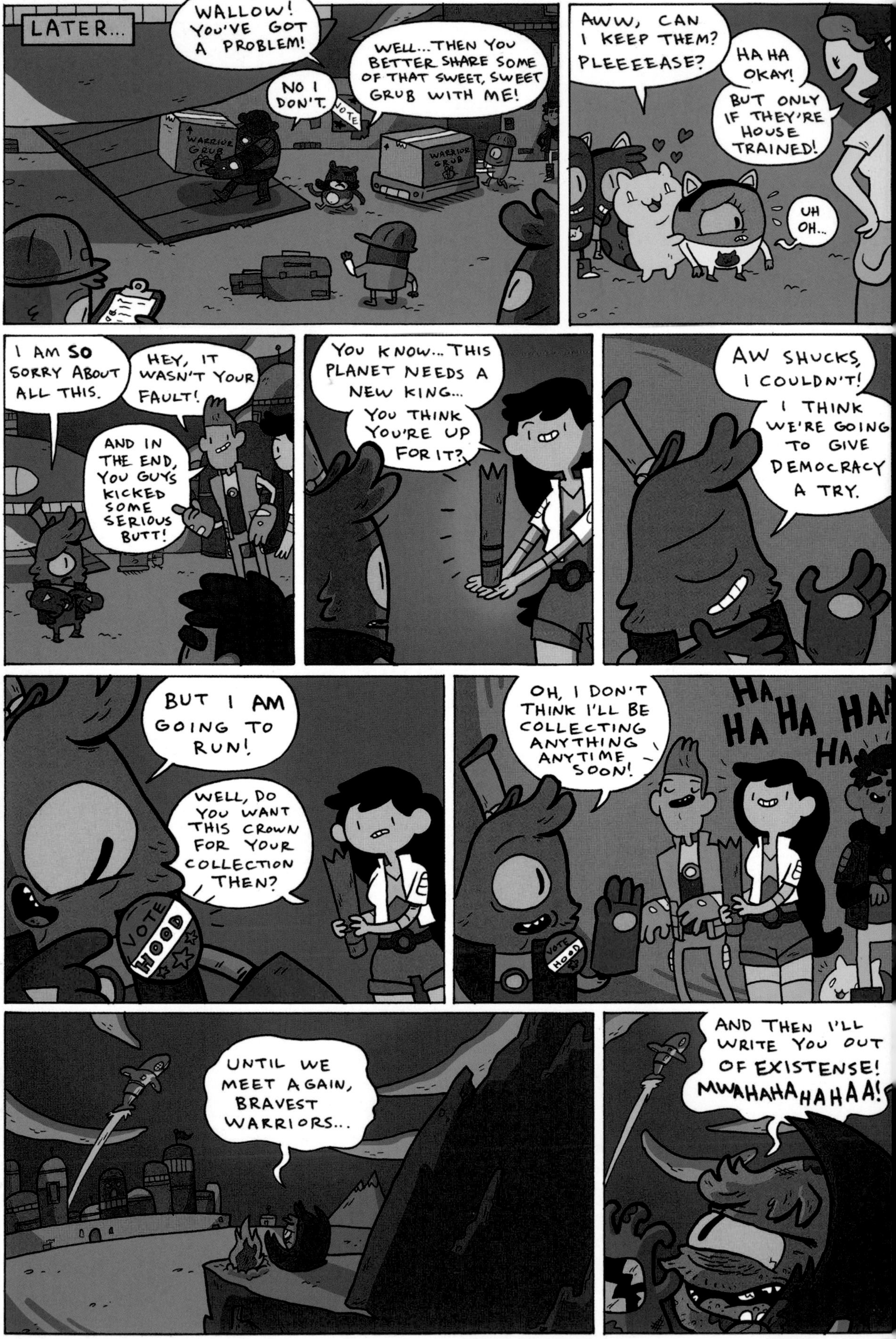
LATER...
WALLOW! YOU'VE GOT A PROBLEM!
NO I DON'T.
VOTE
WELL... THEN YOU BETTER SHARE SOME OF THAT SWEET, SWEET GRUB WITH ME!
WARRIOR GRUB
WARRIOR GRUB
AWW, CAN I KEEP THEM? PLEEEEASE?
HA HA OKAY!
BUT ONLY IF THEY'RE HOUSE TRAINED!
UH OH...
I AM SO SORRY ABOUT ALL THIS.
HEY, IT WASN'T YOUR FAULT!
AND IN THE END, YOU GUYS KICKED SOME SERIOUS BUTT!
YOU KNOW... THIS PLANET NEEDS A NEW KING...
YOU THINK YOU'RE UP FOR IT?
AW SHUCKS, I COULDN'T!
I THINK WE'RE GOING TO GIVE DEMOCRACY A TRY.
BUT I AM GOING TO RUN!
WELL, DO YOU WANT THIS CROWN FOR YOUR COLLECTION THEN?
VOTE HOOD
OH, I DON'T THINK I'LL BE COLLECTING ANYTHING ANYTIME SOON!
HA HA HA HA HA HA
VOTE HOOD
UNTIL WE MEET AGAIN, BRAVEST WARRIORS...
AND THEN I'LL WRITE YOU OUT OF EXISTENSE! MWAHAHAHAHAHAA!

THE END...?

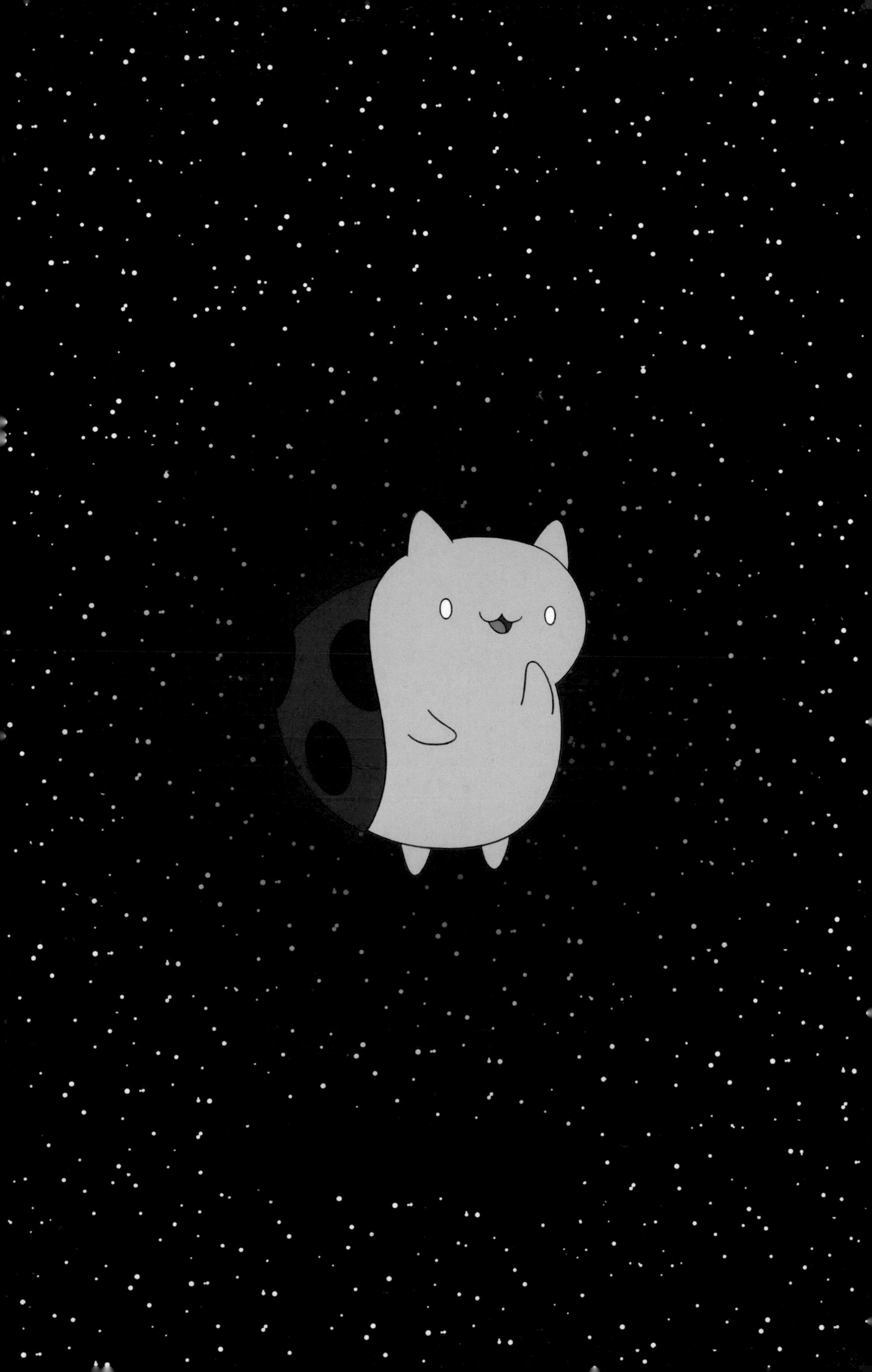

COVER GALLERY

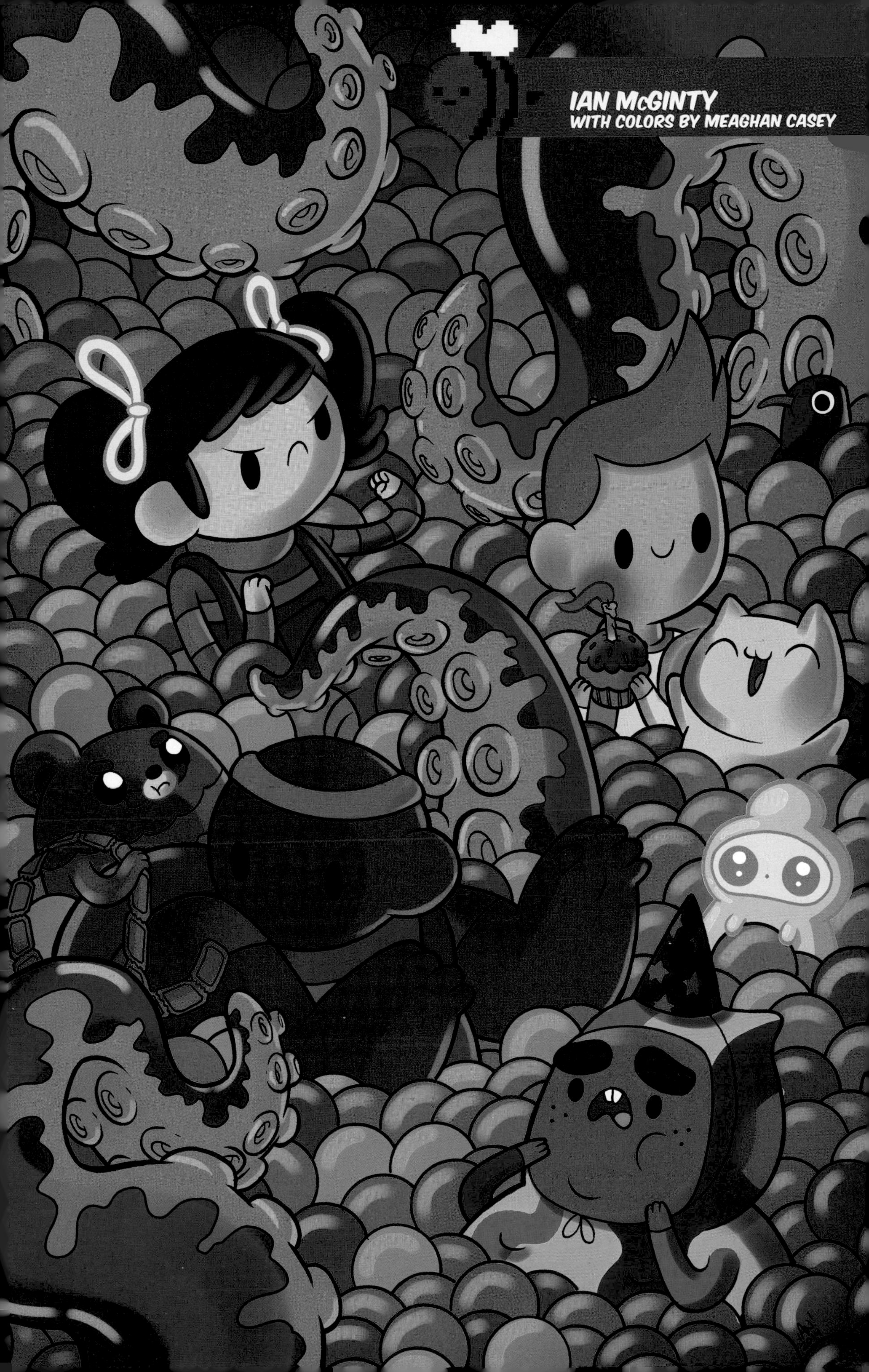
IAN McGINTY
WITH COLORS BY MEAGHAN CASEY

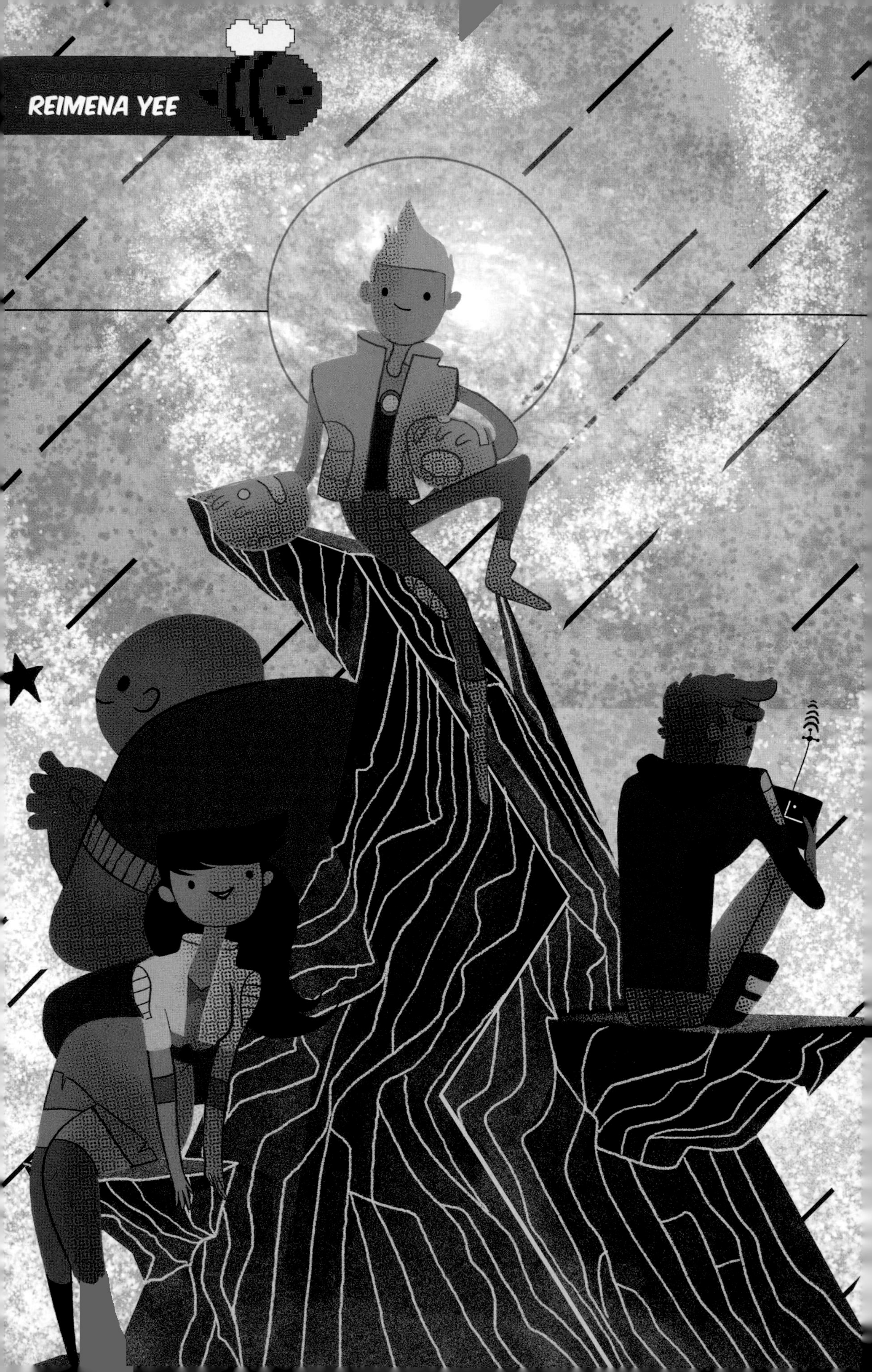
REIMENA YEE

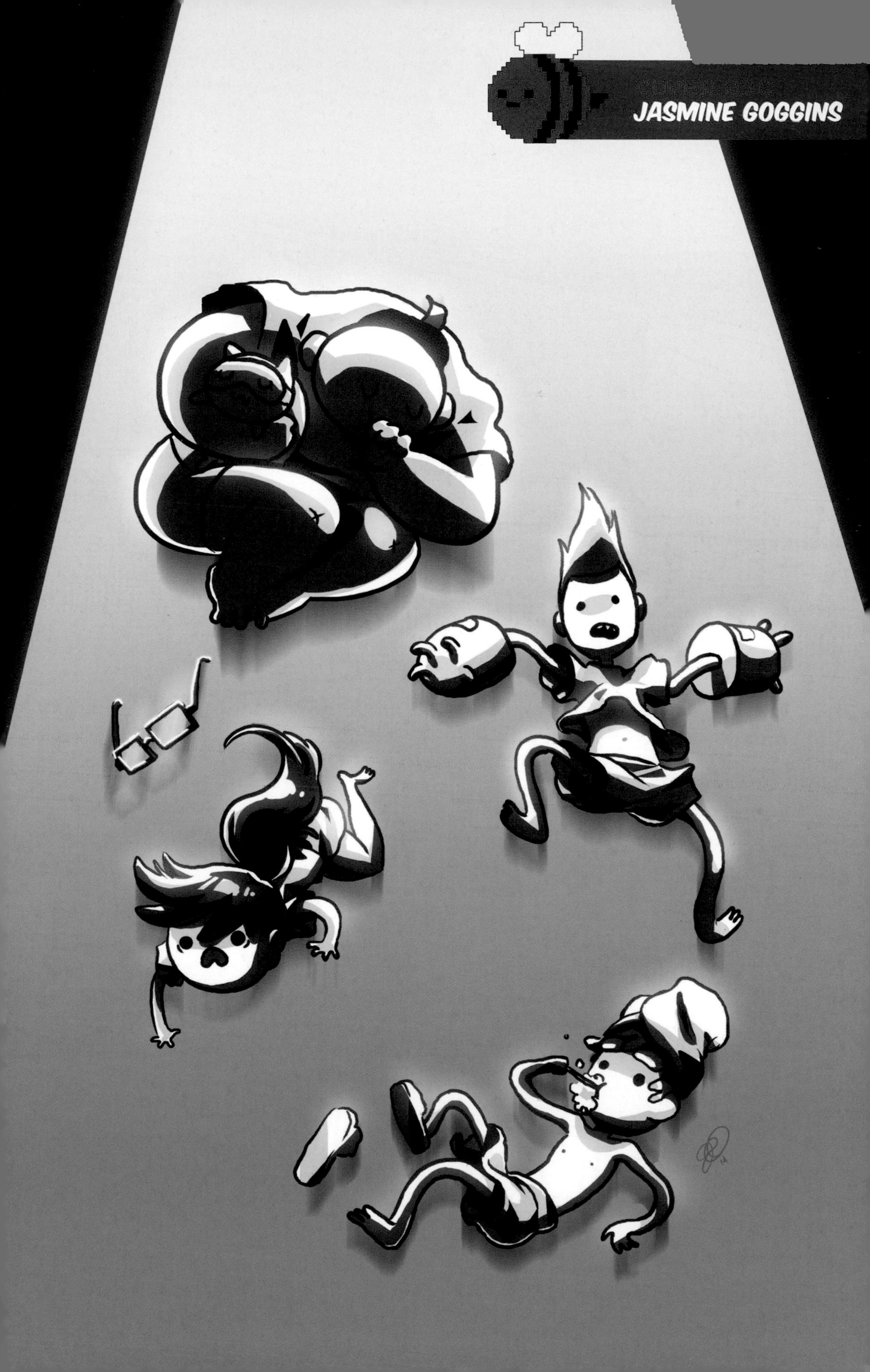
JASMINE GOGGINS

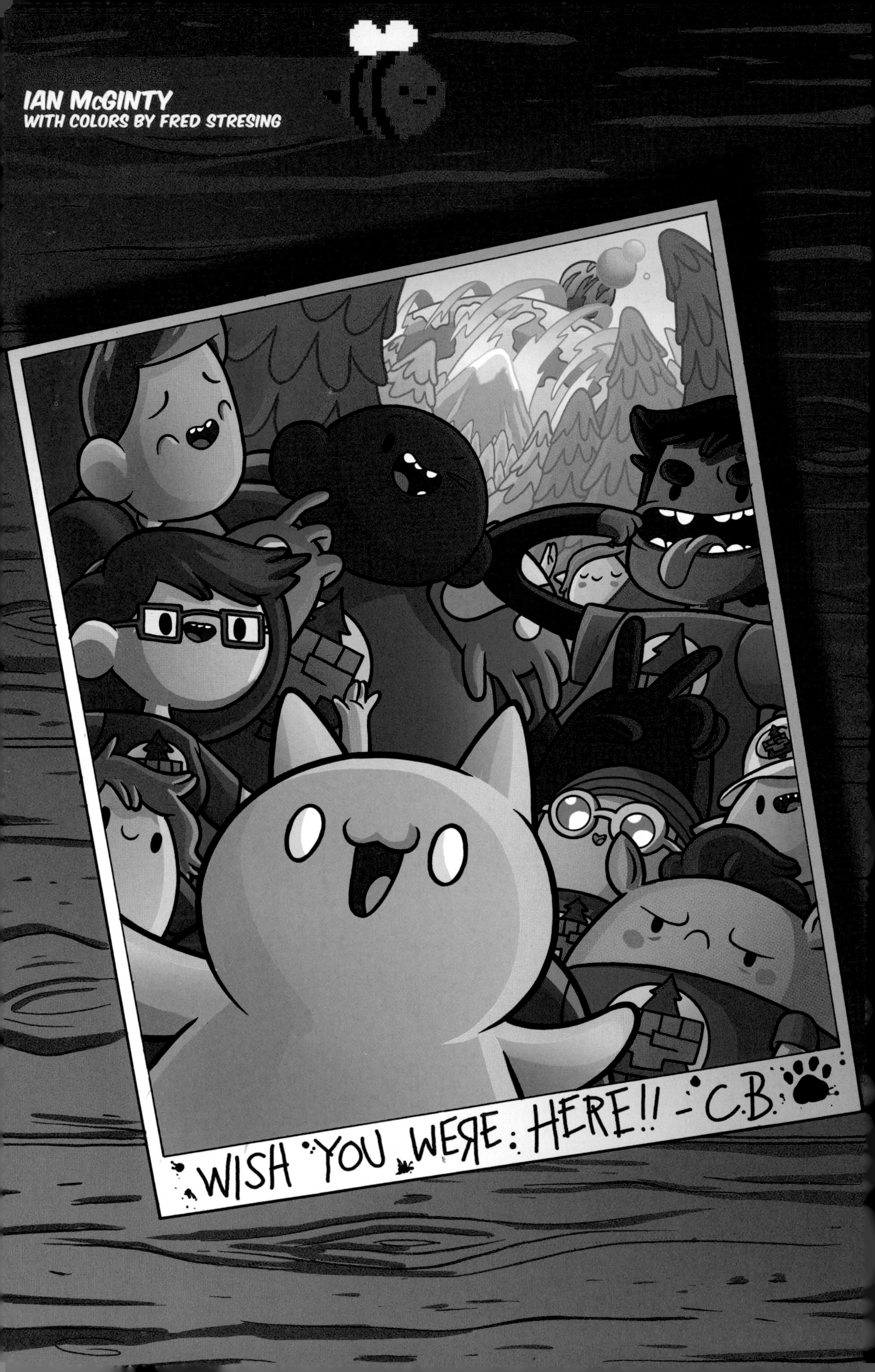
IAN McGINTY
WITH COLORS BY FRED STRESING
WISH YOU WERE HERE!! - C.B.

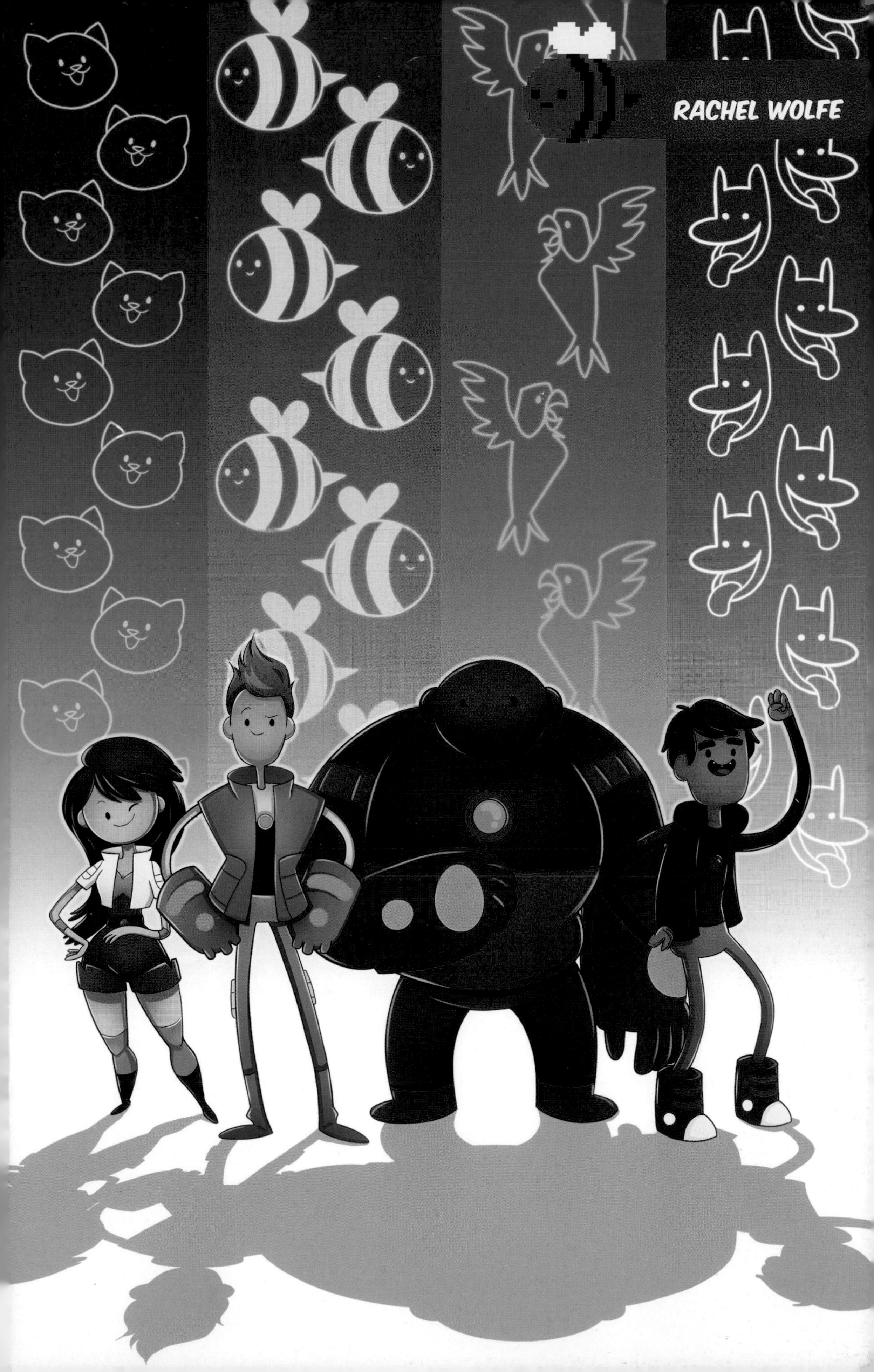
RACHEL WOLFE

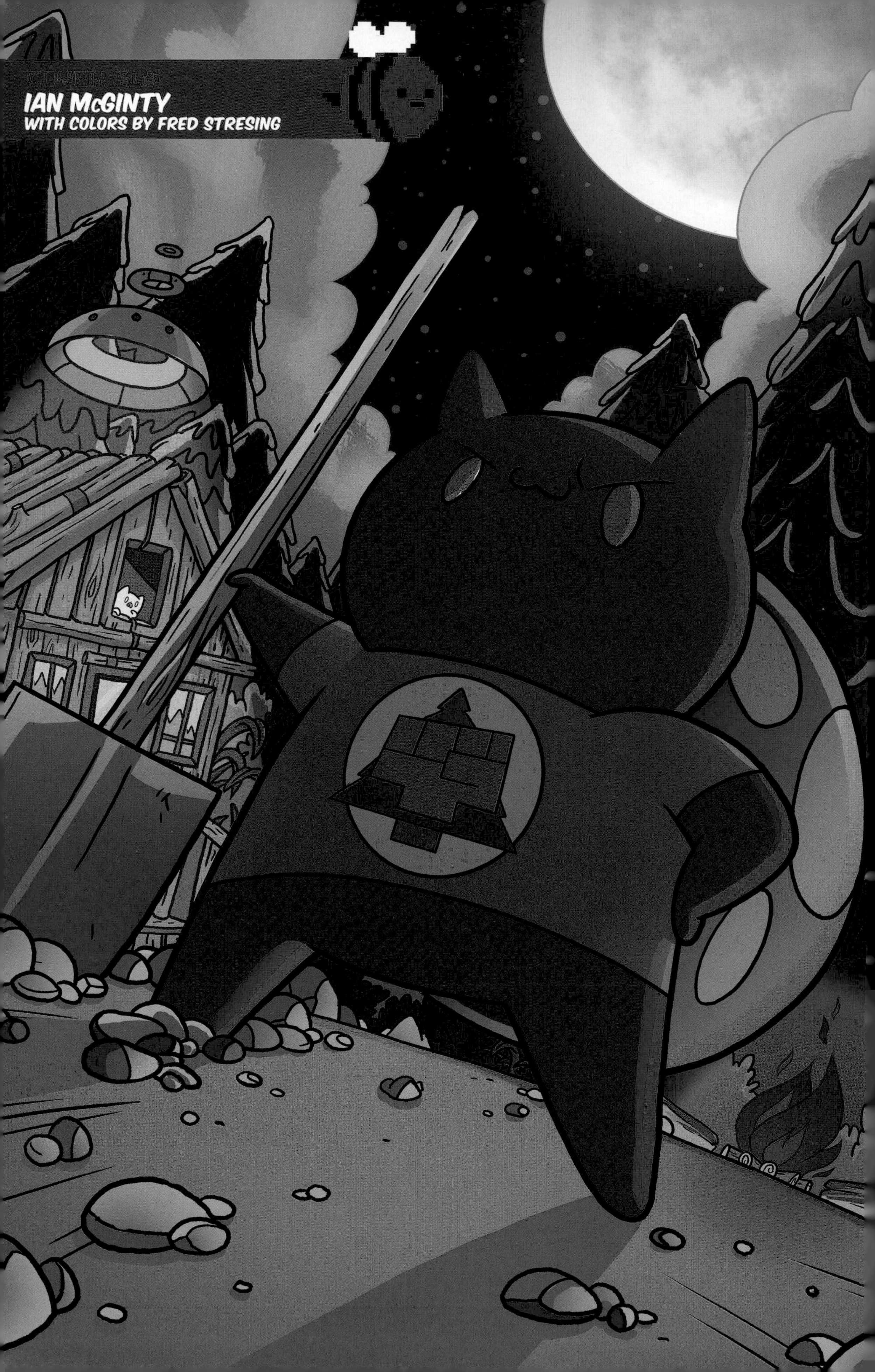
IAN McGINTY
WITH COLORS BY FRED STRESING

REED BLACK

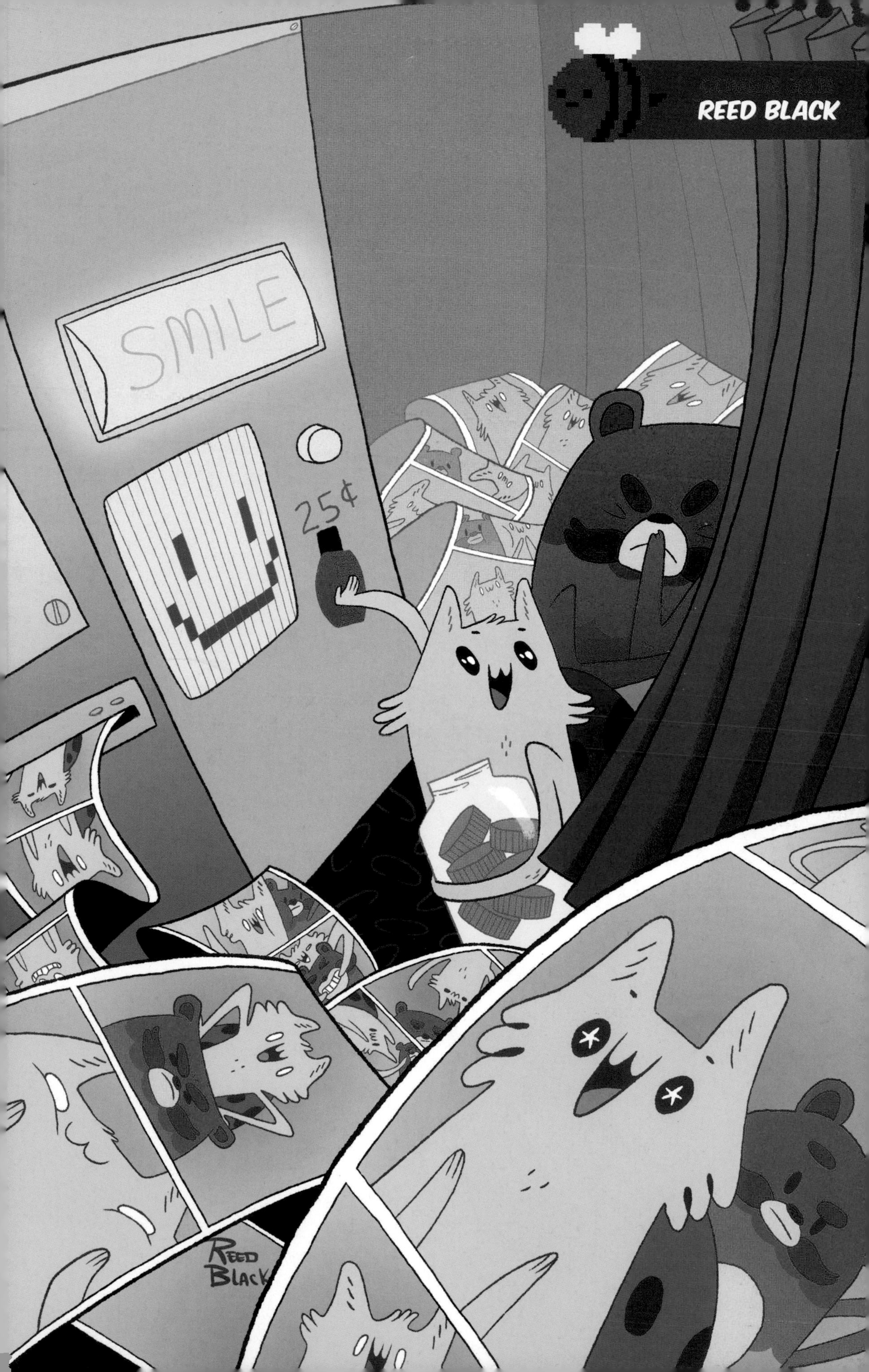
SMILE
25¢
REED BLACK

IAN McGINTY
WITH COLORS BY FRED STRESING

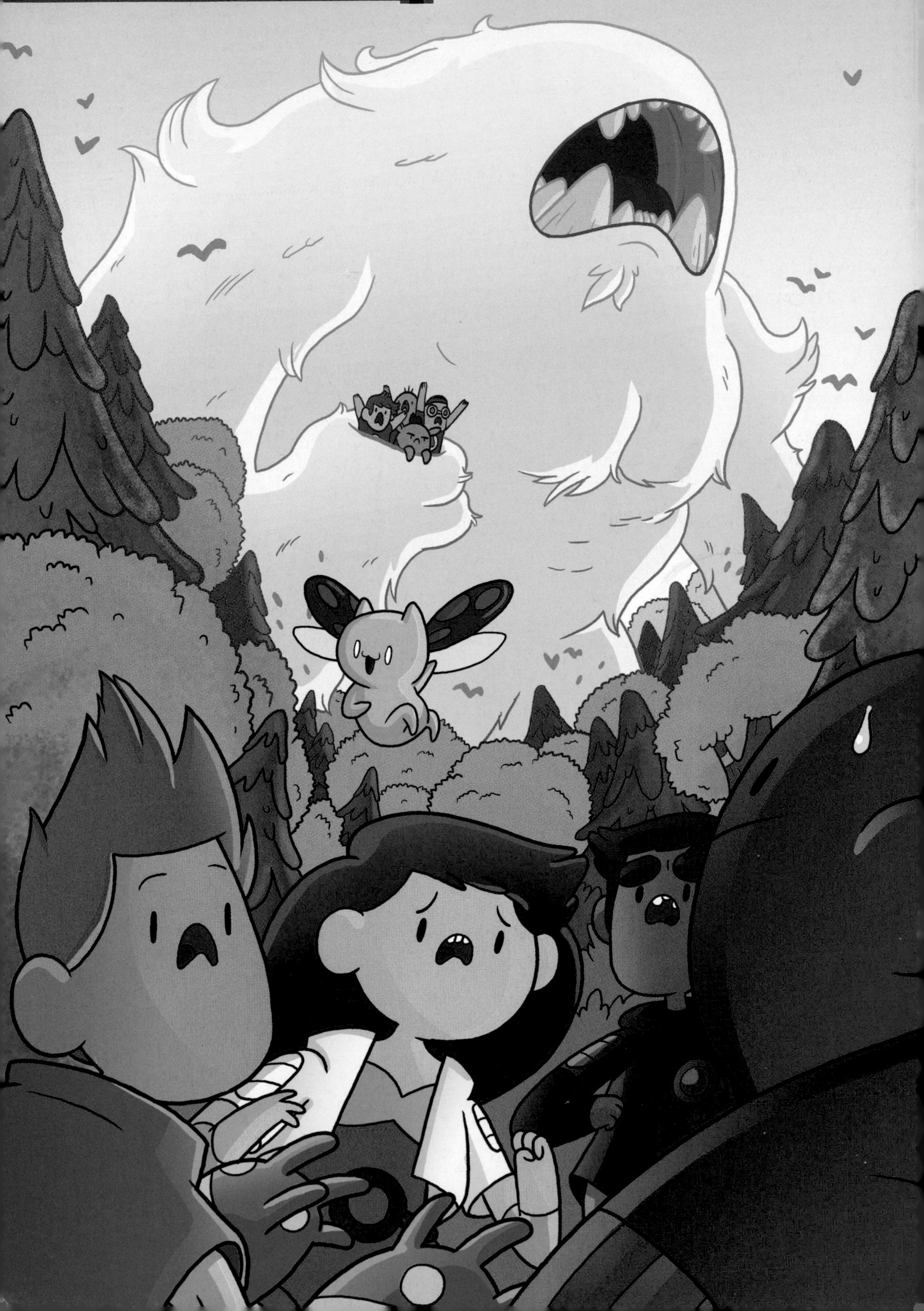

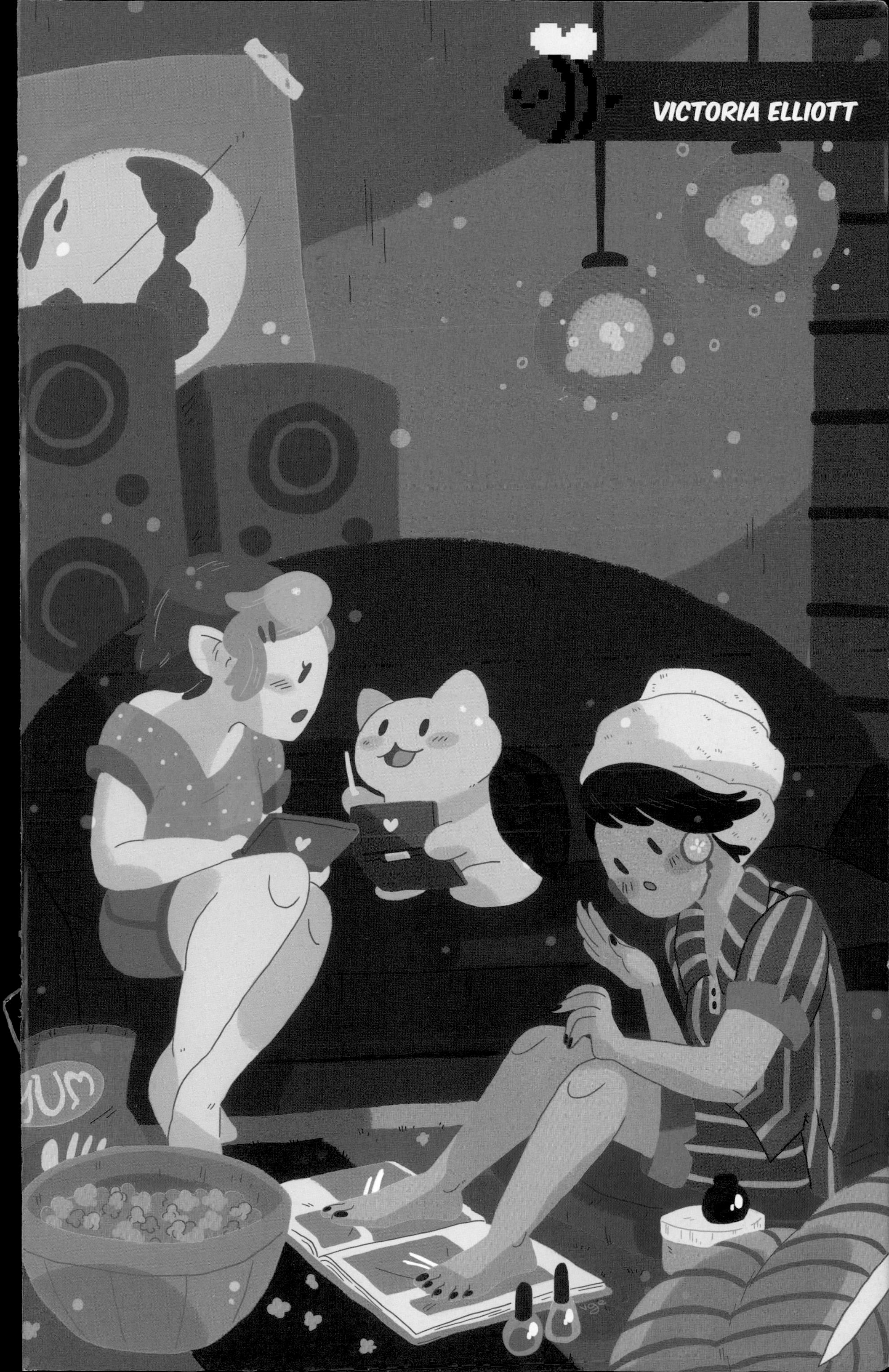
VICTORIA ELLIOTT